Booker's Bliss

Divergent Omegaverse: Paranormal
Gay Romance - Book 3
JP Sayle

Booker's Bliss

One decision was all it took to open a hideous can of worms—and give alpha bear Booker Starling a new perspective on his PA, Frey Abbott. Now all he has to do is get Frey to entrust him with something of vital importance—his heart. But first, Frey has to know Booker is the only alpha who will keep it safe.

Booker has suffered the cruelty of rejection, so for protection, he keeps his big heart hidden under a gruff exterior. He will do anything to protect what he holds dear, even if that includes honoring the code of not poaching someone his brother has slept with. Despite his feelings, Booker keeps his distance—until his father's sudden retirement renders that option redundant.

Coming home was bad enough. Now his hands are full 24/7 dealing with a flirty fox. He sets himself three rules, but can he stick to them?

An overheard conversation gives Booker the opportunity to see the real Frey, and resisting him proves futile.

The only option is to throw his cautious nature to the wind. Booker wants everything—including a mate. As for his rules?

All bets are off.

Dedication

Inspired. I'm totally in love with Booker and Frey, a world developed and captured on page after many conversations with Monica. Book friendships happen over the love of words, passages on pages and more often whole books. For this, I'll be eternally grateful for a little potato called Frenchie, who rolled his way into Monica's heart and brought her into my life.

To Tal, your cover for this book truly captures the essence of my boys and makes my heart sing with joy. You are a wonderful talent I want to keep to myself because I'm greedy, only your work needs an audience to be appreciated fully.

You, my friend, rock.

Contents

Chapter One
Frey

The entire building was buzzing with the gossip that Lane and Derick Starling were retiring and their eight sons were going to take over. They were all going to return to town and work in the same building as Frey.

Fiddlesticks!

Frey ran a hand distractedly through his hair, nodding at the folks he passed, offering a smile he didn't feel but forced to his lips. It was expected. He was the smiley, flirty fox. Only right now, with this news having been confirmed by his boss, Hollis Adice, and Derick's personal secretary, Monica, he wasn't able to put on a real front of fun and friendly.

He listened to the snippets of conversation as he went.

"All of them in the same building?"

"Can you imagine the chaos?"

"How will this impact our jobs with so many people issuing orders?"

He didn't stop and add his thoughts, keeping to himself his own speculation on the impact such a decision would have on everyone. Scared was what he was. There were many reasons for this and none he could or would talk about with anyone when it would mean he'd have to share some secrets he'd told no one except his doctor.

The fears he had were all about Booker coming back into the office full time and potentially what that meant for him. Fashion design, trends, and working with design concepts was the area Frey had majored in at college. These were Booker's assigned part of Starling Enterprises. He could add up the same as everyone else when he recalled what changes these were and Hollis's words.

"I haven't really said anything, other than that I won't be a walkover. And that I was honored, 'cause I am. As for keeping them in check, you've been doing that for years. As for listening to us... that's tricky to say when we barely get to see them, except for important meetings and new business that relates to their particular area of interest. Then it's usually just one or two of them, not all eight."

It all made horrible sense and left him conflicted. Because it stood to reason, Hollis would pair him and Booker together—*in close confines.*

Please, can you lay off?

His fox was in its damn element. It had taken a liking to the big bear shifter from the beginning and over the years they'd gotten to know him, his fox had set his sights on the bear. He believed they'd make a perfect pair. The bear, though grouchy and growly, had a big heart, which Booker wasn't always able to hide. He'd endeared himself to his fox side.

Frey had not had the same—

Tell that lie to someone who might believe you.

Something else his fox had started to do was interrupt his thoughts and read them when Frey didn't want him to. *I'm not listening to you.*

The loud snort got ignored as Frey sniffed and continued on, hoping he could catch Hollis alone to talk about his minor—major issue.

Frey's step faulted. Shit, would Hollis continue with his current role, or would that change with his new position in the company?

There was little that got past Frey. He'd overheard Monica, a PA, talking on the phone about Hollis having a vote on what happened at board level. It had to mean he was going to be crazy busy if he had to work closely with all the brothers who, up to now, only visited Hazardville a few times a year for important meetings, but were now returning *permanently*.

A shiver ran up Frey's spine at the thought of seeing the bear daily. It was selfish to think only of himself, but right now, with these sudden changes and a recent visit to his doctor and the subsequent tests he'd needed, Frey had too much worry for himself.

Frey did work with Booker, but until now, they'd not worked too closely together and he'd behaved in such a way the bear hardly tolerated him, and for good reason.

He sighed dejectedly as he trailed down the corridor, trying to figure out how to approach Hollis to explain he didn't want to work with Booker and come up with a reason that didn't make the actual reasons too obvious.

Frey had spoken to no one about his past. He had a work persona that he'd perfected to hide his insecurities, and it had succeeded. With everything in life, nothing stayed static and what he'd avoided—Booker—was about to land on his doorstep in an unceremonial fashion.

He should have anticipated everyone else would have the same idea as him when he got to Hollis's office not a minute later, to find Isley, Monty, Bowie, Ziggy, Lennon, and Wilder crammed in the office.

"Let's take this to the coffee lounge. There are more seats there and we won't feel crammed in like sardines," Hollis demanded, shaking his head at them.

Frey noted how others working on the floor stopped as they passed, curious looks aimed their way. Frey suspected that whatever official announcement came out, it would be too late, as gossip spread like wildfire.

Ushered inside, Frey perched on a colorful padded seat close to Hollis as a hush fell and an air of expectancy came. Frey took none of his usual enjoyment at being in the coffee lounge with its sweet smells and cheerful atmosphere, one Lane Starling had created to make staff feel relaxed when taking a break.

Frey didn't take his gaze off Hollis after he shut the door and gave them his full attention. He looked the epitome of a smart, no-nonsense business executive, suited and booted with dark-rimmed glasses. "Lane and Derick are retiring.

They have asked all their sons to return to Hazardville and run the company jointly."

Monty's chuckle held no humor. "As if they'll be able to do that!"

"Yes, well, that's not for you to worry about. For now, your biggest concern is that for the transition to happen smoothly, you will each find yourself allocated to one of the sons who work in the area of your expertise."

It was exactly as Frey expected, but the sucker punch came nonetheless, and the wince he'd noted Hollis did while talking was now his own.

"What... no... you can't be serious," stuttered Bowie.

He didn't look at Bowie as he waggled his thumb in Bowie's direction, working to maintain his cool. "What he said! You know I—"

"I know perfectly well your opinion of a certain brother. You have made that abundantly clear. As I have said before, that is not my issue. My job is to ensure that my team, who are paid a princely sum to do their jobs," he met each man's stare, "do it. If you are unhappy, then I'm sure there are other firms looking to hire."

"Hollis, do you really need to be an A-hole?" Frey questioned, finding it impossible to sit still so lounged back on the padded chair, doing his best to convey none of the anxiety forming into a hard ball in his guts. His hand rested on the arm of the seat, moving continually to release some of his tension.

Hollis gave Frey a stare that expressed his displeasure, which he hated but was too up in his own head about his fears coming true to worry about.

"Leave him be, Frey. This applies to him too," Bowie pointed out, looking at Hollis sympathetically.

The remaining conversation flew over Frey's head as he remained focused on one thing. *Booker would be here—all the time!*

How the hell was he going to avoid him now?

Chapter Two

Booker

Booker had always enjoyed his freedom to do as he pleased with his role in Starling Enterprises. And he wouldn't argue that his adoptive parents didn't deserve to retire after forty years of raising a family and managing their successful business. Hell no, they deserved to take things easy and do whatever retired folks did. He tried not to think about that when Popi and Dad appeared to have found a new lease of life that revolved around removing their clothes... a lot.

Booker blew out a breath and tried really hard not to think about the sounds and smells that drifted down the hallway at home. He was going to need to find a place to stay, and fast, if he wanted to keep his sanity. In reality, that wasn't what was pissing Booker off, either. They'd handed over the company to their sons and as there were eight of them and they couldn't even agree on something simple like where to go eat, his dads had to come up with a Hollis shaped solution.

He couldn't say he didn't like Hollis Adice, the head of the PAs, because he did. The guy had strong ethics, but Taylin, one of his brothers, had the serious hots for him. To Booker's way of thinking, that meant they were all gonna get hit with the shit stick when it all blew up if Taylin—now home like the rest of them—acted on feelings he probably thought no one had noticed. Booker suspected the only one who hadn't witnessed his mooning was Hollis. The guy was clueless.

But if Booker was truthful with himself, spending a few days back in Hazardville was fine when he knew he'd be leaving. Staying long term meant the likelihood of running into one of his old bear family, something he avoided like the plague when he remained conflicted by their betrayal, was pretty high. His past was not something he wished to confront on any basis. Like any sane bear, he'd put that shit in the forest of nowhere, where he wanted it to rot to nothing.

The steward, Sarah, on their private jet he'd boarded forty minutes ago to head home to finalize the rental of his house, released her seatbelt, signaling that Booker could turn his Wi-Fi back on. Eager to give himself something else to think about, he opened the email that pinged into his inbox when he saw it was from Hollis.

Reading the first three lines had Booker cursing loudly.

Sarah, pausing on her way past him to the small kitchen, got him glancing up to witness her alarmed expression. Too angry to read on when he'd seen flirty Frey's name connected to his, he offered her an apologetic smile.

"Sorry," he muttered, pushing the laptop away, only to bring it back a second later when his anger drove him to check who his brothers were unfortunate to get.

A sliver of humor returned at Kari ending up with Bowie, a miniature bull who spent most of his time appearing lost, despite his ability to do his job.

When he read on and saw who Hollis had paired himself with—Taylin—Booker wasn't sure if he should be amused or not. His gaze traveled back to Frey's name. He groaned under his breath at having the sexy fox in his space long term. Was it selfish to throw a spanner in the works and ask for someone else—anyone else?

Pushing the laptop away once more, he sat back and brooded when it was too late to contact Hollis. Friday, at two minutes to five, was the perfect time to do a hit-and-run email. Hollis clearly understood that his brothers could have issues with their permanent PA, and how to avoid too much push back. In the past, Popi or Hollis had assigned a PA depending on what they were working on. It worked, so why did that have to change now?

His grump increased as he reached into his suit jacket pocket to retrieve his phone and open the group chat—Alphaholes. This was Jupiter's newest name for the group chat all the brothers shared. Jupiter had a weird sense of humor for damn sure and Booker hadn't bothered to listen to the reason he'd picked this name. Whatever it was, Booker was sure it was derogatory towards them all!

Alphaholes

Booker: *So who wants to talk about the damn hit and run that Hollis just did to us? Tay? Anything to say about your assigned PA?*

Silas: *As if he's gonna complain 'bout his good fortune.*

Kodi: *Good fortune... yeah 'bout that...*

Kari: *Lennon is sweet.*

Laken: *If not a little quiet.*

Rue: *Anyone want to swap? Monty, he sometimes smells of fish... my rhino doesn't like fish.*

Booker: *I never got a whiff of fish from him and my bear loves fish. Are you sure it's not for another reason?*

Rue: What reason would that be? Are you trying to piss me off?

Jupiter: Little brother on a stampede, that'll be fun. Remember the last time you did that, you spent a week without any privileges. LOLOLOLOL

Rue: Fuck you! It was your damn fault.

Jupiter: Is it my fault you can't resist a dare?

Silas: Jup, it's always your fault…

Jupiter: That's right, pick on me. You did see who I ended up with? Wilder! I mean, have you seen how often the guy shifts into his raccoon?

Kodi: He's cute as fuck.

Jupiter: Then you take him and I'll have Bowie.

> **Booker:** *You think it's gonna be that simple? That Hollis will just allow us to swap about when he's listed the damn reasons why we have the assigned PAs?*

> **Silas:** *Tay… your silence is fucking telling. I bet he's dancing naked around whatever effigy he has of Hollis.*

> **Booker:** *Honestly Silas, if I never read this again in any lifetime, it would be too soon and I'm out before you give me anything else to fucking think about.*

Closing the group chat, Booker brooded and stared at his laptop for the longest time before he pulled it back towards him. His hand hovered over the keyboard. He needed to set some ground rules for Frey—for himself—and make sure they stuck to them.

1) No fucking his assistant.

He eyed the screen. His attraction to Frey was an inconvenience, one Booker had in the main ignored because of the distance between them. Jupiter, his brother, had some sort of something going with Frey that automatically put him off limits. Poaching was not cool, despite how many omegas passed through Jupiter's bed.

Half the time, Booker could lead himself to believe the attraction wasn't actually real. If he ignored the fact he enjoyed the company of other fox omegas when he had an itch to scratch. A time or two, he'd signed up to fuck omegas in the clubs they had for single omegas looking for someone to help them through their heats. He'd always picked blond, pretty foxes. His bear had a preference.

Blame me...

The sarcastic tone from his bear got an eye roll from Booker, because he didn't need to justify anything.

2) Spend no time alone with the flirty fox where things could get out of hand.

How workable was that going to be?

Laughter filled his head.

Fuck off!

So adult of you.

You want to go there? His threat got more laughter, and he snarled at the screen, typing on when his bear was rolling around in his mind, clutching his furry sides for effect.

3) Keep him so busy he doesn't need to come with me on any trips.

Booker reread that last one with a sinking heart when Hollis had given them access to all the omega calendars for planning work related trips. They were an essential part of their job. There was no way to avoid them with the change to their workloads. He closed his eyes, rubbing at his throbbing temples.

Screwed... *royally screwed!*

Chapter Three

Frey

Plastering his best flirty smile on his face, Frey tugged on the hem of his pastel green fitted shirt that he'd left untucked over his forest green skinny legged slacks and walked towards Booker's secretary.

He'd given himself a solid two hour talking to, while he'd formulated a plan. He was going to act like he usually did. It seemed to annoy Booker, so he'd lay it on thick. Then it would only be a matter of time before Booker would beg Hollis to switch Frey with one of the others. His smile dimmed a little, but his shoulders rolled as if he was preparing for a fight. In a way, he was because his secrets needed to remain just that. Booker, wanting him permanently, wasn't ever going to be on the cards. The sinking feeling that came with a bout of nausea left him more conflicted but determined when no one wanted to be rejected because they...

"Morning Pam, is his graciousness in?" he greeted the secretary, with as much forced joviality as he could manage.

Pam was a rather frumpy looking woman who liked way too much floral for Frey, especially when she wore differing patterns that clashed horribly. The skirt, which had bold orange and purple hibiscus flowers on it, didn't go with the black, yellow and white daisy top. For someone who worked for a company that was synonymous with high fashion, Pam went against the tide. A part of him cheered her on for being that way, while another part of him remained horrified by the fashion faux pas. Her smile, when she glanced up, made her blue eyes twinkle, revealing her amusement at Frey's choice of name for Booker.

He wasn't gracious. Grumpy suited better, but he wasn't about to go around calling him grumpy pants. Which was often how Frey thought of Booker.

"Why, aren't you looking bright and... green," she said, her gaze skimming down and back up. Crinkles appeared at the sides of her eyes. "If you're looking for Booker, he's not here."

One quick glance at his watch and Frey frowned. "It's after nine."

Pam's flowery shoulders shrugged, and she flicked at her bangs. "He's emailed to say he'd be working from home today."

"Home?" Huh? What the hell was that about? How was Frey supposed to start initiating project 'get Booker to off load him' if he wasn't even in the damn building?

"Yes. He told me he's sent instructions for things he wants you to get started on."

"Has he now!" Frey snapped. His temper flared to life, which was a rare thing for him. He wasn't going to be ignored. No siree!

Pam's brows rose. "Erm... yes." Something about her expression said he'd be the center of office gossip if he wasn't careful. "Is there a problem, Frey?"

The head shake was immediate, Frey giving her an extra wide smile. "No, I'm just thinking while the bear's away, the fox can play."

"I wouldn't let Hollis hear you saying that," she said in warning.

"I was joking," he explained quickly. Clearly Pam didn't get the joke and took him literally. He made his excuse to return to his office via the coffee lounge to check what cake Monty, an otter who could out bake them all when he chose to, had made.

They had a rotation for baking, something that Lane Starling, the owner of the fashion business and his previous boss, had started a couple of years ago. At the same time, he'd also started a group chat on WhatsApp that was part cake chat and part vent. The vent part was usually about one of Lane's eight sons, not that he seemed to mind. In fact, at times, Lane actively encouraged them.

In the beginning, everyone, including Frey, had been wary, but as the weeks and months slipped by they'd kind of forgotten—in the main—that Lane was related to the alphas they complained about.

Back in his office with a wedge of pecan pie, Frey kicked the door shut and went to his tidy desk. He opened the bottom drawer and pulled out the little cake fork he used when he ate at his desk. He didn't like to get his fingers sticky. Placing the plate down next to his keyboard, the fork he sat next to the big slice of pie.

He went to the small cool box he kept a supply of soft drinks in and took out a bottle of Mountain Dew. He poured a drink into the glass he'd washed Friday evening and left on his desk, then he eyed his computer, ready to start.

Frey enjoyed the challenges of his work and, from a young age, became fascinated with how decisions got made around what ended up on the high street from fashion shows. For him, it had led to his choice of degree. He didn't have any talent to create fashion, which was a minor disappointment he lived with when he got to work on bringing runway fashion to the everyday person on the street. Working with Booker would surely allow him to be a part of the process from beginning to end.

Then why are you thinking about sabotaging yourself?

Why do you have to be so sensible? It really wasn't fair.

One of us has to be.

Frey switched on his computer and did what he usually did when his fox annoyed him with reason, shut him out.

The first email in his inbox was from Booker. He opened it.

Frey,

I've attached a list of projects I'm working on for the spring fashion show that Jup is planning to connect with the launch of the season's fashion accessories. The priority right now is what our Native American designer comes up with. Sourcing the materials

and checking with our existing manufacturers, we need to see if
they can produce the level of detail in the designs he's sending me
this week, so we can figure out how to achieve them...

Frey read it through twice, making himself a priority list,
intrigued at what the new designer was going to produce.
Frey had only seen a couple of sample designs and he'd been
majorly enthusiastic at thoughts of owning one of the pretty
leather belts, or a pair of shoes with the design detail on the
sides. A perk of the company was that they could get a dis-
count on new fashion items and obtain them before anyone
else.

When he finished, he was grinning with excitement. His
plans to annoy Booker were forgotten amongst the challenge
of helping the grumpy bear achieve his goals to make the
Milan fashion show an absolute knockout.

"Yeah," he called out absently at a tap on his door.

"You busy?" asked Bowie as he slipped into the room,
looking utterly miserable.

Frey gave him a scrutinizing look and pushed the piece of
pie, which he'd not yet touched, toward the edge of his desk
where there was a spare seat. "You look like you need this."

Bowie was an absolute sweetheart. He wasn't trendy or
kept up to date with what was happening in the world. He
always appeared to be one step behind everyone, but he was
good at what he did, despite that.

His sneakers dragged over the carpet and caught on the
rug. Wide eyed, Frey jumped up and grabbed a hold of
Bowie's arm before he ended up face planting the corner

of the desk. "Bowie," he exclaimed, his pulse getting some morning exercise it didn't like.

"Sorry," Bowie mumbled, looking close to tears.

"It's okay," Frey assured, tugging him down into the empty seat and shoving the plate into his hands, minus the fork. He didn't like anyone licking at his things. "Want to tell me what's got you upset?"

Frey perched his ass on the corner of his desk and stared at Bowie, who was looking at the plate he held. He shrugged his wide shoulders, then looked up at Frey from under his eyelashes. "I heard Kari and Kodi talking..."

The twin brothers looked a lot alike, but they had very differing personalities. Kodi was more of a hothead and Frey had witnessed on more than one occasion Kari work to contain his twin brother's volatile nature.

"Were they talking about us? Who Hollis assigned them?" It was a natural thought process when it was what everyone else was talking about.

A loud sniff and nod were Bowie's answer. His big brown eyes gleaming with tears.

Frey sighed at the urge to go and kick an alpha in the butthole. He came off the desk and wrapped his arms as best as he could around Bowie's broad shoulders, avoiding the plate he clung on to.

"What did they say?"

The tension that came from Bowie got Frey bracing. "Kodi said he felt sorry for Kari getting the dumb one."

Frey jerked back, nearly knocking the plate out of Bowie's hand in outrage. "He said that!"

"Sort of," he mumbled, picking up the pie and taking a huge bite.

Eyes narrowing on Bowie, Frey softly said, "Either he said it, or he didn't?"

"He said I was always a step behind everyone," he mumbled around the mouthful of pie. He swallowed thankfully because pecan pie in someone's mouth did not look appetizing at all. "That makes me dumb."

As the 'a step behind everyone' comment was kind of true, Frey considered how best to deal with the situation. He would never be cruel. He rubbed Bowie's shoulder when he took another bite of the pie.

"You go at your pace, you always have. Answer me this, do you get the job done for the alphas in the allotted time frame?" He did. A plodder by nature, that worked for Bowie well enough. He never missed a detail.

His reply came in the form of a nod, thankfully keeping the pie to himself.

"There you go. How does that make you dumb? You're thorough and definitely a details person. If you don't keep step with others, is that wrong?"

Bowie stared at Frey, his head tilting to the side as he finished chewing on the pie. "I've never thought of it like that."

Frey grinned, pleased to have helped. "Whatever works. No one way is right for everyone. Be you, Bowie. You're absolutely adorable." Frey came forward and kissed Bowie's head.

He sniffed at it.

Bubblegum!

Bowie gave Frey an odd look and touched his head where Frey had been sniffing.

"Your hair smells of bubblegum!"

"It's a new shampoo I found." He clutched the plate in front of him. "Erm... you aren't flirting with me, are you? I like you an all, but... you know... not like that." He was bright pink by the time he'd finished and was back to staring at the plate of half eaten pie.

Frey ran a hand over the silky scented strands and teased, keeping a straight face. "Are you sure?"

At Bowie's alarmed look, Frey gave in and laughed. "I'm joking. I like big, hot alphas."

He lied... *kind of.*

Chapter Four

Booker

Two weeks later...

Life fucking sucked, and Booker had a wealth of frustration stored up inside him. Taylin—or it was purely Frey and his flirty behavior—needed to stop. Booker had already been at boiling point after the trip on the jet at how many times—thirty, he'd counted—Frey had smiled at everyone but him.

Staying away from the office hadn't lasted long when Dad and Popi had pointed out working from home wasn't the best way to work with his brothers to achieve a common goal. He had no argument that wouldn't alert them to his 'Frey problem', so he'd gone back into the office and put up with Frey's sexy sassiness that... irritated him no end.

Yep... irritation is what is causing what's happening in your pants.

Don't even start with me. Didn't you see how weird Taylin was being around Frey?

Taylin was acting fucking odd and not just around Hollis, which was normal for him with the whole 'I'm pretending not to be interested in Hollis, but so wanna get him naked'. Booker hadn't missed how Taylin had done his best to avoid sitting next to Frey. This was what he usually did around Hollis and raised some suspicion on Booker's part. Was Taylin now interested in Frey, too?

He'd gone through their recent group chat on the flight, and nothing stood out to alert Booker that Taylin's obsession with Hollis had changed... but something was off.

He stomped after the porter, pushing their suitcases on a trolley as Hollis handed out room key cards, having been the one to book them in.

Booker stopped at the door and pressed the card to the electronic pad. The click of the door got him pushing it open and freezing when he noticed it wasn't a hotel room but a suite. Three doors led off the main sitting area. He glanced back at Taylin. "What's this?"

Taylin distractedly glanced back, his brows furrowing. "Yours and Frey's suite?" he answered in a way that implied Booker should know this information.

"A suite?" Holy fuck. "We're sharing with who?" he exclaimed, stopping Kodi and Rue, who were ten feet in front of him.

There were some gasps from those behind Booker, but he was too worried waiting for Taylin's response to notice who they came from.

"Your PAs. Rue and Monty, Kodi and Lennon, you and Frey and me and Hollis. It makes sense. You can work with your PA in between visits and not waste any time." The color Taylin's cheeks were and how he avoided looking at Hollis made a whole lot of sense when he had the major hots for Hollis.

For Booker, though, being close was not his idea of fun. Hell no. He wanted to rant about how Taylin was shoving him into a situation he'd, up to now, spent most of his time avoiding.

"We are?" Rue was the first to recover, his gaze narrowing on Taylin. "Why wasn't this shared before?"

"Yeah, Taylin, why is that?" Kodi asked in a sinister tone that suggested he was about to go off on one.

Booker held in his own angry frustration, not wanting a scene in the hallway. "Does it matter? We're here now and I'm fucking knackered." Booker looked back into the room. "We each have our own bedroom, so it's not like we're sharing a bed."

Booker squashed the sliver of disappointment he felt as everyone filed off into their suites. The PAs looked as unamused as Booker, though he'd done his best not to glance in Frey's direction and see how he was taking this news.

Inside the room, Booker decided he needed a big ass shovel to dig a trench between him and Frey at the sight of conjoined bedrooms to the bathroom. Had Hollis arranged the rooms, or had this been Taylin's idea of payback for all his snippy comments about Hollis? He wouldn't put it past his brother, he could be sneaky like that!

Frey's sweet scent was filling the room, and they'd literally only been in the place five minutes. Enough time for Booker to stomp to the minibar and grab a beer. He unscrewed the top and downed it, hoping it would remove some of the images the conjoined bathroom gave him. A naked Frey, all golden skin wet and slick...

"It's alright if I take this room?" Frey asked, his usual flirty tone absent.

A throbbing developed at Booker's temples as he twisted to glance at Frey, the bottle held loosely in his fingers. He wanted to kick Taylin's ass for organizing a trip that required Frey to come with them. Now this! How was he supposed to stick to the rules? How?

When Frey gave him an arched look, Booker shrugged. "Makes no odds to me, take whichever one you want."

Frey's cute little nose wrinkled, and he sniffed loudly, flouncing off into the bedroom and slamming the door.

What was his fucking problem?

This wasn't Booker's fault.

Booker plonked down the empty bottle and reached to grab another beer. He could see it was going to be a long night. They'd already eaten on the jet, so it wasn't like they needed to leave the suite and it was late.

Going to the sofa that was big enough for someone like Frey to sit on, but not so much for him, Booker sat and felt the base springs poke his ass in protest. He drank the beer and brooded.

The sounds of the shower running got him groaning and his eyes shutting to block images of what lay beyond the door. Was his skin as smooth and silky as it looked?

Booker's eyes fired open, and he got up off the couch to pace the carpeted floor. It didn't take long for his nose to twitch at how Frey's chocolate and spice scent wafted under the door and clouded the entire suite.

No matter where he went, even locked in his bedroom minutes later, where he'd sought refuge, nothing stopped it from invading his sensitive nose.

Why are we hiding in here?

We're not hiding?

You locked the door. His bear was too fucking quick to point out.

The smell of the fox was driving him to distraction. His bear was acting like a dick and that was before it envisioned itself curled around the little fox, rubbing his furry body against the fox's, scenting it. Something that Booker had to take the blame for when he'd decided to research exactly what a Fennec fox looked like.

A moment of weakness, that's what it was, after he overheard Monty and Bowie discussing Frey's animal.

His bear considered the larger ears of the fennec fox to be utterly adorable. His pointy face Booker imagined were similar in both forms. Frey's features were perfectly proportioned *and pretty.*

He snapped his teeth together at how his bear kept doing that. Drip feeding him comments about the fox at the most inopportune moments. Like now when he was dragging off his clothes, trying to cool the fuck down.

He's delectable.

I get it. You like him.

Why can't you just admit it, he piques your interest and has done for a long time.

I'm not having this conversation.

Why? Because you know I'm right.

The knowing chortle that came through left him growling in the empty room.

"Everything okay in there?" Frey asked, tapping on the door that led into the bathroom.

Booker had a moment of concern when he glanced down at his naked body and then back at the door. Was it locked?

He launched himself at the door, his cock thwacking off his leg and making his balls throb very unpleasantly as he hit wood.

The thud resounded around the room and Frey squealed in the bathroom. "What on earth? Are you okay in there? Did you fall?"

"I'm fine," he snarled breathlessly, staying put right against the door in case the fox decided he wanted to investigate. Booker tried to catch his breath, reminding himself of his three rules.

"Are you sure?" Frey asked, sounding utterly unconvinced. And so he should, because Booker wasn't fucking fine at all. The fox was right on the other side of the door, wet and smelling like a little piece of heaven.

"Yep." He would be as soon as he got his heart to make its way down from the back of his throat, where it had lodged itself with the thought of Frey bursting into the room and them both being naked... together.

What's wrong with you?

Nothing... abso-fucking-lutely nothing, he snapped so forcibly his mind rang with the words.

Back was the laughter giving Booker a headache when it took another two minutes—he counted—for Frey to leave the bathroom.

He slumped against the door and blew out a noisy breath. He was going to kill his brother slowly—very fucking slowly.

Chapter Five

Frey

Being trapped in the suite working with Booker, who fluctuated from growly to morose, was wearing on Frey's nerves.

He was doing his best. Counting to ten once more, he worked to keep his tone fun and flirty. "I've already answered that question... twice," he said, adding a big dose of sugary sweetness while his eyes drilled a hole through the top of Booker's downcast head.

He didn't look up from his laptop, which was perched on his knees. He looked very uncomfortable, and the way he constantly moved on the tiny couch suggested Frey was right.

Declining to come and sit at the table by Frey should have relieved him, only he couldn't forget exactly how vehemently Booker had refused the day before. Frey forgot himself and sniffed indignantly.

It didn't matter that Frey hadn't wanted the bear to sit next to him in such close quarters when he smelled so damn sexy. Whatever the bear sprayed on himself, it should come with a warning. 'Makes sane foxes want to sit on bears and never get off'.

"What?" Booker finally replied, glancing up, his chocolate brown eyes revealing his confusion.

Was he listening to me at all?

"The Devant account," he smiled brightly, "I filed the invoices back at the office *after* paying the outstanding amount for the handbags we purchased for delivery next month to all the Starling department stores."

Booker nodded, his gaze back on his screen. "Good, what about Rockwell?"

Frey wasn't sure how he kept his cool as he gave Booker the same information he'd given him two hours earlier, and the day before. Was the bear having some sort of 'hormonal imbalance thing' that affected memory?

They continued in the same way, right until they needed to pack their bags to head out for the visit to the factory that was connected to Design Detailing & Co. They were leaving straight after the visit to fly to their next destination. Packing was a relief when it gave Frey some time to gather himself. Being flirty took a lot of hard work, especially when the person he flirted with wasn't paying any damn attention.

They exited the suite when Taylin knocked to let them know it was time to leave. Booker offered to carry their bags to reception, but Frey refused.

"I'm perfectly capable." He could carry his own bags, thank you very much!

He stuck his nose in the air, feeling very aggrieved and not relishing thoughts of what the next hotel suite would bring. But one thing was for sure, Frey wasn't going to put up with having to repeat himself ten times because someone wasn't paying attention. Heck no!

At the two cars they'd organized to transport them, Frey was happy to be riding in a separate car to Booker, away from his smell. Frey sank back against the leather seat and moaned without thought. "Booker is driving me to distraction with his forgetfulness. I never noticed he was like this." He glanced at Monty. "You've worked closely with him before, was he having memory problems?" Frey's fox fretted there could be something seriously wrong with the bear.

Monty pushed back his hair and sagged a second later. "Not that I remember. I'm having some issues of my own with Rue."

"Please, you wanna try working with 'I've got no control over my temper' Kodi. The wolf needs to take a damn chill pill." Lennon's scowl was so unusual. Frey stared at him for a moment longer, then glanced at Hollis when he had no comeback about them being professional.

His taut features gave off a vibe of worry they seldom got from their boss.

"You okay?" Frey asked, shoving aside his own worries when Hollis didn't answer immediately. He might be their boss, but they were all friends, too.

"Just… tired," he finished lamely.

What was this about? Frey glanced at Lennon and Monty, who wore matching looks of concern as he mouthed, "You know what's wrong with him?"

They both shook their heads.

Was this to do with his new promotion? Frey fluffed at his hair, watching Hollis, who stared out the window.

"You sure?" Frey wasn't sure why he was pushing when he didn't like it when others did it to him.

"Of course. It's just with the company delaying us for so long, it's just made things trickier... for the next visit."

Frey could hear that Hollis was fobbing him off. It wasn't like him, and Frey fidgeted in his seat, feeling out of sorts after the last few days. What was up with everyone? Why did Derick and Lane have to retire and upset the balance?

He had no answers and was actually relieved when the car pulled through gates and slowed to a stop in front of a huge factory building, because it meant he could think about something else.

A chill ran over Frey's exposed skin as he exited the car, and his fox whined at the feeling coming from the place in front of them. Frey was sensitive to more than he let on. Their eyesight wasn't the best, but they made up for it with their sense of smell and hearing. He didn't need to step into the building to hear someone issuing threats inside.

Add that to what he could smell, and Frey was left struggling to breathe. Blood, fear and unclean bodies. They hadn't stepped inside, and Frey didn't want to. The place triggered the kind of fear he'd once felt being trapped with an alpha who wanted to...

He released a shuddery breath that hurt his chest and shoved away the horror of the past when Booker, Taylin, Rue and Kodi exited the other car, appearing to have none of his concerns about the place with how they acted. Couldn't they feel something was wrong?

He wanted someone to hold his hand, to help him step inside the building, only he didn't want to ask when they might question the reasons. Frey tucked his hands into his jacket pockets and balled them as he followed, far slower than the others.

Once inside, Frey's innards shook as the awful scent increased and made his fox crazy. Despair... fear, they were all Frey could process.

He tagged on at the back and watched the omegas at the workbenches. There was a stark difference between how he behaved with those he worked with and those in the factory. It made it impossible to ignore there was something majorly wrong when Frey considered the threats he had heard issued.

The place was like an icebox, yet what the omegas wore was threadbare and dirty. They smelled terrible. How could one factory find a whole bunch of omegas that didn't like to wash?

Frey couldn't see how. In fact, he couldn't understand the behavior, not one little bit... unless they had no choice?

Amatus, a huge alpha, bragged about the quality of the work the omegas produced, not once referring to any by name. He never once looked in their direction.

Could Booker, Taylin or one of the others', not see that? It was like they... had no value.

Frey understood that feeling. He understood it all too well.

The alphas stationed around the room weren't working. They were... watching. Watching for what? For an omega to steal something?

Frey didn't think so. They were sinister. His skin crawled from the oppressive feelings.

Booker spoke, but Frey wasn't listening. His attention was on one tiny omega whose hands shook so badly that Frey became convinced he could hear the bones in his rail thin hands clicking together. There were marks on his arms that sent chills through him.

Frey couldn't get a read off the others with him because he was too self-absorbed with what he was terrified was happening to the omegas.

When they left, all Frey could think about was how those omegas had to stay behind with those alphas.

In the car, he shuddered and hugged himself. "Something bad is going on in there," he blurted out, needing to say something now they weren't within hearing distance of those inside the building.

"It smelled so bad." Lennon muttered, his eyes gleaming.

"My animal went into hiding." Monty's voice cracked, and he buried his face in his hands.

Hollis slung his arm around Monty's shoulders. "Let's trust that Taylin and the others will deal with this." He hugged Monty a little closer, rubbing at his arm. "Booker looked like he was going to punch Amatus, despite how positive he was about the craftmanship."

"He wasn't the only one," Frey added, with enough fire that everyone turned to look at him wide eyed. "What? Those omegas were frightened. I could smell it. See it. They had marks on them." Marks that Frey had worn after his escape. Someone was hurting them.

There was a heavy silence for the remainder of the trip to the airport to fly to their next destination.

Boarded and sat on his own, Frey stared out the window after they'd taxied down the runaway and taken off. The city below disappeared, but all Frey's thoughts were on those he'd left behind. He'd listened to the initial conversation going on around him when there'd been mention that Booker had rung Derick Starling, their dad, to find a way to buy the company and the factory.

It was a good thing to do, and that Booker was the one to suggest it, or so it seemed, revealed exactly what a big heart he had. It was gratifying that he'd not been alone with feeling the wrongness of the place or those alphas. Yet Frey couldn't get past the fact they'd walked away.

Hours later, booked into their next hotel for the next visit, Frey hadn't shaken off a thought that clung to him.

"Do you think those omegas in the workshop get to go home?" The quiet question slipped out before Frey could reconsider where they were. They'd come to the restaurant in the hotel as no one had been hungry on the jet.

"What do you mean?" Booker stared at him, and Frey could see the worry in his taut features. Frey heard the chair groan under Booker's enormous bulk and where he'd usually find some amusement at that, he had none.

The tears Frey had been holding on to decided now was the time to make an appearance, like a prima donna. He looked around the table that was tucked into the corner of the restaurant that offered them more privacy for conversation.

"They were so... lost." His nose wrinkled, and he cursed under his breath at the tear that rolled down his cheek, plopping onto his plate. He used the back of his hand to dash at the next tear that fell without his permission. He hated crying in public, but couldn't seem to stop when it came with a huge dose of suffocating sadness.

"That atmosphere was full of despair. Couldn't you smell it? I thought we'd talk about it. Why aren't we?" He hiccuped out a sob. "How do they cope with it?"

Booker wordlessly laid an open palmed hand face up on the table, offering it to him. Never more had Frey needed the touch of an—alpha—Booker. He'd need to think about that later. Right then, he didn't overthink 'the why' and reached out. Booker's meaty fist engulfed his hand, revealing just how much of a size difference there was between them. The fear Frey lived with about such things didn't come, and that was something else he'd need to think about.

Frey didn't take his shimmery gaze from Booker's, for once he gave in to the need and touched Booker like he wanted to.

"I don't know," Taylin replied solemnly.

"We're gonna fix it," Booker said with a fierceness that made Frey have to resist squirming in his seat with the effect it had on him. For the first time in years, he felt his body respond with sexual attraction.

Ohhhh.

"Dad is working on it now. And we weren't talking about it because"—his gaze went to the tables close by—"having this type of conversation where it can be overheard isn't how we do business. What we need to do is have a little patience."

Booker's words floated right over Frey's head when he stroked his big thumb over the back of his hand, looking solely at him. "I promise you we'll go back and fix those shitheads." The growl he released was full of menace.

Frey gathered himself when a giggle tickled the back of his throat at how menacing Booker sounded.

Why wasn't he scared?

He dropped his fork to swipe at his tear-stained cheeks, holding on to the roughened palm. "It's so hard to think they don't have any choices." He used the anger that fought past the sadness. "Just make sure to let me know when you are going to do some head smashing. I'll want to watch."

Those around the table laughed, but Booker's gaze became thoughtful as he eyed Frey in a way that made his heart beat a little faster.

Hollis's loud groan when he nudged Frey's shoulder shifted his attention to Hollis. "How can you look so cute and love violence?"

Knowing what they expected from him, he tucked the sadness away for now and gave his usual flirty grin. "There's something hot about watching an alpha kick ass." Frey glanced at the other PAs. "Don't you think so?"

He returned his attention to Booker, when no one an-swered him. Which he kind of expected. "Big and fierce is..." he licked at his plump lips, "hot." He added enough sass to cause Booker to cough hard enough that the table shook.

Frey's hand landed with a thud on the table with the speed Booker let go. Frey hid his grin when Booker didn't appear to notice because he was rubbing both hands over his rather flushed face.

Were his hands trembling?

Have I done that?

A curl of excitement at the prospect left Frey unnerved as he eyed the big bear. His worry about being trapped in an-other suite for a couple of days didn't seem so bad, if maybe it gave him time to... test the theory.

Chapter Six

Booker

Frey's emotional outburst during dinner left Booker having a hard time trying to disassociate himself from the feisty fox who wanted him to go kick those shit heads in the balls. But that wasn't the only thing on his mind, fuck no.

Taylin and Hollis were...

He unbuttoned his shirt and hooked it on the back of the bathroom door, doing his best to avoid thinking about exactly what Hollis and Taylin were getting up to. Who the fuck goes on a work trip knowing they were going to go into heat?

Hollis's announcement about his brother going to help him get through his heat had floored them all. Rue and Kodi hadn't noticed what was going on, so Booker was pretty confident nobody noticed his distraction over Frey.

He did not need his brothers getting on his case. He was already struggling with seeing this other side of Frey. What they'd found at the factory had given Booker a new insight into Frey. He'd believed that Frey was fickle. That he was only concerned about himself and getting naked with whomever was interested. There was no faking the emotions he'd displayed and now Booker thought about how he'd behaved in the factory, it gave him a whole new perspective on the little fox.

He ran a hand over his bearded jaw and stared at himself in the bathroom mirror. What the fuck was he going to do? Resisting Frey was much easier when he thought he was shallow... now... fuck!

To top it off, he now couldn't decide if he was envious of Taylin or terrified for him about what it all meant. It was a hard call and now, back in their suite with Frey on the opposite side of the door, Booker's head was a fucked up mess.

Naked, pissed, and needing a distraction, he turned on the shower. He wanted to wash the smell of the factory from his skin, making him feeling dirty long after the visit.

"You going to be long?" Frey's voice penetrated through the door and over the sound of the water.

"Not too long," he called back, not thinking too hard about him being naked near Frey. It was getting harder.

He closed his eyes and groaned in despair when the vision of the omegas they'd found abused and treated like slaves, replaced Frey's sunny smile.

The work they produced on the leather accessories Booker wanted for the next season's fashion launch was stunningly beautiful, he would not deny it. But at what cost to them?

The unanswered questions pounded at his brain.

What were they doing to those men?

Frey was right, they'd left them there... alone and suffering. He'd smelled fear. It burned his nose as he'd walked around, watching as the omegas at the workbenches had cowered away. The silence was oppressive, as were the stares directed at the omegas from the weapon wielding alphas. He fucking hated that they'd had to leave. Despite the call they'd had with Dad to talk over their options, it didn't sit well with Booker knowing something was seriously wrong. Dad had been clear that to achieve their prime directive—buying the place—they had to keep their cards close to their chest. Walk away and fight behind the scenes, especially now they'd found out the place was owned by divergent haters.

Booker had always supported the underdog. It was how he'd found his way into Lane and Derick Starling's family. How they'd become his life raft in a storm of his own making by fighting to protect his friend—fighting his family.

Seeing where his thoughts were headed—right down the toilet—he stepped into the shower. The hot, steamy water poured over him from a rainfall shower head and he growled in pleasure, impressed that he could indeed stand tall and not have to bow like normal in hotel room bathrooms. At six foot six, he often had to slouch, which he hated.

Reaching for the shower gel, he flipped the lid and rolled his eyes when the spicy scent was all Frey.

Was life going to cut him break?

He eyed the bottle and cursed when he realized he'd left his own wash bag in his room. He held his breath and washed himself super-fast. Out of the shower, he dripped on the floor, grabbing a towel to drape around his hips. Water drops caught in his chest hair and ran down his stomach. He went into his bedroom and grabbed his toilet bag. Back in the bathroom, he brushed his teeth and plopped his toothbrush into the glass on the counter, next to Frey's. At the intimacy of such an act, he snatched the toothbrush right back out of the glass, staring at the one sitting harmlessly in the glass. He gulped when an unbidden thought popped into his head.

Did Frey have a boyfriend... several boyfriends?

None of your damn business!

The fox flirted with everyone, and Booker reminded himself Jupiter had already laid claim to the fox, which put him in the 'none of your business' column. He'd never ask Jupiter about it either... it wasn't his business. Frey was off limits.

Not that Booker wanted him to be in his limit zone...

Still staring at the pink toothbrush, he shook himself visibly, when he couldn't decide if he should put the toothbrush back in the glass.

Sad... plain sad.

A loud knocking on the door made Booker whirl and fling the toothbrush in his fright. "Can you hurry please... I need to pee."

A vision of a wet patch on the carpet they'd have to explain got him reaching to pick up the toothbrush and fling it in on the counter, before opening the door without any thought about his attire.

Frey's alarmed squeal was loud enough he made Booker's ears ring and bring forth his protective nature.

"What's wrong," he came past Frey, putting him behind him, searching the room for whatever had caused the fox's distress.

"What is it?" he demanded, confused when he could see nothing that would cause Frey to make a noise like that.

He spun back to Frey, who was staring at him so oddly he had to take stock for a moment. Booker's eyes narrowed as he tilted his head. Water dripped from his hair onto his shoulders... *his bare shoulders.*

He glanced down at his hairy chest.

Shit!

When he returned his attention to Frey, he hadn't moved or replied and continued to eye him... hungrily?

Booker's cock stirred at the idea, intrigued. He tested the theory by moving a hand to stroke down the wet fur on his chest.

Frey's eyes tracked the move, his Adam's apple bobbing when Booker's hand stopped at the treasure trail that led beneath the knotted towel. He paused and watched closely as his hand took the path back up his chest.

Frey blushed a pretty pink, the tip of his tongue coming out between little white teeth as his eyes hooded.

Interesting!

Shagged your brother!

The reminder got him lifting the hand to wave in front of Frey's face. "What's with you?" he asked, tongue in cheek. The fox liked to flirt. That had to mean he enjoyed what happened after that, didn't it?

Frey blinked and looked at Booker directly, the color in his cheeks darkening as he hopped from one foot to the other, reminding Booker why he'd come out of the bathroom in the first place. "I... erm... yeah... what?"

Booker bit the inside of his cheek to hold back his laughter and pointed to the open door. Frey looked at him nonplussed until Booker nudged him toward the bathroom. "You need to pee."

"Ohhh..." he muttered, and darted for the door, slamming it shut behind him. When Booker heard the lock click, only then did he release the laughter tickling the back of his throat. It felt good after the day and evening they'd had.

His amusement fled as he looked about and realized he was in Frey's bedroom. He had scattered his personal things about the room. There on the bed was a pale pink set of what looked like silky nightwear.

Booker backed his way to the door, his cock tenting the towel as he never took his eyes off the bed. He reached blindly behind, hearing sounds in the bathroom that said he needed to escape, and now. Out the door, he ran—yep, ran like the devil was chasing him—back to his room, where he slammed the door and leaned against it, panting.

If his brothers could only see him now! Running from a tiny fox... what the fuck was happening to him?

Chapter Seven

Delicious & Vicious

Monty: *I've left Nutella cheesecake in the coffee room if anyone is interested.*

Frey: *Do bears shit in the woods?*

Isley: *What is your fascination with bears? Guys, scroll back, is it just me that can see a theme?*

Frey: *I work with a bear, of course I'm gonna use bear references… it's natural.*

Bowie: *If that's the case, then why isn't everyone using their alpha brother animal half?*

Wilder: *Maybe Hollis is 'cause he's getting all the 'wolfy' love and Frey can only imagine getting naked with Booker's big, hairy ass?*

Frey: *How do you know Booker's ass is hairy?????*

Wilder: *He's a bear… of course his ass will be furry! Why am I feeling like I'm missing something here? You aren't…*

Frey: *I am not.*

Wilder: *You sure about that?*

Frey: *What's that supposed to mean?*

Wilder: *What do you think?*

Hollis: *Is this the time to play twenty questions? We all have deadlines to meet for the upcoming fashion show. A fashion show you all requested to attend...*

Frey: *Point taken.*

Bowie: *Sorry, Boss.*

Isley: *I don't think I wanna go anymore because Laken will be going, and he's mean!*

Hollis: *Isley, please come to my office. We need to talk about this.*

Ziggy: *I'll plate up some cheesecake and take it to Hollis's office. That'll help.*

Bowie: *I wish I liked omegas. Ziggy, you'd make a great boyfriend.*

Chapter Eight

Frey

"I can't stay for the meeting with Sawyer's lawyer, I've an appointment. I'll only be gone for about an hour."

Frey knew that the energy Booker released could fluctuate dramatically with his mood, so he had learned to read it like a barometer. It was the only way to try and get a feel for what might come his way. Right now, it told him that there was a storm brewing, and it was heading right for him. Why couldn't Booker, just for once, check his calendar in advance?

"What do you mean you've got an appointment and can't stay? It's your job to be here for these types of meetings." Booker's snappy growl was enough to bring a burning to Frey's nose. Yup, he had totally pegged Booker's mood.

Everything he feared about this appointment and what it meant for him was ready to pour out of him in a flood of tears that Booker would absolutely hate. Frey was struggling more and more with his emotions, just as his doctor had said would happen if he continued taking the heat blockers beyond their recommended five years.

He sniffed, just once, but it was more than enough to get Booker out of his seat, towering over his desk. His hands slammed down on the papers scattered over it and he shook his head, making his dark waves move. "Not in here... you hear me? No tears... this is a workplace... not a... not a nursery for sniffling foxes."

Frey wanted to see the funny side of the absolute panic coming off the enormous bear at the mere threat of a tear. Only he couldn't. There was nothing funny about his situation and he needed to attend his appointment. He had to look at least partly in control if he wanted to argue his case for continuing the drugs. They had become his lifeline to continuing the pretense that all was well.

He sucked in a shaky breath and boldly looked Booker in the eye. "I never cry at work," Frey insisted, because in the past this was the absolute truth... not so much of late. "And I put this appointment in your calendar last week so you would know in advance I wouldn't be available."

He sniffed again, this time more in indignation. "It's not my fault you didn't check it and as I said, I'll only be gone for about an hour. I'll be back in plenty of time for the four o'clock meeting with Laken."

Met with suspicion at the crack in his voice, Frey chewed on his lower lip, holding Booker's gaze.

Booker thumped his ass into his seat and jabbed a finger at Frey, looking less than impressed. "Make sure you are."

Frey didn't wait to see if he was going to say more. Darting for the door, he slipped out, closing it behind him and carrying on down the corridor. He avoided making eye contact with anyone, trying his best to give off the vibe he wasn't in a hurry.

He didn't breathe easy until he was in the underground car park and headed to his car. The lights flashed as he approached, signaling the doors had opened. The fob in his pocket automatically did its job when Frey couldn't get his mind to work in any semblance of order. He slipped inside, hands trembling.

He did everything on automatic pilot, his mind utterly chaotic, making focusing on anything impossible. Panic did that to him, and it was probably best when thoughts of what would come in the doctor's office would be something that could derail the life he had created to hide the truth about himself.

Shivers came as he started the engine and headed to his appointment.

Exiting the car park, he groaned at the heavy rain bouncing off the hood. The sky was dark and moody, matching his mood perfectly. Rain lashed down on the windscreen, ensuring he took his time and paid attention to what traffic there was.

The doctor's building was five minutes by car from his office and traffic was light. Frey suspected that was due to the storm that had blown in that morning, as the weather reporter had predicted.

Parking in the near empty lot next to the two-storey office, Frey didn't bother grabbing his umbrella when the wind would whip it inside out in seconds. No one wanted to look like Mary Poppins flying with an inside out umbrella, despite how cute he'd look in his sparkly sneakers and bright pink raincoat.

He darted for the door and even though he was but two or three seconds outside, his hair became plastered to his head and rain had seeped down his collar, wetting his sweater. The receptionist, Clare, glanced up from the computer screen with a ready smile. She'd worked here as long as Frey could remember. And since he'd been coming since he was a toddler, it was a long time.

"Frey, so lovely to see you." She glanced at the window, furrows appearing between her brows. "It's wild out there. I can see the rain hasn't eased at all. Do you want me to get you a towel to dry your hair?" Up out of her seat before she'd finished speaking, she skipped to a cupboard that Frey knew held all manner of things a person might need.

It never failed to make him smile the way she moved. Frey long since convinced himself she put springs into her shoes to make her bounce that way.

"That would be great," he replied, although she was already grabbing him the towel.

"Dr. Hockings is on time, so he shouldn't keep you waiting more than a minute or two. His last patient left ten minutes ago, so he'll be writing up his notes." She handed him the towel, offering him a sympathetic smile.

Two swipes to catch the offending drops, he returned the damp towel to her waiting hands, then Frey sat in one of the comfy leather chairs that had originally been a weird mustard color but were recently updated to the classy brown they were now.

He cast an eye over the varied selection of magazines on the coffee table in front of him. Most came from Clare and her husband, he had learned in one of the many conversations he had with her when the doctor ran late. An eclectic taste from motor mechanics, muscle cars, fashion and beauty, along with one or two on planes and trains.

Clare, if not busy, would sit and gossip with him about models. He could see today wasn't one of those days as she went back to work at her computer.

Too nervous to bother to read, Frey pulled out his iPhone and scrolled through Delicious & Vicious group chat, finding none of the usual humor at reading the threads of conversation.

The phone rang on Clare's desk and Frey swallowed hard, figuring out it was to say he could go on up and see the doctor. He got up when not two seconds later Clare said, "Yes, your next appointment is here, I'll send him right up."

Frey smiled his thanks and walked to the door leading to the second floor. The smell of the place, a little disinfectant and a lot of air freshener, didn't help with the nerves doing a swing dance inside him when he reached the second floor.

Hyperventilating, his hand continued to tremble. Frey quickly tapped on the white door, like ripping a plaster off just to get it over with.

It opened to reveal a gray-haired and bearded man with a weathered face that spoke of the many hours Dr. Hockings spent outdoors. He loved to keep fit through cycling and hiking.

As usual, Dr. Hockings wore a gray suit and white shirt. Not once had Frey seen him in anything else in all the years he could remember. It was like his doctor's uniform instead of a white coat. Which Frey didn't mind, not one bit as it made the doctor appear more human and allowed Frey to feel a little more relaxed. Today, that was not the case.

"Hi, Dr. Hockings. It's good to see you," he lied. "You must be glad to be working inside with how awful the weather is out there today."

Frey knew he was waffling, but his nerves wouldn't let him stop as the doctor stepped to the side to allow him into the consulting room.

An examining couch, a chair, and a desk with a computer on it were all the furniture in the room. The pictures on the cream walls were all of body parts and descriptions of how they worked. On the one large window sill below the frosted glass window sat a hip, a knee and a spine model.

"You too, Frey. Take a seat and let me pull up your blood work."

Frey sat fidgeting with the cuff of his raincoat, determined not to jump to any conclusions about the results and whether he could persuade the doctor to give him more medication. He'd spent most of last night stressing about it and hadn't slept at all. Something Booker noticed this morning and pointed out.

"So, I'll get to the point of why I asked you to make an appointment." Dr. Hockings reached for the cup of water on his desk and took a sip.

Frey didn't need the doctor to tell him the blood results were bad. Dr. Hockings only ever took a drink of water when he was collecting his thoughts on how best to deliver news that was mostly unpleasant. Everyone thought Frey was flighty, which he was, to a degree, but his past also meant that he was excellent at reading people. It was a knack, and if he was correct, Dr. Hockings was worried.

Glass down, he wet his lips and gave Frey a sympathetic smile. "As I explained last time you were in, it's been nearly six years since you started taking the heat blockers. You have all the literature on the side effects, so I won't bore you again with those." His expression became very serious. "My problem, Frey, is that I was right to worry about continuing with the drugs after your insistence last time. What I hoped wouldn't happen... has. Your hormone levels are very low. So low that I'm doubtful they will return to a level that would allow you to conceive when you choose to find a mate."

Frey blinked slowly, digesting what he'd secretly worried about for the last six months. "I won't ever be able to get pregnant."

"I can't say never, but with your blood picture and your long-term history of taking the drugs to prevent your heat, I'd say it's unlikely. I'm sorry."

"It's not your fault. It's mine. I knew the risks." Saying it aloud made reality sting like he'd stumbled into a bee's hive.

"Does that mean I won't be able to have any more? Drugs, I mean?" This was Frey's biggest fear.

Pregnancy. A person had to be having sex with an alpha for that to happen. He had no alpha, nor was he having sex of any kind, even alone, so it was a moot point.

"You are now susceptible to other ramifications such as mood swings, emotional outbursts, decrease in sex drive, to name but a few if you continue to take the drug. In good conscience, I am no longer able to prescribe them for you."

Even knowing it was coming didn't help the physical blow those words landed, causing him to jerk back in his seat. Horror etched into his features as the first tear rolled down his pale cheeks.

Dr. Hockings leaned forward and patted his knee. "I can refer you to a therapist... to talk about your past so you can—"

"No." He sniffed and scrubbed at his wet face. "I've had therapy and their suggestion to... yeah, I can't do what they want." He could, but only with one person he trusted implicitly—Booker. And Frey didn't have the courage to ask the bear to help when he really wanted... *more than someone to help him through a heat without scaring the hell out of him.*

Ask him.

No!

He rose, needing out before he broke down and begged when he already knew that was useless. "I'll figure it out."

His fox remained pushy and focused on the bear. *He's interested, I know he is.*

Booker would never want us.

Frey quashed the idea even as his fox made a rude noise.

The gentle bear would never be interested in a defective fox, not in a million years.

How do you know if you don't ask?

Chapter Nine

Booker

If there was steam coming out of his ears, then who could blame him?

Who?

First Taylin remained AWOL after going off with Hollis doing who knew what and now Frey was doing this, *'I've plans and it's in the calendar'* routine. Who the fuck looked in someone else's calendar? He knew having to take on the responsibility of knowing what someone else was doing was going to blow up in his face. And here he was, being proven right.

The problem with being right was that whatever put the light of fear in Frey's eyes meant Booker now carried a huge fucking knot of anxiety in his gut. It persisted as Frey left, darting out the door, reeking of fear.

Booker's bear was as stompy as him as he stalked out of his office. "If anyone is looking for me, tell them I'll be back in an hour. And postpone the meeting with Sawyer," he added as an afterthought as he passed his secretary's desk, not once looking at her. He didn't have time to get into a conversation, not when Frey was rushing off.

Seeing Frey head for the stairs, Booker frowned, doing something he'd kick his own ass for later. He followed.

What had Frey acting out of sorts... frightened?

Booker had somehow, since they'd come home from the trip, become more attuned to Frey's moods. He had picked up that morning that something was bothering the fox. Despite his groaning desk full of work, he headed after Frey, keeping his distance. Regardless of his size, Booker could, when he needed to, blend with his surroundings.

He caught Frey driving away and contemplated for two seconds what he should do before he got in his car. The driving need to make sure he was okay had refused to release its vice-like grip around his heart.

It was fucked up.

A tiny fox fucked him up!

How had that happened?

He cried. He'd fucking cried...

Booker was defenseless against tears, they did something funny to him. They had to be to blame for what he was doing! They had to be.

Rain bounced off the windscreen and it was hard to tell if Frey had noticed Booker's car or not, with so little traffic on the roads. He stayed back as much as the traffic lights allowed.

Minutes later, Frey pulled into a car lot. Booker circled around the block before coming back to find Frey's car empty. Booker pulled over into a space just far enough down the street not to stand out.

He reached into his suit jacket and pulled out his phone and put in the address.

He stared at the information on the screen, then back at the building, rubbing at an eyebrow and feeling an ache develop at his temples.

Why did Frey need to see a doctor?

Was he ill?

Was that what the fear was about?

He had no answers, and the questions didn't quit. Who would Frey confide in?

He quickly opened his WhatsApp.

Alphaholes

> **Booker:** *Dad is Popi around?*

> **Silas:** *You could just ring the house bozo.*

Booker cursed at not even considering that. It showed how messed up he was.

> **Dad:** *Your popi isn't home, he's at the office. I'll message him and tell him to come to your office.*

"Fuck," he exclaimed, typing back quickly.

> **Booker:** *I'm not in the office.*

> **Laken:** *Why the fuck not? We have a meeting in less than an hour, or had you forgotten? This is important Booker!*

> **Booker:** *Hold on to your fucking hair. I'll be there, I just needed to pop out and do something.*

He hoped like hell no one asked him what, especially Dad. Booker hated lying, and the truth wasn't an option when they'd all judge him and make assumptions as to his reasoning. Assumptions he wasn't ready to talk about or face.

> **Laken:** *You better be, one brother dipping out of work is more than enough.*

Booker shut the group chat, not wanting to think about Taylin or Hollis, not when his ire at them paled against his worry about what brought Frey to this place.

He sat for another ten minutes, debating about what he should do.

Go in and find out what's wrong. His bear's thoughts on the matter were simple.

Booker knew it would never be that simple. *If I do that, he's gonna get upset with us.*

We need to know he's alright, he insisted.

How do you figure we do that and not piss him off? Tell me, I'm all ears.

That's your side of things. Unless you want me to go in?

Did his bear sound hopeful?

Jeez, you'll frighten the fuck out of him.

He'll love us. His bear was adamant about that.

He's never met you.

You are me. I am you. What's the difference?

There's a big hairy ass difference.

His bear growled at him. *Your ass is as hairy as mine.*

In your dreams.

He sniggered at himself and shook his head, glad that his brothers couldn't see him sat in his car, having an internal debate about whose damn ass was hairier. Maybe the pressure of everything was finally getting to him?

Go with that. In fact, better yet, let's go in there and let Frey judge whose bottom is hairier.

And I'm out! He shut out his bear and started the car, pulling back into the traffic, trying his best to ignore the feeling in the pit of his stomach that his bear was right, and they should go in and find out exactly what was going on. Or better yet, do something utterly ridiculous to make Frey laugh and ask him to judge whose ass was hairier, his or his bears. Would that distract him from the fact he'd gone all stalkerish?

As fucking if!

Back at the office, Pam eyed him in such a way he sucked in a breath before he apologized. "Sorry for earlier, had to slip out for something urgent." It wasn't a lie, and that reality got Booker rushing on. "Was Sawyer understanding?"

Pam continued to eye him, this time with a look of speculation, while nodding. "Yes, I've had to move some appointments around. Sawyer can only do tomorrow morning at nine am when you had the conference call planned with Cross Leathers and switching to Brand Alliance. So I've had to move that to five-thirty in the evening. It was the only available time Malcom could fit you in."

Malcom had worked with Booker for the last decade, and they had a solid working relationship. He hated that he might have inconvenienced the other man. "Good. Thank you."

Booker slipped back into his office and groaned at the sight of his desk. He muttered about flighty foxes as he set about trying to find some order to the things he should have done while running off to follow Frey.

His phone rang, and he absently reached for it. "Hello, Booker Starling."

"What's going on?" Dad asked without preamble.

He paused before replying, working on regrouping. "Nothing... I'm not sure what you're getting at?"

What had he given away in the group chat? He ran frantically through what he'd said.

"You skipped out of the office right before a planned meeting. So I'll ask again, what gives, Booker?"

He groaned. "Who snitched on me?"

"Popi came to see you and was concerned when Pam advised you'd hightailed it out of the office after Frey."

"I didn't hightail it after Frey," he blustered, flushing bright red despite the empty office.

"Is that so? Then can you explain where you were going?" Dad didn't sound convinced, and Booker didn't blame him.

His sigh was full of frustration as he slumped back in his seat and stared unseeingly at his office. "Frey's acting like he's frightened, and I followed him because... because..."

"You were worried," Dad supplied.

"Okay, yeah. It's not a crime to be worried when one of your employees looks terrified about something," he defended, glad no one could see him.

"Terrified... that's a strong word? Are you sure that's what you're picking up?" Dad's genuine concern helped settle Booker.

If he displayed the same level of concern, that had to mean Booker's meant nothing more than a boss worried about an employee? Did it?

"It's what fits, Dad. I can't explain it any more than that. He went to a doctor's office." He licked his drying lips, about to voice a fear of his own. "Do you think he's sick?"

Booker gave some thought to how Frey had smelled. Nothing came to mind that suggested there was anything amiss. Frey's fragrance was his usual chocolate and spice.

"Does he smell different?" Dad asked, as if he'd plucked Booker's thought from his head.

"No."

"What about... his heat scent?"

The denial was instant, and Booker had to stop himself. They'd only been working together for a few weeks and omegas had a heat on average once every two months. He searched his memories of the times he'd worked with Frey in the past. "I can't recall having been around him when he might have been preparing to go into a heat."

Was that odd?

Now he was thinking about it, he'd scented other PAs' change in scent, even Hollis's while they were away.

"Not even once?"

Dad's question gave him a weird sense of missing something... but what, Booker couldn't fathom. "Nope."

"Probably just wrong timing."

Was it?

Chapter Ten

Frey

There was so much going on in his head, Frey wasn't sure how he could find his way out of the maze of questions when all he wanted to do was hide from reality. Booker spent so much time staring at him, Frey had convinced himself he'd gotten a smudge on the end of his nose and had gone to the restroom to check.

It gave him something else to focus on. Since his doctor's appointment, Booker was acting... nice? The word didn't quite fit. The bear was fussing? Frey couldn't come up with a better word for it.

The press conference the week before had shown yet another side to Booker. When he'd gone all growly, protective bear over Hollis, Frey had started having vivid dreams. Ones where it was Frey, not Hollis, who'd received that kind of display. They'd announced Silas was the new figurehead of the company, but Hollis's blossoming relationship with Taylin had become the focus. With Taylin a divergent, the slurs they'd cast at him had upset everyone. Then it came with nastiness about Hollis being a 'true shifter'—non-divergent, somehow implying he was better than Taylin. This resulted in all the brothers standing literally and figuratively with their brother.

Frey had gotten tearful. His hormones were wreaking havoc on him, and he'd had to leave. His body was doing things it hadn't done in years, and it was why he was hiding from Booker's all-seeing eyes in the coffee lounge after the last attempt at holding back tears for no apparent reason other than Booker saying 'thank you'.

Standing in the coffee lounge, he lifted a big slab of cake and instead of nibbling, he rammed it between his lips, eating his feelings. The chocolate gooeyness hit his tastebuds, and he groaned despite his inner turmoil. He cupped a hand under the other as crumbs fell from his mouth.

He sighed in distress when, seconds later, the chocolate gooeyness no longer distracted him, so he shoved an enormous chunk in his mouth, then worked to close his lips to chew.

"What's this? A cake eating competition where we see how much we can get in our mouths?"

Frey blushed hard and glanced sheepishly at the man who entered the coffee room so silently that he hadn't heard him.

Frey chewed and watched Ziggy head straight to the counter where there was always a pot of fresh coffee. Ziggy's striped shirt, with the sleeves rolled up over his elbows, revealed tattoo covered forearms.

Frey would never be brave enough to get one, never mind so many. The idea of needles being jabbed into his skin sent icy shivers through him.

He swallowed what he had in his mouth, taking a second to savor the last few crumbs by licking them from the palm of his hand and fingers. Before he finished, he eyed the last bit of cake in the box. He shook his head at his own greediness, but mainly that was just because there was someone there to witness it.

Frey turned his attention back to Ziggy, who was busy filling a mug. "It's a magnificent cake. Isley out did himself with it. I could eat the whole thing in one sitting." It was the truth, but not because it was so good—or not the sole reason.

Ziggy's chuckle came with a head shake. "You'll make yourself sick."

"You do know me, right?"

The chuckle turned into deep belly laughter. "I forgot, how silly of me!"

Frey leaned against the counter, watching Ziggy, needing a distraction from work, Booker, his life, heck with everything.

"How many tattoos do you have?" he asked with genuine interest. He liked Ziggy, he wasn't anything like how he appeared.

Ziggy, the newest recruit to the PAs after Derby had quit, had been the one to suggest changing the original boring name of the group chat to Delicious & Vicious. When they'd first been introduced, Frey had found himself wary of the snake shifter, who looked a little like a thug. It couldn't be farther from the truth. He was sweet, kind, and very caring.

Despite the vibe the tattoos gave off, that didn't fit any of what Frey had taken the time to discover about his work colleague and now friend. His arms weren't the only place that was tattooed. They peeked out of the collar of his shirt, going part way up his neck. He'd shaved off the dark blond hair at both sides of his head and he had a mohawk type hair style with a trimmed beard adding to the bad boy look. His dress sense was unique enough to gain a lot of attention. Smart shirts and slim legged slacks were paired with heavy boots, and then he added in cardigans instead of jackets. It shouldn't have worked all together, yet he looked hip. Trendy, even.

"Not sure…" He shrugged, eyeing the remaining piece of cake in the box. "Thirty maybe?" he reached in and plucked out the cake and Frey held back a sigh at losing the opportunity to have the last slice.

"Why are you asking? Interested in knowing who does mine? I can make recommendations if you want one." He brought the cake to his lips, paused as he sniffed it, then nibbled at the top bit where the icing was.

Frey waited and grinned when Ziggy groaned obscenely. "Fuck, that's good!"

"I know, right? Isley needs to make this a regular bake." He really was regretting that he hadn't taken that last piece.

"Umhum…" Ziggy answered, taking a bigger bite.

"No, I don't have the balls to get a tattoo. I also am not sure how my fox would feel about being marked that way. Does your snake like it?" Frey asked, returning to the conversation.

Ziggy swallowed the mouthful of cake, took a sip of his coffee, and eyed him thoughtfully. "I'm not sure I ever thought about how it would affect my animal. I've wanted tattoos since I was old enough to understand what they were."

Frey picked up something that gave him pause. "Why?" he asked hesitantly.

Back to shrugging, Ziggy didn't reply and took another bite of the cake. "This is so good," he mumbled around the next mouthful.

Seeing he was changing the subject, Frey sighed and worked to come up with something else to distract himself.

"You've got something worrying you. Wanna talk about it?" Ziggy's quiet question had Frey deflating like the air being released from an airbed.

"Is it that obvious?"

"You've a real sunny disposition, and if someone is paying attention, it's easy to see that you've not been yourself these last few days. I'm a good listener."

He debated for all of three seconds before he caved. None of his skulk would understand his dilemma. They all shunned him for his past choices.

He glanced at the open door and walked over, pushing it too. One glance at the padded colorful seats Lane had selected so they could be comfortable in the bright space, he opted for them versus standing.

He'd contemplated talking about his issue in their WhatsApp group chat, then he'd not be face to face with anyone. At how chill Ziggy was, he realized this could work better. Ziggy just might be the right person to discuss his... dilemma with.

He patted the seat next to him as he plonked himself down. "Okay. But you asked for it," he stated, knowing what he was about to share would change Ziggy's perception of him. Everyone thought he was this flirty fox who loved sex... they couldn't be more wrong.

He had... he shuddered, pushing away any thoughts of what Rally had tried to do to him when Frey went into his first heat.

The cushion depressed and a worried looking Ziggy tapped at his leg. "You look like you swallowed a hive of bees and they're stinging you inside... you sure you wanna talk about this,"—he glanced at the closed door—"here?"

"I'm crawling out of my skin. I need to do this or else I'm gonna get the sack because I can't concentrate for toffee."

Ziggy settled, tucking a leg under him as he twisted to face Frey, giving him his full attention. Something else that Frey liked about the snake. He paid attention.

Inhaling Ziggy's zesty scent, Frey released a breath before meeting the other man's gaze. "I'm a virgin." Ziggy's brow quirked up, but that was the only outward sign he'd shocked Ziggy. "I know I act all flirty and interested in sex... don't get me wrong, I am..." or he was of late when he had thoughts about Booker. "It's just..." he blew out a breath. This was so much harder than he thought when it meant going to places he hated to go willingly.

Ziggy placed a gentle hand on his thigh. "In your own time."

Frey nodded and slumped back against the comfy cushion. "Once upon a time there was this fox whose skulk was overrun with alphas. Omegas, there were very few of." His mind drifted of its own accord. "It meant the omegas had the pick of alphas. When an omega came into heat, the alphas fought to be the one to mate." As he spoke, his color drained from his cheeks and his palms grew damp at the memory.

The press on the hand on his leg gave comfort and Frey found he could continue. "My first heat..." he sucked his lower lip between his teeth after he released a shuddery breath. "It was... traumatic." The word never seemed to really fit.

Harrowing.

Horrific.

Life changing.

"Do you need to stop?" Ziggy asked, so gently it brought with it the urge to cry.

He shook his head, sniffing back the tears. "No... I need to get it out. I don't have a choice." That knowledge made his innards tremble. "My heat is due soon."

When he met Ziggy's gaze, his brows pinched together.

"I'm running out of time," Frey explained. "I was taking heat blockers. Which, because I've taken them for too long, have caused me some issues." Understatement, but *that* he wouldn't talk about until he'd come to terms with his own lack. "So my doctor has stopped them, which means I'm going to have to go through my heat. I haven't done that since..."

"What did the alphas in your skulk do to you?"

Once more, Ziggy's gentleness brought tears with it, Frey didn't want to spill them, not when he'd have to go back to the office and face Booker. "One of the biggest alphas, the leader in our skulk, got it into his head that I belonged to him. I just ignored him, I wasn't interested in him. I never had any inclination to think he'd be the one I'd want around when I went into my heat."

A ball formed in Frey's throat as the memories tumbled out of the box he shut them away in. "Having never experienced a heat, I was a little clueless about what was happening to me until it was too late." He rushed on, working to escape what chased him. "Rally knew. Must have scented me. It gave him the opportunity to manipulate others to leave me alone. He timed everything to perfection so no one else was home when he... when he cornered me—"

"The fucker!" Ziggy exclaimed angrily, while he continued to keep his touch gentle.

"Yep." Frey shuddered. The simple acceptance of his version, which had gotten rejected by the other alphas in the skulk, helped settle his nerves and gave him the courage to continue. "He attacked me... ripped the clothes off me and rough handled me, trying to fuck me when I wasn't ready." Frey's body hadn't quite reached the point where his slick would have allowed the alpha to fuck him with wild abandon. The attack had somehow prevented Frey from reaching a natural progression.

Rally had stopped Frey's first heat dead in its tracks. Something, with hindsight, he was grateful for because he had no clue what the outcome would have been otherwise. His doctor couldn't fully explain Frey's bodily reaction. Only to suggest the fear—fight-or-flight response was so strong—had prevented his heat. Frey didn't care, only that he'd never wanted to be in that position again. Vulnerable.

A light flashed in the snake's eyes and Frey could almost believe Ziggy was preparing to strike. "You... he didn't..."

"Rape me?" Ziggy nodded jerkily. "No. It was close, I was in the bathroom trying to find a way to cool down when he attacked. I managed to grab a can of deodorant and spray it in his eyes after we'd fought for a minute or two." He let the memory of Rally's screams settle his tummy and he giggled. It felt good that he could see the funny side... sort of... possibly, after all these years.

"I hope you blinded the fucker."

He said it with such menace, Frey's giggles increased. "I wish, but it sorted him out long enough to allow me to get out of there."

Ziggy wore a thoughtful look as he continued to stare at Frey to the point he had to resist fidgeting. "So your problem is that you need help with your heat?" he asked tentatively.

"I do and I don't wanna..." Frey winced, at a loss for what to say or if he wanted to actually bring Booker's name into the conversation. With how he reacted recently to Booker, attraction wouldn't be an issue. The dreams about Booker's bear and what Frey had seen of his chest... yeah, that had left him toying with the insane idea of asking Booker to help him.

His fox was insistent the big bear was the answer to all their problems.

He is.

Shut up!

"I could help. I'm sure we could figure it out between us."

"You'd do that... for me?" Frey asked, wide eyed and feeling a wallop to his chest at such a generous offer.

"Frey, I like you a lot. It could be fun, and we can get inventive. We can do a google search to find things for omegas to use on each other. There has to be some, they have everything else on the internet these days." He gave Frey a cheeky grin.

The dread and gloom that had shrouded his day disappeared. And okay, he wasn't Booker, but it might give him time to figure out if Booker would be interested. "I'd like that... and thank you."

"My pleasure."

They looked at each other and both burst into fits of giggles. Frey had no interest in Ziggy, and it was clear from Ziggy's expression right then he had none in Frey, which suited him. Frey's interests—he could not deny—lay in the enormous bear who hid his kind heart behind a gruff nature. If Frey was a little disappointed that he had ignored his fox's idea to have this conversation with Booker, then that was just tough.

Chapter Eleven

Booker

Booker, driven out of the office, gave Pam an absent smile as he walked past. His bear was scenting the corridors for Frey, who had left fifteen minutes earlier, looking dreadful. He'd been off all morning and Booker's bear was antsy enough to get him going in search of the fox. They'd been keeping watch since he'd returned from the doctor, looking like he'd been crying and trying to hide it. Nothing made sense. Nothing.

Up to now, he had resisted searching for information from his brothers. Gossiping might not work in Booker's favor if his brothers got wind about his growing affection for Frey. He'd considered he might have to seek Jupiter out to clarify exactly what he and Frey had together. Only, the outcome of bashing his brother's teeth down his throat at actually confirming a fling wasn't something he relished explaining to everyone else.

At the sound of voices on the other side of the coffee lounge door, Booker paused. Realizing one was Frey's made Booker grin, so he raised his hand to the wood, about to push it open when Ziggy's voice stopped him dead.

"So what you're saying now is that you need help with your heat?"

Booker shook his head at the meaning behind Ziggy's question. What the fuck was this?

"I do and I don't wanna..." Frey answered in a tone of voice that was thick with emotion.

What. Was. This. About?

"I could help. I'm sure we could figure it out between us," Ziggy offered.

Booker's eyes narrowed on the door, imagining ripping the head off the snake for daring to make such an offer.

"You'd do that... for me?" Frey's reply sent Booker's heart into a tailspin, driving his blood pressure so high his head felt like it might explode.

"Frey, I like you a lot. It could be fun, and we can get inventive. We can do a google search to find things for omegas to use on each other. There has to be some, they have everything else on the internet these days."

Say no.

Say no.

"I'd like that... and thank you."

Motherfucker!

Booker drew his hand back from the door like it had burned him, refusing to believe his own ears until Ziggy answered, "My pleasure."

Quite positive he had smoke coming out the top of his head, he breathed hard as he held back his bear and spun around to charge off down the corridor, away from the couple. The fact that he was considering killing Ziggy with his bare hands was actually a little frightening! He needed someone to talk some fucking sense into him and soon, or else he might receive a life sentence for murder.

Large fists clenching and unclenching at his sides, he stomped angrily down the hallway in the direction of the stairs. Confined in a small metal box wasn't a chance he was going to take if someone decided they were going to get in the elevator with him. Booker knew himself, knew his limits, and he had gotten pushed right to the edge of them by a fucking flirty fox.

Yeah, murder wasn't a big ask right now.

He climbed the stairs three at a time, his long legs eating them up in no time. He didn't even debate about whether it was sensible to go and talk to Silas—rage about the injustice—when he could and had stopped him from doing something rash when life got kicked off balance. It didn't happen often, but when it did, he needed someone to get him back on an even keel, and fast.

At Silas's office door, his secretary gave him an alarmed stare when she looked up. He never gave her a chance to speak. "Is he in?"

"Yes—"

He didn't wait for her to say anything more and barged straight into Silas's office, coming to a halt at the sight of

Wilder sitting next to Silas with an iPad, tapping at the screen.

Silas's eyes narrowed on him and his brows arched up. "Whatsup?"

"Wilder, get out," Booker growled impatiently, ready to burst a blood vessel.

Wilder, the cute raccoon who Booker was usually polite with, gave him a wide-eyed stare at his demand.

"If you wouldn't mind leaving us, Wilder? We can finish up later." Silas didn't look away from Booker as he frowned.

"Erm... yeah... okay... but there's a deadline of five pm to submit the electronic application if we want to secure the date we want for that venue," Wilder stuttered, getting up as he gathered two notepads off Silas's large, messy desk. He clutched them to his chest like a barrier as he moved around the desk and skirted past Booker.

"It's fine, I'll do it."

Booker didn't sit, he couldn't. He was so restless he paced to the window, waiting for Wilder to leave, doing his best to contain a fury he really had no business feeling.

"If you're sure."

"Yes, go for now and maybe catch up with Ziggy? Ask where he filed the paperwork for Cresta."

At the mere mention of the snake shifter, Booker snarled ominously, swinging back around. His bear pushed him to shift and hunt the fucker down for daring to...

"Wilder, leave now!" Silas was out of his seat and across the room before Wilder had the common sense to hightail it out of the office. "Breathe Booker, come on."

Silas placed his hands on Booker's forearms, squeezing, then releasing. He repeated the move as he lowered his voice to a soothing tone. "Slow your breathing, that's it. Match mine."

Booker had no clue how long they stood facing each other, working to get him under control. It was only when his bear receded enough that he could think without the red haze of fury that he nodded at Silas.

"What was that? Fuck Booker, that was close! Who got you so riled up that you were about to go scaring the natives with your big, hairy butt?" Silas went with humor, but Booker could see nothing funny about his current situation.

"When did other damn omegas offer to fuck omegas during their heat? When?" he ground out angrily.

Silas's frown was back, his brows touching as he stared at Booker. "I'm lost? Who's offering to fuck who? And why would that make you and your bear angry?"

Booker stomped around the office. It was the only way to get rid of some of the excess angry energy making his blood boil as he recalled word for fucking word what he'd overheard. "Ziggy and Frey!"

"Stop fucking pacing a minute and explain," Silas insisted with enough force it registered somewhere that his brother sounded as pissed as he felt, but Booker was too mad to consider why. "What is it with Ziggy and Frey?"

If he'd taken a moment to think, Booker would have questioned why Silas sounded off as he spun to face his brother, but he was too angry at the world and jabbed a finger at Silas. "Ziggy is fucking Frey."

Silas visibly paled and staggered back as if Booker had actually punched him. "You're wrong," he replied in utter disbelief. This time, Booker registered his brother's weird expression. "Ziggy is no way offering or fucking Frey." His lips curled into a snarl.

"Little you know!" Booker snapped angrily, spoiling for a fight, rolling his eyes at Silas's stupidity. "I've just heard them talking about it. Frey has his heat soon and Ziggy was talking about going on the internet... googling shit to find ways to make it fucking fun..." he swallowed, feeling as if he'd drunk a cup of sand the way the words tore at his vocal chords. "To fuck Frey."

The mere thought of the omega touching Frey... using toys to pleasure him left Booker in a cold sweat and his bear ready to tear Ziggy's head off his shoulders once more.

He was so lost in his head, when Silas came at him and gripped the front of his shirt, fisting it so tightly he could hear ripping, he could only gawp.

What was this shit?

He was the offended one!

Booker looked down, staring aghast when he had no answer to what Silas was up to. They hadn't had a fight... fuck in forever, not one where they'd laid hands on each other. He brought his hands up to cover Silas's shaking ones.

"What's your fucking issue!" he exclaimed, his fury building at the injustice of whatever was bugging Silas that clearly had something to do with Ziggy... or was it Frey?

Booker was clueless about which it could be, so he tugged hard enough to bruise Silas's fingers when he didn't release him.

"You've got it all wrong," Silas snarled, right in his face.

"I've got fuck all wrong. And if you don't get your fucking hands off me, you're gonna see my damn furry ass!"

Silas let go so suddenly Booker staggered back, making him angrier. "What am I missing here?"

"Nothing!"

"Yeah, right?" Booker twisted to the side, digging his fingers into the ripped seam of his shirt. "It sure fucking looks like it," he scowled, thinking about how he'd look leaving the office and what gossip it would create.

Silas's angry gaze landed on the torn shirt and a flush of color flooded his cheeks. "I'm sorry," he said, in a stiff, formal tone that was unrecognizable to Booker.

He threw up his arms, deciding he was absolutely done with this day. "Right, whatever. But you better not be fucking interested in Frey!"

Back to stomping, he didn't even look back at Silas as he swung out of his office, wondering what the fuck had happened to his orderly life. A life that had been near perfect before he'd returned home to this fucking madness.

Omegas fucking other omegas... a violent shudder ran through him. He'd have to figure it out himself, and he would, but there was no way in hell he was going to *allow* Ziggy to snatch Frey from him and his bear. Hell would freeze over first.

He might not have wanted to be in this situation...

Attracted to the flirty fox, his bear side supplied, none too helpfully.

It's your fault I just had a fight with Silas, so you can fuck off, too.

No two ways is that snake smooching with our fox. You need to figure your shit out, and fast.

My shit! He growled menacingly and realized a little too late that there were folks coming towards him.

He needed out, now!

Who knew if he'd start blubbering like a damn baby next, the same way Taylin had over mating with Hollis...

He shuddered at the horror of it as he stalked down the stairs.

Fuck work.

Fuck Silas!

In fact, fuck everyone!

Chapter Twelve

Delicious & Vicious Chat

Wilder: *I don't know what's going on, but I was in with Silas finalizing details that should have been Jupiter's job, but he still hasn't shown up for work yet! Any-wayyyyy, I've just got kicked out of Silas's office when Booker came in looking fit to murder someone. Does anyone know what happened?*

Isley: *Busy over here being drowned in emails!*

Lennon: *I haven't seen anyone except you know who… he's in a foul mood and it doesn't matter what I do, he has to find fault with it… I think I'm gonna quit.*

Hollis: *What? You will do no such thing. Come to my office Lennon, let's see if we can figure it out.*

Bowie: *What's happening? Why would Booker go all bear? He's been really sweet lately. Did you see the flowers he gave to his secretary for her birthday? They were beautiful and her favorite.*

Wilder: *We weren't talking about flowers here. Let's figure why I got shouted at by Silas and him hightailing it around his office desk to get a grip of Booker when he looked as if he was going to shift?*

Hollis: *Are you exaggerating what happened, Wilder?*

Wilder: *One time I over egged the pudding.*

Bowie: Why would you knowingly over egg any pudding? I don't understand.

Wilder: It's a figure of speech. Like I may have exaggerated one time and now everyone assumes I do it all the time. I can tell you, I'm not over egging the pudding. Booker was madder than a bear dragged out of hibernation.

Hollis: Are you positive?

Wilder: Absolutely.

Frey: Maybe he went to the coffee lounge and found there was no cake left. That would make me mad.

Hollis: Yes, let's not rake up the last time you got cross with Monty over eating the last slice of tart.

Monty: Do I hear my name being called in vain?

Bowie: *Why can't you guys talk normal, so I understand what it is y'all meaning. What has vanity got to do with anything?*

Hollis: *I'll explain later, Bowie. For now, let's get back to work.*

Wilder: *So that's a no then…*

Chapter Thirteen

Frey

At first, when Ziggy had sent Frey a link to this place and suggested it as their Friday evening entertainment, he hadn't loved the idea. That he was now through the door was entirely Booker's fault.

Frey scratched his ear, momentarily distracted from what was happening around him by thoughts of Booker. The bear was away with Taylin, back at Design Detailing & Co to finalize the deal. Frey was over the moon about that, especially as Booker had been acting like his shadow all week. He'd barely even had room to piss in peace.

It was like he needed Frey joined at his hip, though Frey was clueless to why. It was like torture to his drug free body and had driven him to agree to the extreme of visiting a sex club. Why he'd insisted everyone come with him, Frey tried not to think about. His friends' reactions when they walked through the sex club and gotten the full effect were as bad as his own.

Sex... folks were having sex in public! Like, right there for all to see. Who did that?

He gulped audibly, doing his best not to stare wide eyed when he listened to the conversation between Bowie and Hollis. He gave Ziggy a 'what the heck have we done' look, before his head twisted to Hollis, pulling up his big boy pants and sucking it up. "We're not leaving. We just got here, and this is a great idea. No one has to do anything except drink and watch the fun. That's what the information on the website said."

He pointed it out partly to remind himself of the fact. There were huge alphas situated around the room, monitoring those getting frisky with each other. The website said the security of its patrons was very important.

"They'll stop anyone from doing something we don't want." Frey prayed they were telling the truth. No one wanted to see his fox freaking the hell out, not even him.

The place looked high end, with plush carpet and black padded leather booths lining three of the walls in the large space. The middle of the room was filled with chrome and glass topped tall tables. Most of the tables had men drinking at them, watching those in the booths. Classical music played in the background, which unfortunately didn't disguise the low hum of noises filtering out from the booths.

Uncertainty filled Frey. Had he made a massive mistake by suggesting this to the others? This was supposed to be him working to get comfortable with alphas getting jiggy with omegas, but currently he was doing his best not to hyper-ventilate. He was supposed to be here so he could see how it wasn't as scary as part of his past self still believed.

This was all part of Ziggy's big idea to plan for beyond his first heat. Neither of them wanted it to be Ziggy's long-term job to help him. They decided, once they'd done a little research, that this place was a step in that direction. The direction of asking... *Booker*.

He lost his train of thought when his eyes landed on a couple in the corner. He paid no mind to what the others were saying as he whispered frantically in Ziggy's ear at the sight of an alpha holding an omega by the throat, "I'm not so sure this is a good idea."

"We're here now, so let's just see. I'm not suggesting you do anything or interact with anyone. But it won't harm to see there are alphas who love to let the omega take control," he hissed back, giving Frey a *'we're gonna be fine'* look.

Frey wanted to believe him. Give this a go. As much as he needed help with his heat, he didn't think... *ohhhh*.

His gaze got caught once more on the big alpha as the omega being held by the throat came forward and kissed the alpha with undeniable passion.

"Watching can be fun," Ziggy said pointedly and loudly enough for the others to hear, staring fixedly at Frey when he'd seen where he'd been looking. Then Ziggy took a firm hold of his elbow to guide him to a free center table, like he got that Frey might bolt at any second.

"Have you been here before?"

Ziggy didn't answer Hollis, and Frey had to wonder, not for the first time, if Ziggy was a little more out there than he'd initially thought.

"Drinks. We need drinks," Frey announced, waving his cell phone around, doing his best to keep the mood light. One quick scan of the QR code on the top of the table brought everyone closer.

"Can I have a cocktail?" Wilder asked, coming to peer over Frey's shoulder at his phone screen.

Heck, he needed a cocktail, maybe two, as he eyed the menu, seeing they had a great selection. "I'll get us all a cocktail, as this was my idea." He reeled off all the different choices on the menu.

"Oh... oh, I'll have the cherry one," Wilder said excitedly.

"Me too," Lennon interjected, looking at Frey.

"Sounds good to me, too," Monty added distractedly. "Shit. Is that Jupiter?"

"Where?"

Wilder's demand sounded off to Frey as he glanced at the other man, spinning so fast his hair bounced around his head when Lennon pointed at a booth tucked into the far corner of the room.

Frey couldn't bring himself to look, he just... no, it was *Booker's brother*, that would be just plain weird.

"Let's go say hi."

Wilder's suggestion got Frey staring at him like he'd lost his mind, as Hollis said fervently, "No. We are staying right here, having one drink and then we are all leaving together."

"Spoilsport," Wilder moaned, looking to Frey like a man who'd gotten denied his dying wish. "Hey, where's your glasses?"

"In the safest place. I do not need to see my mate's brother... doing whatever he's doing... in public," Hollis muttered, flushed and fidgety.

Fuck... this was all getting out of hand. "Isley, what do you want to drink?" Frey questioned, a tickle of hysteria developing at the back of his throat.

"I'll have the cherry thing too."

Frey nodded, turning his attention to the two men who hadn't ordered yet. "Hollis, Ziggy, what about you two?"

"I'll take the cherry one, too."

"Might as well make that a full house," Ziggy supplied.

"Great," Frey murmured, tapping at the phone and selecting their choice. "I'll put in the order."

"Is he getting his cock sucked?" Wilder exclaimed loudly, and Frey winced, not once lifting his eyes from the screen.

"Dear gods, he is," exclaimed Bowie. "Is that even legal?"

"The club has a license that permits it. A bit like the places omegas can go to and hire an alpha to help with their heat, I suppose," Ziggy answered Bowie.

Frey was doing his very best to act his usual flirty self, but it was getting harder by the minute. Eventually the drinks arrived, and the conversation continued around him.

You can do this.

You can do this.

You can do this.

Frey took a sip of his cocktail, keeping up his chant, and let the hit of liquor do its job. It gave him the courage he needed to actually do what he'd set out to do. Watch the couples do... stuff.

"Holy cow, look at that alpha with the omega sat on his lap!" he exclaimed, so loudly, he embarrassed himself and caused Hollis to choke.

"Please, keep your voice down," Hollis hissed at him when he stopped coughing.

Getting he was pretending by acting up, he didn't cringe the way he wanted to. "No one's paying us any attention." Frey hoped that was the truth as he hissed back, opting at sounding miffed. "Stop being a killjoy, Hollis. I just wanna see... how alphas behave with omegas."

He realized his mistake at his wording when Hollis's expression became worried. Hollis was a great boss, thoughtful and paid attention. Right now, Frey needed him to pay a little less attention.

Thankfully, Ziggy moved in and did what he promised he would do; have Frey's back. He reached out to put a hand on Hollis's sleeve, mumbling something quietly to him. What was said stopped Hollis from doing whatever he'd intended to do.

Frey half listened as he sipped at his drink and forced himself to look back at the second couple who'd drawn his attention. The alpha had his hands on the padded seat, not touching the omega who got to do the touching. He stroked and caressed anywhere he wanted. There was no conversation between them. Not verbally, anyway. What struck Frey as he finished his drink and ordered another one was the way they looked at each other. The intensity of it was... beautiful. Nothing about it was threatening... *it wasn't threatening.*

The thought stuck, and he drank his second and third cocktail, paying no one else any attention as he watched with fascination. When the omega finally got down on his knees in front of the alpha, it was absolutely his decision. He was in control.

A breath shuddered out of Frey, his body reacting to how much he wanted to try... *to get down on his knees and lap at Booker's cock.* There, he'd admitted it to himself. He wanted to try to overcome his fears with the enormous bear.

"You doing okay?" Ziggy murmured in his ear. "You've been watching them pair,"—he pointed to the booth—"for a long time."

"They're so attuned to each other," he replied honestly, the liquor helping to say what was on his mind. "The alpha isn't pushy." Frey shook his head in amazement. "Not even a little, and the omega is in... control."

"He is." Ziggy's warm chuckle made Frey glance from the couple to Ziggy when he continued on. "It's fun to have an alpha by the balls in such a way they will do anything you want."

"Do you do that?"

The sexiness of his smile was an answer all in itself, but Frey waited for Ziggy to reply. "Yes. It takes a special alpha to relinquish control to an omega unless it's in a kink situation and the omega is the Dom."

"Huh?" Frey gave Ziggy a startled stare. "Are you a Dom?"

Ziggy's eyes glittered and Frey's breath got caught in his chest. "Not in any traditional sense. But I like to be the one who takes charge during sex."

"Wow." Intrigued by the idea, Frey asked, "Is it easy to find alphas that like you to be that way?"

"I've not struggled, let's put it that way." His shrug was offhand.

"Have you got an alpha now?" Frey questioned, feeling he already knew the answer. There was a slight hesitation—or in his tipsy state, he thought there was, before he nodded. "Do you come to places like this with him?"

Ziggy burst out laughing, a joyous sound that brought the attention of the others. "Nope. Not his thing."

In his inebriated state, it took Frey a few seconds for a thought to sink past the cocktails. "Won't he be mad you're doing... you know what with me?"

Ziggy's laughter continued, though Frey thought it sounded off. "Not his business. He wants to keep things casual. He's been very clear 'bout not wanting anything long term."

Frey was about to question how Ziggy felt about that, but Isley slipped an arm around his waist.

"What's you two laughing 'bout?" The little sugar glider rested his head on Frey's bicep, too small to reach his shoulder.

Frey didn't point out he wasn't laughing, instead he grinned at Isley. "Sex, of course."

"I wish I was as bold as you, Frey," said Isley, with a heavy sigh.

"Not everything is as you believe," Frey murmured, his gaze wandering back to the couple he'd been watching. "But maybe one day I will be," he said to himself.

Soon! It better be soon, his fox insisted grumpily, making Frey stifle a drunk giggle.

You're so pushy.

Chapter Fourteen

Booker

How had his actions created this?

"What do you mean, you shifted and attacked other shifters in the street? Why would you drag our good name into the gutter like this? Break your curfew when I strictly stated you needed to be here when your mother placed dinner on the table? What part of that fits with my expectations?"

Each question came at him like a bullet, creating just as much devastation given his father's refusal to so much as acknowledge the two men who'd insisted on coming into his home to explain why Booker was late.

Booker stood dressed in the hospital gown he'd had to wear home because he'd shredded his clothes in his hurry to shift. Worrying about them hadn't been on his mind when he'd chased after the group of bullies who'd gone after his best friend, Silas. He gulped as his father's fury rolled over everyone in the room, although his father hadn't raised his voice. He didn't need to, to make his point. He never had.

The tiny, smartly dressed man who'd insisted on bringing Booker home, took a step closer to him and rested his hand on his arm. The quiet acceptance and support he'd always found in the Starling family didn't have the same effect when it brought Lane Starling closer to the angry man, looking at him with something that kicked Booker in the gut. Derision.

He'd always worked hard not to overstep all the boundaries his father set for them. He'd spent his childhood working hard to get his father's approval. Right in that moment, it dawned on him that to be what his father wanted would mean he'd have to turn his back on people he loved. It made answering impossible.

The pressure on his arm increased, as if Lane had sensed his inner conflict. "As I explained and apologized for, Booker was defending my son against six other teenagers who were attacking him. I wanted to ensure Booker got checked out at the hospital before we brought him home, so the lateness of the hour is our fault." Lane, an omega, added a little more snap to his voice than when they'd arrived a couple of minutes ago.

Derick Starling, Lane's husband, stood silently at his side. They had both wanted to come and offer thanks, but Booker could see now he'd made a vital error of judgment by agreeing to this.

His father towered over Lane and jabbed a finger that was twice the size of Lane's, right in his face, nearly touching his nose. "I wasn't talkin' to you."

Oh, no! "Dad—"

The hand flung out with force in his direction and made contact before Booker could second guess what was happening. The slapping sound left a stunned silence in its wake. Though the slap stung, it didn't hurt as much as Booker's pride. The man ruled the house with an iron will. A feat that could bring everyone in the family to heel immediately, just with a look.

Booker's mom winced but said nothing. It was Derick, a wolf shifter, coming one step forward that set off alarm bells. The tension in the room was volatile, leaving Booker dry mouthed and conflicted. He'd never once considered that he'd have to defend someone against his father's wrath. But these men represented the goodness Booker secretly wanted to be measured against.

"You come into this house, acting like your divergent son isn't the reason Booker broke the rules," he spat, acting as if it was an everyday occurrence to hit his son in front of others, "like I'd be proud. He beat up shifters! Where the hell is the pride in that? Where?" he snarled in Lane's face.

As small as Lane was, he never moved a muscle as he held Booker's father's furious gaze. "Am I permitted to speak now?" The icy contempt Lane fired back came with a helping of fake pleasantries when he smiled.

This time, Booker anticipated his father's reaction and stepped in front of Lane before the punch could touch a man he respected. He rocked on his bare feet at the force at which his father delivered the punch. He couldn't catch his breath from the impact to his chest and wheezed, coming forward only to receive two quick jabs to the head, knocking him back onto his ass. His vision waved and blood trickled out of his mouth from his busted lip.

He blinked rapidly, and then wished he hadn't when he watched in horror the pandemonium that broke out in front of him.

Body jerking, Booker woke with the sudden, violent urge to defend. He blinked in the dark and worked to calm his breathing as he relived the horror of a night that had changed his world. A cold sweat coated his skin as he rolled out of bed and snapped on the lamp. Pushing the nightmarish visions from his head, he walked into the bathroom. His hand trembled as he filled the glass he left on the counter with cold water.

He shivered, drank deep and avoided looking at himself in the mirror, knowing all he'd see were haunted eyes. He filled the glass again, this time sipping it before plonking the empty glass down and going back into the bedroom. With a sweeping look around the room, he saw the tumbled sheets on his bed, evidence that he'd been thrashing around. He sighed quietly and listened out to hear if he'd disturbed anyone. His nightmares had receded over the years, but with recent events, he should have expected it might trigger one. The violence of that fateful night, when he'd been declared dead to his family, haunted him. Dead to people who only saw the value of those who could shift. What they'd discovered in the factory's basement when they'd gone to kick those shithead alphas out of Design Detailing & Co had cut way too close to Booker's past inner turmoil. He loathed with a passion the world's injustice and use of threats and violence to control others, and hated even more that nothing had superseded it.

He released a shuddering breath, knowing he was done with sleeping for the night.

His past family had put paid to that.

They aren't your family. Not the one that counts, his bear grumbled and settled back down.

It was an argument they'd had a time or two—three hundred—over what came before and after. Booker hated his father, it was deep-seated, and he lived with it... accepted it to a degree. But losing his mother? That hurt, cut too deep to heal. Nights like tonight, where he traveled back to that night in the alleyway, to what came after... yeah, he had regrets.

He headed to the door, knowing he needed to escape his thoughts as they weighed heavily on him.

He quietly padded down the hallway lit by a small lamp on the table near Silas's bedroom. It was comforting to see some things never changed. Lane had always wanted his boys, if for whatever reason came out of their bedrooms at night, didn't encounter darkness.

Booker's bear had no problem with moving in the dark, but he'd discovered Silas suffered with night blindness. He didn't sleep in the dark because he had trouble going from light to dark, his eyes didn't adjust well. The glasses he'd worn as a child were now contact lenses, so people didn't know of his problem.

It was a weakness that Silas hated and one he had blamed on being divergent until Lane had made a point of finding evidence to disprove that notion. That shifters could—and did—suffer from the same condition.

Silas... they hadn't spoken since they'd laid hands on each other the week before. Going away had given Booker breathing space... despite the unexpected kick in the teeth from the awful discovery of chained omegas in a basement not fit for rats.

At the bottom of the stairs, he tilted his head, listening out, sure he could hear someone moving around. Keeping his steps light, he headed in the kitchen's direction and stopped in the doorway at the sight of Popi setting out two mugs and, by the smell of it, making Booker's favorite hot chocolate.

"How do you do that?" he asked resignedly, coming into the room when he realized he'd woken Popi up. His feet chilled on the cold tiles, but he didn't question that Popi was indeed making hot chocolate for him. It wasn't the first time he'd had a bad dream and come down to find Popi there, waiting for him with his favorite drink.

"I'm a mind reader," he said, keeping a straight face for all of three seconds when Booker rolled his eyes at the silly response. Popi grinned and nodded to the seat he had placed at the front of the counter so Booker could sit right opposite him as he stood in front of the stove. "I know my boys. Sit, talk to me."

It had been years, and still this man could ease his troubled heart. "I had a fight with Silas." He went there first, not sure he could talk about what he'd shared with Derick when he'd gotten home last night. Not yet, not when Popi had such a sensitive soul.

"It wouldn't be the first time." Popi added three enormous lumps of chocolate to the milk he was heating in the pan.

Booker's mouth watered as the chocolate melted into the milk releasing a heavenly smell, distracting him for a moment. The tap on the counter top brought his attention back to Popi. "What's different this time?"

He slumped in his seat and dropped his eyes to the counter, where he used a fingertip to rub at the marble, trying to figure out how to evade answering directly. "We fought over a guy—an omega."

"Do you both like this omega?"

"It's not like that," he mumbled, hating having to explain how overhearing part of a conversation brought about the epic fight he'd had with Silas.

"Then what's it like, tell me," Popi encouraged, stirring the milk and chocolate mix.

He sucked in a breath, blew it out, then found himself going with the truth. "I overheard Ziggy talking to Frey about a problem he was having. Only I didn't hear all the conversation—"

"You mean you didn't clarify what you overheard," Popi pointed out, giving him a sympathetic smile.

Booker cringed on the inside. "Possibly... I don't know for sure."

He didn't. As much as he'd glued himself to Frey, he'd been no closer to discovering what was going on. He'd checked that the trip away hadn't coincided with any days off Frey would need to take for his heat. So whatever was happening between the pair hadn't happened yet. If he discounted the fact Ziggy had taken Frey to a sex club. A sex club... to the bear gods, what was the man thinking, letting his little fox into a den like that?

"What do you know?"

Popi's question diverted his attention, and he scowled at the simmering pan.

"What I know is that what I heard made me mad. You know, the way I need to blow off steam." Popi nodded, offering that wonderful, understanding smile as he stirred the pan. "I went to see Silas."

Booker wanted to bury his face in his hands, recalling how mad he and Silas had been at each other. "I stupidly blurted out that Ziggy was fucking Frey—or offering to. A big difference when it appears that there is something going on between Ziggy and Silas."

That was the only conclusion that Booker could come to when Silas wasn't speaking to him, or Ziggy for that matter. He'd caught Ziggy attempting to talk to Silas, and Booker had recognized the wall that Silas used when he was protecting himself.

"Not that he'd so much as mentioned it to me. Not once, so in my defense, how could I be to blame for firing up Silas when I didn't know in the first place they were doing whatever it was they are doing?" He grumbled, building back up a head of steam. He grew more and more furious that he'd been unable to deal with his frustration at upsetting Silas—his brother, because a big part of his anger he aimed at himself.

He slumped forward and banged his head on the counter. "It is all very fucking confusing. How the hell did I get myself into these situations? Why can't folks just be honest about what's going on in their lives? Tell me," he groused.

Popi's laughter brought his head up. "It's not a laughing matter, Popi!" His eyes narrowed on the man, giving off a vibe of someone who looked way too pleased by the situation. "How did I get myself in this situation!" he demanded in utter exasperation.

Popi filled a mug with the steaming, divine smelling liquid and gave Booker a beautiful smile.

"Because you're such a wonderful, helpful boy," he supplied, making Booker push the mug aside to bang his head back on the counter again, embarrassed enough to blush at the words he'd never gotten used to coming out of Popi's mouth, despite how they warmed his chest.

"Stop that, you silly boy, you'll hurt yourself. Drink up your hot chocolate, it'll make you feel so much better."

He scowled as he lifted his head. "Helpful... I'm a damn sap, is what I am."

Rich, deep laughter came from the doorway behind him, and Booker held back the curse word when he glanced back to see Dad. "Who is turning you into a sap, son?"

Booker didn't answer because of how amused Dad was.

Wearing only pajama bottoms, he ran a hand through his graying chest hair as he came to a stop at the counter and eyed the hot chocolate Booker hadn't touched. "I thought this might be what you were doing when I woke to an empty bed."

Booker reached out and nabbed his mug, seeing the interest in Dad's eyes. "Popi made it for me." He took a sip to make his point, then made an appreciative sound when the flavor hit his taste buds.

Dad smiled widely at Popi, and without asking, the mug slid over the counter. "We can share it," Popi said as Dad lifted the mug and sniffed.

"Yeah." He drank a sip and made a similar noise to Booker.

Their gazes met, and they grinned at each other. "There are perks to you being back under the same roof, Booker."

Booker gave an exaggerated huff. "Is that the only perk to me being home?"

Dad didn't answer straight away as he went and grabbed a stool to sit next to Booker. He took another sip before relinquishing the mug.

He glanced sideways at Booker, raising a brow. "So, who has turned my boy into a sap?"

Chapter Fifteen

Derick

Silas and Booker had always been thicker than thieves. If one was in trouble, the other was right there for them. Booker's fidgeting in his seat indicated that they needed to switch the topic of conversation because he was clearly done talking about it.

Derick set aside his thoughts on what reasons Silas might have had for laying hands on Booker. He would need to find a way to figure out what was going on with Silas, who was no more likely to discuss what was bothering him. Their oldest son was much like Derick and kept his own counsel. Only sometimes that was not the best thing, as Derick had learned as he'd gotten older. Thankfully, Lane had pointed out the error of his ways.

"So what else is bothering you?" Lane asked softly, leaning on the counter, the mug of shared hot chocolate cupped between his hands. They both knew it had to be the discovery at the factory, but they wanted to encourage Booker to talk about what was on his mind. It was how Booker worked.

An ache developed in his chest as he watched Booker wrap both hands around the mug in front of him, looking forlorn. "Do you think the fuckers will get out of jail?"

Derick acknowledged the fatherly love he had for Booker, his adopted son. The bear had come into his family because he'd attacked the bullies who'd set out to murder Silas. Then, he'd had to defend Lane against his own family and lost them all because of his ethical code. One Derick applauded. There was nothing he wouldn't do to protect this boy—man, who was as much his son as his own blood. The man had a big heart, which many never noticed due to his size and overall grumpiness.

He reached out and placed his hand over Booker's, whose gaze lifted. The sorrow Booker wasn't able to hide gave Derick a kick to his gut with the knowledge he couldn't always ease his son's suffering the way he wanted to. It was too late to berate himself for not following his instinct to go with Booker and Taylin.

Retirement... yep, it could suck too.

"They won't get away with what they've done," Derick stated forcefully. "I'll use every resource at my disposal to ensure that they pay for their crimes. Buying the company has shone a light on everything they've done. They can't escape what's coming despite the divergent haters who might support them."

The thought that Jupiter might have been the one who'd found such a situation was a constant source of dread for

Derick. In all this mess, it was the one positive. Had Jupiter been present, he may have revealed more about his past, to those who were previously clueless, than he would have wanted to.

Derick was thankful Taylin had Hollis to comfort him, which lightened his heart. But Booker wasn't ready to admit he had feelings for the cute fox that Lane had pointed out was perfect for their grumpy boy. So for now, Derick and Lane would do what they'd always done for Booker.

Derick squeezed Booker's hands as Lane slipped around behind them, his arms going around Booker's middle and pressing his cheek to his broad back. They both offered comfort to their boy. Unfortunately, Lane was so small his hands only just met, making Booker shift slightly so Lane could get a better purchase.

Derick kept his smile to himself at his husband's frustration at being so little.

Booker sighed, his head dropping between his shoulders moments later. "How does anyone get over what those fuckers did to them—to the omegas?" His dark head lifted. His eyes glistened with tears that Booker would see as a weakness as they met Derick's stare. "How?"

"I don't know." Derick hated to admit it. "But know this, we'll do everything in our power to give those omegas back the right to choose. Give them their freedom and support in whatever way that is needed."

"I know *we will*... I just needed to hear it." Booker released a shuddery breath before moving, so Derick let go.

Booker gently stroked the back of Lane's hands. "Thanks, Popi. Your hugs are the best."

"Hey," Derick complained good-naturedly.

The grin, this time, held genuine amusement as Booker slowly got up, allowing Lane time to let go.

Each of his sons had a sensitive side, one that Lane nurtured, not that any of them would openly admit it to the other.

"You have nothing to thank us for. You were the one who set those omegas free by wanting to visit this new place, Booker. Don't you forget that."

Lane spoke the truth. The omegas they'd discovered chained up and held hostage, forced to work for a pittance that was then taken off them for their 'accommodation and food' were now in a hotel receiving care. They were safe and Derick planned to make sure it stayed that way.

What their sons had discovered was the reason Lane, for the last couple of nights, had slipped out of bed to head to the kitchen and wait for Booker. He always found sleeping hard when feeling troubled and those were the times the nightmares would start again. Derick suspected it was a nightmare that had driven Booker from his bed tonight. The haunted look his son wore earlier suggested the nightmare was a bad one.

Booker's cheeks flushed a dark pink. "Popi,"—Booker cracked a giant yawn—"Dad, I think I'm gonna head to bed, I might catch a couple more hours as I've got a full day ahead of me tomorrow."

Derick stared after Booker as he left the kitchen, his dark eyes narrowing. "You were right, as always, my love."

Lane's chuckle was very telling, and Derick switched his attention to his husband. "I don't know why you doubt me." Lane smirked, wiping the counter after clearing up the dirty mugs, his expression growing serious. "It doesn't take a rocket scientist to see how much Booker is suffering right now. He's so big that many don't notice the soft heart that beats inside his chest. I knew he'd suffer after what they found down in Drinkwater."

Lane's knuckles turned white as he waved the cloth he held between them. "Chained... those animals... they should be chained for what they did to those poor divergent omegas. What if Jupiter had been there?" Lane shuddered violently, his thoughts matching Derick's earlier ones.

The catch in Lane's throat and shimmering eyes brought Derick from his seat. He took the cloth from his husband, dropping it onto the counter and taking him in his arms.

"You promise me you'll make them all pay? That they'll suffer for what they did to them?" Lane asked quietly.

The scent of chocolate and the faint scent of sex they'd had earlier lingered, and Derick nuzzled Lane's hair. "They will, my love. I swear to you, they will." Retirement plans didn't matter, Derick would make it his business to take every last fucker down. Every person involved, no one would escape. He'd make damn sure of it.

No one hurt his family *and got away with it.*

Chapter Sixteen

Delicious & Vicious

Bowie: I think I've made a mistake...

Frey: I'm sure you haven't. What is it you think you've done?

Bowie: I read an email from Kodi to Kari about what happened in Drinkwater, and I mentioned it during a conversation with Jupiter.

Hollis: *I'm confused. Bowie, what's wrong with talking about it with Jupiter? It's not like he won't be aware of what they found in the factory. He's on the board of directors.*

Bowie: *I don't know about that. But Jupiter went nuts after I spoke about it.*

Wilder: *More nuts that he already is?*

Bowie: *I'm not sure what you mean, Wilder, but he was… kinda wild and crying.*

Hollis: *Sorry, he was crying?*

Frey: *Are you sure? That doesn't sound like Jupiter.*

Wilder: *I second that. He doesn't have a heart, more a stone!*

Hollis: Wilder, behave.

Bowie: Erm… yep. Kodi had to sit on him, and Kari demanded I ring Lane and Derick to get them to come into the office. That can't be good, so it has to mean I did something wrong. Do you think they're gonna sack me? I need my job.

Isley: I heard the commotion. I didn't realize it was Jupiter. Sounded like a crazed animal had got in the building. Bowie, Hollis wouldn't let anyone sack you.

Hollis: Exactly. Bowie, you've done nothing wrong, I'm sure. It's probably not connected at all to what you said.

Bowie: Sure seems like it… but if you're sure, I'll believe you, Hollis. You've never lied to me.

Wilder: Isley, can you sneak in and see what's going on?

Hollis: *Isley, please do no such thing. Wilder, behave!*

Frey: *I'm sure Wilder's not the only one who wants to know what upset Jupiter like that. I mean, really, we're all like a big family… aren't we?*

Hollis: *No one likes an interfering family.*

Lane: *Bowie, it's not your fault and thank you for calling us. I've left a mars bar cake in the coffee lounge… enjoy.*

Chapter Seventeen

Frey

The hallways were full of staff members gossiping about the incident. There was no other word for it, given how Jupiter lost his shit with his brothers. Then there was the switch around of the PAs. Jupiter now had Ziggy, and Wilder was working with Silas. The conversation in the coffee lounge at lunchtime on that Monday had been very interesting. That, however, was not what was on Frey's mind as he stared at Booker, who was glowering hard enough to make him sweat.

"I won't be here from tomorrow, Friday, through to Tuesday. I've had it marked on the calendar for weeks," he explained, blushing like crazy, but doing his best to act like there was nothing to see.

"We have some very important work to finish up," Booker ground out through his clenched teeth.

Nothing about his tone suggested this conversation was going to be an easy one, not that Frey could understand why. It wasn't like Booker was to know that he'd never taken time off for a heat before. He'd filled in the calendar the same as everyone else, then worked from home to avoid suspicion.

"Yes, I'm well aware of that." Frey forced his lips into a beaming smile. "I've shared what needs dealing with. Monty is fully up to date with the projects I'm working on. This will ensure there is no disruption to them," he rushed to reassure. "I've given Monty access to all the information on my computer. He's more than capable of stepping in while I'm *away*."

"Away where?" Booker's lips curled into what came across as a grimace.

Frey coughed, blushing even harder. So much so that he felt hotter than the one time he'd decided a tanning bed was a good idea. He dropped his gaze to the desk between them, looking at the clutter instead of the bear.

"It's in the *other* calendar."

Lane had established an omega heat calendar long before Frey had started working for the company. It made it easy for all the omegas to add the times they need off, so there wasn't any debate or discussion around having the time when their bodies demanded sex.

"Which calendar?" Booker's expression portrayed none of his emotions, making it hard for Frey to determine if the bear was being obtuse on purpose.

He stood straight and glowered back at Booker, unable to stop the challenge when he was feeling miffed and frustrated. He had neither the daring nor the courage to actually ask for what he wanted, so he added a big helping of flirtyness to his next words. "The steam version of a sex calendar." His grin was all teeth as he finished. "You know the one where we get to plan to go—"

"I... *stop*," Booker growled, his teeth making a clicking sound as they snapped together on the last word.

Frey fell into silence, his eyes narrowing on Booker when he now looked as flushed as Frey.

When the uncomfortable silence continued, Frey's nerves forced him to speak. "What?" he asked innocently. "I thought you were interested."

"I..." Booker growled once more, and it lifted the hairs on the back of Frey's neck as Booker got out of his seat and stalked to the window. Hands on the sill, his whole body was rigid with tension as he stayed staring out the glass. "Fine. Whatever." He lifted a hand in a dismissive gesture, not once looking back at Frey.

Booker didn't witness Frey's shoulders slump or how he trudged to the door and left, closing it quietly behind him. He gave Pam a grimace of a smile and quickly returned to his own office to hide.

Whatever he'd expected from deciding to discuss his heat with Booker and his time off, he admitted it hadn't gone the way he'd secretly hoped it would. Booker had gotten pissed about the disruption of his work and nothing more.

What had I really expected?

Some undying declaration that Booker would be his—*forever.*

He was being stupid. Not a little stupid, but utterly stupid to get his hopes up after listening to his fox. Who, after the whole clingy thing Booker had done before the trip to Drinkwater, considered the bear was definitely interested in him.

Now he was...

Frey couldn't decide because Booker was too damn confusing.

Had Booker heard about his trip to a sex club? Was that what was different? Although Frey couldn't fathom why. It wasn't like he'd done anything except watch, and he wasn't even sure Jupiter had noticed them to report back.

He sighed, disheartened by the whole situation, and shut himself in his office. His gaze landed on the files on his desk. Work, he'd concentrate on that. At least it wouldn't confuse him.

The nerves had taken hold the second that Frey had started to feel overly warm the evening before after leaving work. He'd spent two hours sniffing himself, trying to figure out if he smelled different. Up to now, all he'd got was that he felt like he had added extra layers and turned up the heating, making it hard to catch his breath. His doctor had informed him that this first heat after having none for years—and Frey couldn't remember how he'd felt because he'd blocked it out—could be unusual. It wasn't helping Frey decide whether or not he was reacting normally.

Why couldn't they have just given him more pills?

They made us infertile.

No! They said it was a possibility, not that it was a sure thing.

He had clung to that knowledge since the conversation. He was hanging on to the little ray of hope because he never considered not having babies. He wanted babies in his future... little cute bear-foxes...

"Oh jeez! Is the heat going to make me only think about Booker?" There was no one to answer him, not that he wanted anyone to know he was pining for the big bear. Working so closely and constantly with Booker, Frey got to see how much Booker cared... about everything. He worked harder than anyone Frey had met, even Derick and Lane.

Was he trying to prove himself?

Frey, even after some digging into Booker's past, remained uncertain around the reasons and circumstances why Lane and Derick adopted the bear. Nothing suggested Booker was bad, or had done something awful to warrant his family disowning him. To Frey's way of thinking, Derick and Lane would never have someone in their family that was say... a mass murderer, or something like that.

Why don't you call our bear and ask him? his fox side wheedled. *Then we can have his big hairy body wrapped around us.*

Why are you torturing me this way? What did I ever do to you to deserve this? What? Isn't it going to be hard enough to get through the next few days without you bringing the big hunk of furriness into the equation?

We're both suffering here, not just you!

Frey blew out a breath, then sucked a big one in and tried not to think about the way Booker looked or smelled in the hotel suite they'd shared. He focused on being calm, finding his Zen. It hadn't worked up to now, but that didn't mean it wouldn't happen.

He searched for something else to focus on when he failed, like every other time. He ran through what Ziggy had said when Frey had asked him numerous questions, along with his doctor, about what was going to happen to him. Neither had mentioned anything about having endless thoughts of a certain bear doing...

Come on, you were just getting to the fun parts, imagining all those muscles covered in fur as we rubbed ourselves, naked, all over him.

This right now, you gotta stop it? You're a very naughty fox!

His fox's laughter grated on Frey's last nerve because as much as he wanted it, some part of him remained scared he'd freak, and his head would take him back to being trapped without a choice. Which meant that part wanted to lock himself in a room and not come out until this entire ordeal was over. Did anyone die if they didn't have sex during a heat?

It wasn't a question he had asked his doctor, maybe he should have.

Instead of worrying about that, Frey did his best to block his fox when his fantasies got Frey feeling hotter and more bothered, although his ass wasn't dripping or soaking the pair of specially made underwear he'd found for the occasion. Underwear he'd bought from a specialist website, which allowed for some modesty for omegas during their heat. They had a slit in the ass section, meaning they could stay on and keep his cock covered, which, in the circumstances, was for the best. He didn't want Ziggy touching him there.

This wasn't about attraction, only need. And Ziggy didn't really want to touch his dick, either. It was going to be weird enough without being fully naked and there being touching beyond the use of toys. They'd agreed all Ziggy was going to do was use whatever toys they'd found online to get Frey through, and nothing more.

Would it work?

Frey was terrified to think it might not... because he had no other options when coping alone wasn't something his doctor had recommended for his safety, after not experiencing a heat for years—or really at all. What he'd meant by that, Frey really didn't want to find out. Images of him haring down a street, naked and begging any old alpha to fuck him were what nightmares became made of.

He jerked towards the sound of the doorbell and his palms grew sweaty as he clasped his shaking hands together to go to the door. He stared at it, willing himself to open it after looking through the peephole and seeing Ziggy with a bag slung over his shoulder.

I can do this.

I can do this.

I can.

The doorbell chimed again, and Frey's shoulders slumped as he opened the door, not looking at his friend.

"Hey," Ziggy murmured, coming in so Frey had to step back.

The door clicked shut and Ziggy slipped the deadbolt into place, setting off Frey's already erratic pulse.

"Erm... do you still wanna do this?" Ziggy asked as Frey continued to stare at the now locked door and not directly at the man who dropped his bag to the floor.

He gulped and nodded, only it wasn't quite a nod, more a half nod, half head shake. "I..." he gave Ziggy a desperate look. "What if..." he threw up his arms, unable to put his fears into words.

They'd done lots of talking, but the reality part? They had nothing.

"How's the sexual urges right now?" Ziggy's gentle approach helped. He was so patient and a fantastic friend.

"I took my temperature, and it's steadily climbed since last night. So the doc's predictor thingy has worked."

"So the urges?" Ziggy gently prompted again.

Flushing for a whole new reason, Frey shook his head. "No urges... or not, like, I want to hump the first alpha I might find to assuage the need."

Everything made him fret, and this was no different. "I have thoughts about an alpha... sexy ones... where I..." he waved a hand in front of his face, attempting to create a little breeze to cool him off, "shimmy over his furry body."

Would that description tell Ziggy who it was? The night in the sex club, Frey had vague memories of sharing, but Ziggy had said nothing, so Frey had kept quiet about it.

"Do you want to go find that alpha, hunt him down and..." Ziggy's cheeks filled with color that Frey considered matched his own, "let him fuck you?"

Frey sighed, disheartened at being unable to really verbalize exactly what he was feeling when he had a rational, thinking brain. Something both the doctor and Ziggy said would disappear when his heat hit. So should he be feeling like that now? And because he wasn't, did that mean there was something else wrong with him?

He scratched his head in frustration, then tugged his hair. "Why can't it be simple? I know that I'm attracted to..."

Ziggy's eyes narrowed, and he wore an expectant look.

"You know, don't you?" As he said it, Frey became more convinced when Ziggy tried and failed to hide his amusement. "Alright, Booker. I'm attracted to Booker."

Ziggy's lips twitched before he turned his back on Frey, taking off his jacket to hang it up on the hooks by the door that led into the apartment. "You're right. You might have mentioned it once or twice at the club. And sometimes I can see it in the way you stare at him. Or how you sometimes talk about him in the group chat."

"Great!" Frey tossed up his arms when Ziggy turned and came deeper into the room, aiming for the massive couch that faced into the room. "So that means everyone knows!"

Ziggy lounged back, stretching out over the back of the couch. His plain black T-shirt showed off his tattoo covered arms, and the intricate designs never failed to fascinate Frey.

"Does it matter who knows? I'm pretty sure you aren't the only PA who is interested in their paired alpha."

Ziggy's observation brought Frey's attention away from the tattoos. "Are you interested in Jupiter?" Frey questioned when the thought entered his head after the recent change that everyone in their group chat had avoided mentioning. Frey wasn't sure why, but he suspected there were others who didn't want to swap around and end up worse off. He for sure was one of them. There was also Lane. No one would want to upset him with him being the alphas' father, that was for sure.

Ziggy laughed aloud. "I've barely had time to get to know him. But I'd say from what I've seen of Jupiter, his tastes aren't mine."

"Huh? What tastes?" A furrow developed between his brows as he stared at Ziggy, failing to understand what he was getting at, unless it was to do with what they'd seen at the club.

Ziggy gave a kind of half shrug. "Let's say he has interesting activities in and out of work." He ran a hand over his beard, his attention fully on Frey. "Shall we get back to you and Booker?"

"What's there to say?" Frey blew out his breath and gave in to Ziggy's silly grin. "Okay... I took one look at his big hairy chest—which I totally blame Hollis for, when he had us sharing suites on the last trip—and all I could think about was what it would be like to lick the fur and slide naked against him."

Frey spun around and marched around his living room, his ass getting twitchy, but not damp, with his train of thought. "I've never wanted to do that with anyone else. And I'm not sure I want to do it with anyone other than Booker."

He looked back at Ziggy, hating his frustration. "But see, that makes little sense to me. Is this because I stopped the pills? Or is it because I want him... like, really want him? He's there in my head." He tapped at the side of his head to demonstrate, now he was letting it all out. "Digging in and staying put like a damn tic, sucking on my thoughts, making his presence felt."

The chuckles coming from Ziggy didn't help Frey's mood now he was on a roll and coming to terms with what had been playing on his mind. He liked Booker.

He really liked Booker, enough to get naked.

Jeez!

His legs turned to jelly, and he staggered more than walked to the big armchair closest to him.

Ziggy rose, darting to him, looking concerned, and helped him to take the last couple of steps when his legs totally gave way. "What is it?"

"Don't panic, but now I've admitted how much I want Booker... I kinda feel like I wanna find him and maybe demand things..." he released a shuddery breath. "I'm doomed!"

"It's the heat. Your biological reaction."

Frey would not kid himself, it was not that. His ass wasn't slick. His thoughts weren't all about sex. The sites he'd visited said he'd have no logic. They were wrong. "No. I don't think so," he muttered, more to himself than to Ziggy.

"What did the doc say about your reactions after suppressing for so long?"

"He wasn't sure. The inhibitors could have made me uninterested generally in wanting... sex. I don't want only sex with Booker... I want more." There, he'd said it aloud, and the world hadn't imploded.

Ziggy's blond brows rose, and he blew out a noisy breath. Frey didn't miss the concern clouding his eyes. "Your fox might not want me touching you if you've... connected sex and—"

"Please don't say it, don't," Frey begged.

Ziggy's expression made Frey's tummy dance unpleasantly with the truth of it. "What are we gonna do?"

Frey refused to cry and shrugged. "I don't know."

We want Booker.

Please... we just need to get through the next few days.

We want Booker.

Obstinate fox. It's too late to do anything now. We have to get through this. I swear that for the next one, I'll speak to Booker. If he ever got the courage up.

He felt the moment his animal side blocked him. *Great! Now what was he supposed to do?*

Chapter Eighteen

Booker

Booker sat opposite Silas in the sunroom and pretended like he wasn't about ready to crawl out of his skin as he listened to the minutes tick by on the wall clock. What were Frey and Ziggy doing right now?

If you refuse to go to our little fox, then keep your thoughts to yourself!

You can block me, remember!

His bear was being a testy fucker and Booker had struggled all day, knowing that Frey was in heat... without him.

Your choice.

No, it's Frey's choice.

You never offered or gave him an option, did you?

"—you look at it?" Silas's attention was on the laptop sitting on his knee, where it had been for the past hour.

He never looked up, so he didn't see Booker frown. "Say again?"

Silas arched one brow as he flicked a glance at Booker. "The information from Design Detailing & Co on the employees. I sent it to you and our HR department. *Did you look at it?*"

He spoke slowly, enunciating each word like Booker was deaf.

"I replied to your email."

They still weren't speaking, or not the way they usually did. Booker was at a loss on how to broach the subject. Not when he continued to brood over Silas blowing up so spectacularly at him for mentioning Ziggy fucking Frey. Like that was his fault!

Silas didn't respond, his fingers clicking over the keys, offering the top of his dark head to Booker.

Infuriated, Booker got up to stalk out of the room, muttering, "It's not like I wanted to fuck someone you were interested in, is it?"

There was the sound of something slamming down on wood and before he could register it fully, a large hand grabbed the back of his work shirt he'd not bothered changing out of. Pulled to a halt, he staggered back into the solid body behind him.

"What did you say?" Silas demanded angrily.

Booker wrenched free and spun, getting right in Silas's face. "I said it's not like I wanna fuck someone you're interested in," he spat out in fury. Not all of his anger belonged to Silas, but he was the only target Booker had right then.

"What the fuck are you talking 'bout?" There was confusion, along with annoyance, as Silas met his stare.

Booker's growl was all menace. "You never fucked Frey, did you? That was Jupiter! So what gives you the right to be pissed at me? I didn't do anything."

"I never fucked the flirty fox," Jupiter exclaimed from behind Booker. "Who told you I did? And when did you become interested in who graces my bed?"

Booker swung around to stare at Jupiter, who was lounging against the wall, casually dressed for a Friday night. "You said you fucked him." Booker jabbed a finger at him. "I heard you."

"I was probably winding one of you up. I've fucked none of the PAs. I don't shit where I eat, man."

"What kind of saying is that?" Booker asked, baffled and totally getting off topic while he processed what Jupiter had said. Had he really not touched Frey? Was this another wind up? Jupiter, although he'd been out of sorts since he'd found out about what had gone on in Drinkwater, could remain a wind up merchant despite his mood.

If he hadn't any interest in Frey, regardless of when, then that left Booker where?

Free! It stops your silly human side throwing excuses at us. His bear actually did an ass wiggle.

What. The. Ever. Loving. Fuck. Was. That!

"Don't think I'm gonna let you change the topic of conversation when this is so juicy." His brother broke through his thoughts as Jupiter looked pointedly at Silas. "I figured there was something up between you two, and with Popi staying schtum, I guessed it was major. I can see I was right, although what it's got to do with me fucking anyone is be-yond me."

"It's got nothing to do with you," Booker snapped

Right as Silas answered, "The world does not revolve around you, as much as you like to believe it does."

Booker saw pain flash in Jupiter's eyes before it got masked with Jupiter's 'go to smirk'. "Oh, big brother, it total-ly does." He thumbed his nose at Silas before disappearing as quietly as he'd arrived, leaving a heavy silence in his wake.

Booker blew out a frustrated breath. "Why did you have to say that to him after..." Booker couldn't make himself say it.

Jupiter's past was something no one talked about, not unless he brought up the subject, which he never did.

"I wasn't thinking." Silas gave a haunted look in the direc-tion Jupiter had gone. They'd both been witness to Jupiter's state when he'd first arrived at the house. Not something either of them would ever forget. "Fuck, he makes it too easy to have a go at him."

Booker heard Silas's sorrow. "Go say sorry."

Silas stepped closer, his attention on Booker. "Seems he's not the only one I need to say sorry to."

"He's more important right now." Booker nodded in the direction Jupiter had gone. "Go sort it out and then come find me."

Silas hesitated before he nodded and disappeared.

Booker stood for long seconds, staring into space, coming to terms with just how happy he was that Jupiter hadn't touched Frey. It was stupid really, when he was damn positive that Frey would have had many alphas touch him. The guy was gorgeous, who wouldn't want him?

He'd taken one step and abruptly came to a halt. *Then why was Frey using an omega to help him through his heat?*

Booker had witnessed firsthand Frey's flirtatious side. The way he brought conversations around to sex wherever possible. Wouldn't it stand to reason that he would have lots of alpha options for his heat?

He went to a sex club, goddamnit... yet...

Something felt off. Booker's gut was mincing his supper better than a meat grinder. What was he missing?

Booker rubbed at his temples, his frown deepening.

Omegas with omegas... was that an actual thing? If it was a thing, then why did Frey only really flirt with alphas?

He had no answers and the man who had them was doing... whatever, with Ziggy right now. Booker was so damn confused he didn't know which way was front and which was back.

"You feeling alright?" Popi asked a second before an arm slipped around Booker's waist, making him aware he remained standing in the sunroom's doorway, staring at nothing.

"I was... thinking," he stuttered when he met Popi's gaze and couldn't tell an outright lie and say he was fine.

"About?" Popi asked, guiding a reluctant Booker to the seats in front of the windows.

"Stuff," Booker replied noncommittally.

Lane chuckled and patted his knee when he sat next to him. "You know it's just best to tell me, or I'll only worry." He gave him a practiced look that made Booker want to confess faster than someone in a confessional.

"Popi, do you know anything about omegas liking other omegas to help them when they have a heat?" he hedged, going with a question Popi, being an omega, might have an answer to. One that made sense. As Booker had referred to this before about Ziggy and Frey, maybe it wouldn't come across as odd—possibly.

"Not something I've heard of being a common practice." His slim shoulders shrugged casually in the lightweight, rose wool sweater that suited his complexion. "There are so many things available to omegas to aid with their heats that I can't see why any would wish to get another omega to assist them." He patted Booker's knee once more. "Unless they feel attracted to each other—or are in a relationship. It happens, I'm sure."

Booker's head wanted to explode when what Popi said got lodged inside his brain, and the possibility of genuine attraction between Frey and Ziggy would not let go. "You... really... what... well dammit all!"

Popi reached over and stroked the side of his face, his lips twitching, Booker thought, but then he must be wrong because when Popi spoke, he sounded concerned. "I'm not sure what you are trying to say, sweet boy."

"Neither the fuck am I," Booker answered truthfully. His brain had turned to mush at having 'the Jupiter situation' resolved and now to be met with another possible barrier—Ziggy!

"Maybe if you explain why you asked me that question, it would help? Or maybe I can guess it has something to do with what we talked about before?"

Booker balked at the very idea of going back over the conversation and explaining that he was interested in Frey and that he knew Ziggy was doing the horizontal mambo with him right now.

"I... oh fuck, yes, okay, it is," he said sullenly, when no one in the world could resist Popi's encouraging smile.

"Frey's a lovely man."

"Popi," he fired back in warning. "It's not like that."

Back was the knee patting. Popi was totally humoring Booker, he could tell by the smile gracing his face. "Booker, my darling boy, there's nothing wrong with having feelings for someone."

Booker shot out of the seat in panic, his eyes wheeling around the room to check no one had heard what Popi was implying. He breathed just a fraction easier at seeing none of his brothers as he held up his hands. "No Popi... it's not like that"—the smile never left Popi's lips—"it isn't," Booker reiterated forcibly.

"Whatever you say."

Silas chose then to reappear, and Booker breathed a sigh of relief.

He walked to Silas before he could take more than a step into the room. "Weren't we going out for a beer?"

Silas wore a look of confusion for a second when he glanced between Booker and Popi. "Oh yeah, right."

He gave Silas a grateful smile and hooked his arm. "Come on, then."

He dragged Silas with him as he headed back out of the room, calling over his shoulder, "Catch you later, Popi."

Much later... like five years' time later, when he'd forgotten the silly notion of me having feelings for Frey!

His bear laughed all the way to the car.

Chapter Nineteen

Frey

By morning, Frey figured his body was broken. He stifled a sob, staring at himself in the mirror. He'd slept all night with no issue after his body had done nothing more than stay hot. At two in the morning, he'd sent Ziggy off to sleep in the spare room as he'd struggled to keep his eyes open. Frey had promised that he'd wake him when things changed.

Frey had woken ten minutes ago, at noon, which was a common time for him to wake on a weekend if he'd had a busy or stressful week. He'd had both. He wanted to blame those things for why his body wasn't behaving as a heat predicted.

A shuffling sound came from beyond the door and Frey shoved a fist into his mouth to stop the next sob from escaping.

He stood staring at his glistening eyes for so long; he smelled coffee before he was brave enough to go and face

Ziggy. Although face him didn't quite apply, because the other man wasn't the issue. Frey's body was the absolute problem. He dabbed at his eyes with the sleeve of the top he'd put on when leaving his bedroom.

Ziggy was lounging against the countertop, holding a steaming mug of coffee. His expression revealed none of his thoughts as they looked at each other. "Wanna coffee?"

Happy Ziggy hadn't offered a dollop of sympathy to add to his misery when he felt fragile enough to break, Frey nodded.

"You like three sugars, right?" Ziggy, wearing old sweats, which hung perilously low on his hips, and nothing else, asked, glancing over his tattooed shoulder at Frey.

"Four, please. I need all the sweetness to wake me up." He needed more than sugar, but he'd take what he could get for now.

Moments later, Frey mimicked Ziggy's stance, standing next to him and leaning on the countertop, sipping his coffee. The caffeine hit buzzed through him, sending his anxious stomach into a full on macarena.

"You make wonderful coffee." Small talk, it was all he had when everything else meant acknowledging that he needed to make another appointment with the doctor.

"I'm broken," Frey whispered in a terrified voice.

Ziggy placed his mug down and took Frey's from his icy grip. Ziggy wrapped his arms around him, and Frey sagged into the embrace. The sob came with a full body shudder of despair. "You aren't broken, Frey."

"How can you say that? I don't smell like I'm in heat. The physiological reactions I should be going through... they aren't happening." He buried his face in Ziggy's neck and let the grief come.

He really was broken.

He hadn't listened to Dr. Hockings, and now it was too late.

What was he going to do now?

Ziggy stroked his back and remained silent as Frey cried until his head felt wooly, his eyes ached and had become swollen. Ziggy didn't complain at how wet and snotty his shoulder was as he led Frey into the bathroom, got a cloth and gently wiped his face. "What do you need from me?"

Frey hiccuped, unsure how he'd gotten so lucky to have a friend as great as Ziggy. "I don't know," he confessed. "I'm broken."

"Okay, as your friend, what I'm gonna say comes from a place of love." He placed the cloth down on the sink and cupped Frey's bristly cheeks. "You gotta stop being silly."

He locked gazes with Frey with a look that suggested he was being very serious. "Your internal system is unique. Not broken. The discovery of divergents has shown that nothing is black and white for shifters. Some shift, some don't. Some have more of one hormone than another. Would you say they were broken when all they are is beautifully unique?"

The hands holding him limited his head shake, but Frey tried. "No." His quivering belly settled as he processed what Ziggy was telling him. He clung to the hope that his being different wasn't so bad after all. Maybe his difference gave him time to adapt, to figure out how to accept his body's needs.

"Then I need you to stop saying that about yourself. You're different. There is nothing wrong with being different. Whether that's the drugs you took to survive a traumatic experience. Whether it's to do with your biology. Or even to do with your fox choosing to hide out, none of the reasons matter if you can accept that different isn't necessarily bad... or mean you're broken."

His eyes crinkled as he grinned. "I mean, you kinda won the omega lottery right now with how you aren't governed by pesky hormones, which can remove your choices of when you wanna have sex."

When he put it like that, Frey's lips twitched. "I suppose I did."

Hands dropped from Frey's face, and Ziggy took a step back, giving him an expectant look. "So as we don't need to get jiggy all weekend, what do you fancy doing instead?"

A slow smile spread over Frey's face. "Wanna go get cake, veg out, and find a series to binge watch?"

"Sounds perfect."

On Monday, Frey did what he'd always done. He got up with his alarm, sorted himself out and had come into work on automatic pilot. As Booker stood in the doorway to his office, looking at him like he'd somehow lost something important, it struck Frey what the issue was.

He wasn't supposed to come into work, was he!

Crapola! How am I going to talk my way out of this?

Booker's nose wrinkled as if he was scenting the air, stepping fully into Frey's office. He quickly shut the door behind him and stayed right there with his back against the door and his hand gripping the handle.

"What are you doing here?" he demanded.

Frey eyed the white knuckled hand on the handle before he fired back, "I work here!"

He went on the defensive, scrambling to come up with a valid excuse for forgetting himself and being at work when he was supposed to be going through his heat at home.

Ziggy had left him last night, after a glorious weekend of binge eating cake and watching Reacher in all his gloriousness. He'd had such a 'normal weekend' after his meltdown on Saturday that Frey hadn't thought to turn off the alarm on his phone. So when it went off to say it was time to get up for work, he had.

He really needed to come up with a way to stop his rational self from getting in his way. Fifty questions about his heat wasn't the way he wanted to start his day, especially when it was with Booker.

Booker remained plastered to the door, quite literally. "You said you weren't coming in until tomorrow," he accused, his eyes wheeling all over the place.

"Then why are you here?" Frey asked sweetly, getting up from his desk to move around it, watching Booker closely.

When had Booker become a door hugger?

"I... I heard... someone say they'd seen Zi—you," he stuttered and wore an angry look that Frey was familiar with. It was the one Booker got when he wasn't sure of his footing and anger became his defensive reaction.

Had he been about to say Ziggy?

Interesting.

Frey knew he could trust Ziggy, and would sell his soul to the devil if the snake shifter had gossiped about him. The man was honorable and there was no way he'd have told Booker about their plans at the weekend. That had to mean one of two things. One of the PAs had overheard them and gossiped about him. As the PAs were his friends, they would have come to him directly to ask what was going on. That was how they worked.

They hadn't.

That left Booker having overheard him and Ziggy talking in the coffee lounge, the one-time they'd spoken at work about Frey's heat issue.

What had Booker heard?

He went through the conversation and counted back the days to his doctor's appointment. *Was it after that Booker had glued himself to me?*

Things clicked together and Frey gave Booker a narrow-eyed stare as he walked towards the bear, who remained clutching the handle. Frey's heart thundered in his ears at all the possibilities as he aimed his most sexy smirk at Booker, watching for his reaction.

If anything, the bear appeared to pale and then his hand rose as if to fend Frey off.

His ears actually rang with how fast his heart beat as Frey stopped, his hand going to the hip he cocked out.

"Whatsup?" he asked, doing his best to keep the nerves from his voice. Did Booker like him in a 'I don't want anyone else touching you' kind of way? It sure seemed that way when Frey considered how Booker had been last Thursday, now he saw it through fresh eyes.

"You shouldn't be here!" Booker exclaimed in a strangled, almost unrecognizable voice.

"Why?" Frey questioned, taking another step closer, only to watch Booker appear to hold his breath.

Then Booker put a hand over his nose and mouth, giving Frey a lock of utter panic that gave Frey's pulse another boost.

The bear was worried about his heat scent...

Our bear.

Now you choose to unblock me!

His fox sniffed indignantly.

"Stay back!"

The muffled command got met with a big ass grin. "What's wrong, Bocker."

Frey sashayed closer and watched in utter delight as Booker flung open the door and darted out. He sprinted off down the corridor faster than Frey would have considered possible for such a big man.

"I thought you wanted to talk to me," he called after him.

There was no response, not that he expected one when Booker had already disappeared into the stairwell leading to the fire escape.

"What's going on?" asked Hollis, who poked his head out of his office door, frowning. "Shouting in the corridor, Frey? You know better."

Frey couldn't find it in him to be upset at the chastise he heard in Hollis's tone as he nodded in agreement. "Sorry boss. Won't happen again."

Hollis glanced down the passageway and back to Frey. "Is there something I'm missing?"

Giggling, Frey shook his head. "Absolutely nothing," he answered.

The frown remained as Hollis came fully out of his office. "Aren't you supposed to be out of the office today... recovering?"

Blushing, he beckoned Hollis into his office. "About that..."

Chapter Twenty

Booker

Running away from a damn flirty fox in heat? Booker would feel the mortification once he'd calmed his bear down and spoken to Hollis. There was no way they were going to allow Frey to remain at work with the potential of one of the alphas working in the building catching his delectable scent.

It remained in Booker's nose, the spicy sweetness so powerful it made him hard enough that the zipper on his slacks would become a permanent imprint on his cock. His bear, on the other hand, was ready to tear off Booker's clothes and tuck the tiny fox under his arm to hibernate.

What the heck was Frey playing at, coming to work in heat? Was there something wrong with the tiny fox? He stumbled at the thought but kept going, despite nearly plowing into Monica, who rounded the corner. Her bat-like reflexes saved her, hair flying as she darted out of Booker's way.

Hollis would have to find out!

He ran past an alarmed looking Pam, who caught him mid charge to his office door. He could barely manage a wave to show he was fine. Was he fine? Was he hell.

Panicked, breathless, running and sweaty was so not his normal, in office behavior.

He grabbed his phone with a far hairier hand than usual and, with trembling fingers, dialed Hollis's office. It rang and rang. He counted off the number of times it rang. Only when it reached thirty did he slam the phone down, no calmer, even after the breather.

"Can I help?" Pam asked from the doorway. She hovered in it like she couldn't decide if it was safe to come inside.

It wasn't.

Booker needed Frey out of the building, like now. His bear was close to losing it at thoughts of not being near their fox and anyone scenting him. He wasn't fairing much better, if truth be told. Running hadn't been his brightest idea, but it was that or doing something totally out of character. Throwing Frey over his shoulder and locking him away from everyone was exactly what his bear wanted. He was the more reasonable one of the two of them—just not today.

"Go get Hollis, I need him here like yesterday," he growled past his elongated teeth. "And call Silas first, get him to come."

The doorway was empty a second later and Booker rested his hands on the desk, shutting his eyes and working on taking some even breaths of air that weren't scented with Frey.

"What... argh, shit Booker! What do you need?" Silas asked, his enormous hands slid down Booker's quivering back, offering him the support he needed to keep his mind focused.

"Not sure... Frey is in the building." His teeth dug into his lip as he tried to speak.

"Isn't he..."

A crushing sensation came with Booker's lack of ability to take a decent gulp of air.

"Breathe. Fuck Booker, breathe for me. In and out, slowly. Come on, you know the drill, work with me Booker," Silas cajoled continuously, the time slipping by unnoticed. The hands never stopped from their soothing motion, keeping him tethered to the here and now.

His bear, when in an emotional state, never ever listened to reason when it wanted to protect those he loved. That alarming reality did not help Booker regain his control as fast as he'd like.

How long they stood just like that, Booker couldn't have said. His bear, in this heightened state, never released control back to him easily. The two sides of him became extremely conflicted and though he got his bear wanted to shift and protect them both, it couldn't be trusted with how he felt about Frey. How it wanted to curl its enormous body around the fox and snuggle. This was why Booker had run. His bear didn't listen to reason, not fucking once.

He's ours.

Booker was too damn exhausted to argue back.

"I hope this is…" Hollis trailed off as he came into the office. "What's wrong?"

Booker's eyes opened, and he growled.

"Get Frey out of the building, now!" Silas stated gruffly.

"What…" Hollis frowned and stepped closer to Booker's desk. His gaze swept over Booker, and he blushed. "Oh… *I see*."

"You see nothing," Booker forced out on his next breath.

Hollis quietly shut the door to the office, blocking out those who were in the hallway, gawping at his stupid, over-reactive ass.

"He's not in heat," Hollis advised gently, showing he did indeed know part of Booker's issue.

"He is," Booker snapped back at the man, who gave him a sympathetic look.

"No, he's not. I can't say more than that. It's up to Frey to explain, *if he wants to*."

The cryptic comment wasn't helping when Booker knew damn well what he'd scented in Frey's office. "He is," he insisted.

Silas's hands paused. "Hollis seems pretty sure—"

"I'm telling you, I know what I smelled in his office," Booker stated, not so calmly.

"Don't bite my head off. Think about it rationally." Silas moved to look directly at Booker. "If Frey was indeed in heat, do you think he'd have made it into the building? Through reception and up to his office without one alpha noticing?"

He laid it out in a way that gave Booker time to pause and got his bear receding enough that he found it easier to breathe. To think. 'My nose..."

"Scented what?"

Booker's lips snapped together before he said exactly what was in his head—*my fox.* "I'm okay now," he said instead. It was far safer to say that when he had an audience. There was no way he was confessing he might—*did*—have some sort of feelings for Frey.

"Are you sure?" Silas asked, staring him down.

"Yeah... I'm fine, honest. You can both leave." He lied. He was far from fine, and the reason was on another floor smelling like all of Booker's favorite things.

Doomed. I'm fucking doomed.

Hollis remained where he was, as did Silas.

"Go, I got shit to do."

Neither man moved, and Booker gave a very loud, disgruntled sigh. "Listen. My bear smelled Frey and because we expected him to be home... in heat... we got it wrong. It appears."

No, we did not.

Now is not the time to discuss this.

We will discuss this, mark my words. You aren't going to pretend that was all me.

His bear went silent and Booker almost sagged in relief until he caught both Silas and Hollis staring at him, wearing identical looks of concern. "Seriously, I'm fine. If you say Frey isn't in heat, then great, he can pick up the slack, as Monty isn't all caught up on the list I gave him Friday."

There, that sounded convincing?

"Please don't hound Frey... he's..." Hollis pushed up his glasses.

His bear took notice. "He's what?"

"What he's shared with me... Please, just don't go all bear on him, you might frighten him."

Booker swung around his desk so fast the thing shifted a good inch as Hollis turned to leave. His stomach churned at the implications of Hollis's statement. "What's that supposed to mean?"

Had his behavior frightened Frey? He ran through how Frey had been before he'd left him. Frightened was not what Booker recalled.

His brows drew together. What was he missing?

Hollis shrugged, looking very uncomfortable. Something Booker was not used to seeing. "Be gentle with him."

He left, giving Booker a prickly feeling at the back of his neck as he twisted to glance at Silas. "Do you know what he's talking about?"

"What? Other than the obvious that you can be a grumpy asshole?"

Booker flipped his middle finger at Silas, scowling. "Fuck off. You're as grumpy as me. It's why we became friends."

Silas grinned before strolling to the door. He looked over his shoulder. "You ain't never had to talk me off the cliff, have you?"

"That might be so, but never count your fucking chickens before they hatch," he called after Silas's shaking shoulders.

"Asshole," he muttered under his breath, going and plonking himself back in his seat. One look at his phone and, for a moment, he contemplated calling Frey to his office.

He shook his head.

He sure wasn't ready for that and what it might prove. Burying his head in the sand like an ostrich? Yeah, that was a much better option.

Playing the avoiding game was for teenagers who had the hots and were shy of having any face-to-face conversations, so why was he doing exactly that?

He opened the door and dragged his weary ass inside, thinking about the last week. Booker spent days hiding—working—with Monty, despite Frey coming to his office several times to go over things that needed dealing with. He'd actually told Pam to tell Frey he was too busy to see him. To lie for him.

Booker was aghast by his own behavior, but he was totally in survival mode. He was majorly embarrassed after Monday. He'd also decided to avoid Ziggy. Thoughts of him anywhere near the fox during his heat sent his blood pressure through the roof. It was harder to avoid Ziggy with the time he'd needed to spend with Jupiter tying up loose ends for the fashion week prep that was hotting up the closer they got.

Silas was giving him a knowing smirk after he'd let it slip in front of Popi about losing his shit at work—again. Those two times rankled Booker when it had been years since he'd needed that kind of support. He knew exactly where to cast the blame.

And here he was on Friday, exhausted from all the avoiding, which included Popi. Booker was ready to shift in front of the fire and curl up on his special rug. That meant he could escape any talk about feelings. No, that was the last thing he wanted to do with anyone. He wasn't that kind of bear.

Give over.

You give over. It's all your fault I'm in this mess.

Deep chuckles filled his head as he slammed the door behind him, placing his laptop bag on the hall table to take off his jacket. He left it on top of the table, too tired to go hang it up.

"There you are, my sweet boy. Just in time."

Booker's shoulders slumped and the grump at being caught fed his frustration as he watched Popi stroll towards him, beaming.

"In time for what?" Popi's smile said he could kiss goodbye to his evening plans.

Popi slipped his arm through Booker's, patting his shirt sleeve and leading him down the hallway, heading in the direction of the kitchen.

"Family night," he declared happily.

"Great," Booker muttered sullenly. The last thing he wanted was to spend time with his brothers, poking at him with Taylin not here to take the flack.

Popi slapped playfully at his arm. "Don't act like that. You love family night. I've made your favorite pizza and got popcorn and oodles of chocolate treats."

He perked up a little at that. "Did you get milk duds?"

"Of course I did," Popi answered, like Booker was being silly. "I've got everyone's favorites."

Two steps into the heavenly scented kitchen, Booker hid his grin at his brothers, all sitting at the counter that was made to fit them all. Popi liked to eat messy foods in the kitchen after many disasters in the fancy dining room. The only one missing, as expected, was Taylin.

His grumpiness wanted to come back when he considered how happy Taylin was with Hollis, and his own lack...

He shook his head, warding off where his thoughts decided to take him without his permission.

"About time you dragged your sorry ass home," Laken snapped, giving him a death stare that made no sense to Booker. What had he done to piss off Laken? "Popi's tortured us with divine smelling pizza for the last half-hour, waiting for you to get your hairy self home."

Silas picked up his beer, his brow raising as he looked at Laken. "Who chewed on your ass?" Silas took a sip, his gaze moving between the two of them.

"Don't ask me. I've seen no fucker this week, been too busy."

"Don't I fucking know it. You held Monty hostage while my work has been piling up," Rue stated, sounding as pissed as Laken.

Booker eyed the empty seat between his brothers and contemplated if it would be safer to sit between two crocodiles.

"Boys, behave. I want a nice family evening." Popi's reprimand came with a stern look before he went to the large pizza oven he'd gotten especially for pizza nights. "I want there to be no talk about work tonight."

They'd established that rule years ago.

Dad rolled his eyes at them all, while he said, "Listen to your Popi."

Jupiter rested his elbows on the countertop, a sly look appearing. "Then what are we gonna talk about? Sex?"

Beer snorted out of Silas's nose as he coughed out the sip he'd taken. Booker knew Jupiter would have timed that to perfection.

Silas wiped his face, glaring at an unrepentant Jupiter.

"We can, you know that no subject is taboo." Popi gave them all a glowing smile.

Booker wasn't sure what was worse, talking about the sex he wasn't getting, or listening to Jupiter regale them with talk of his conquests.

"Let's go with baseball," Laken said quickly.

"Like that's much better," Kodi exclaimed, reaching out to nab a slice of pizza before anyone else.

"Only 'cause you support the banana's baseball team," Kari answered, chuckling at the dirty glare he got from his twin.

Taking his seat, Booker laughed with everyone else. "Banana's," he winked at Kari, "how can they play with no arms and legs?" asking tongue in cheek as everyone around him, except for Kodi, fell about laughing. Like usual, Popi was right. Family night was just what he needed.

Chapter Twenty-One
Alphaholes

Laken: Anyone seen Isley of late?

Silas: Why would we? He's not working directly with any of us.

Booker: Lost the little sugar glider again?

Jupiter: When did he lose him the first time? What's this?

Laken: Booker, stop being a dick.

Booker: I'm a bear not a dick.

Laken: You were definitely a dick on Friday over the last slice of pizza.

Jupiter: He's got you there!

Booker: I wasn't the one who nearly cried at the end of the movie.

Jupiter: Just shows I'm in touch with my emotional side.

Silas: You're definitely in touch, but usually it isn't your emotional side!

Booker: Don't encourage him, Silas! I couldn't take another round of discussing how good it was to have the cross eyed supermodel bouncing on his balls.

Jupiter: Massimo is going to be the star of our runway show!

Booker: And?

Laken: Why do you always have to derail the conversation, Jup?

Jupiter: Hey, that was all Silas!

Silas: Guilty. Sorry Laken, what's your concern?

Jupiter: Our little sugar honey not giving you a good… servicing?

Laken: Give over Jup! Silas, I've a ton of work but Islay's gone AWOL.

> **Booker:** Has he booked time off in the other calendar?

> **Laken:** Shit......I forgot about that one.

> **Booker:** How can you forget about it? The damn thing rules our goddamn lives.

Booker shut down the app with shaky fingers and scowled at how he'd gotten carried away. The weekend had given him too much time to think. He'd come in this morning with a plan to face Frey and act normal. He could do that!

Normal.

Yes, normal, he fired back at his bear's snide remark. *I put rules in place, and I need to stick to them.* Yes, he did.

His bear, on the other hand, didn't get with that programme. *Then go find him and let's see how normal you are.*

Is that a threat?

Threat? I don't know what you're talking about.

Yeah right. You better behave or......

Or what?

Booker's teeth ground together as he stomped out of his office, his mission to prove his bear wrong. The battle of wills had started after last week's behavior.

Minutes later, he stared at Frey's empty office. The scent of him was not strong, revealing he'd not been in his office this morning. Booker rammed his hands into his pockets and strode back to his office, muttering and cursing under his breath.

Where was he?

He should have had the decency to tell him if he wasn't coming into work.

At Pam's desk, he came to a halt. "Did Frey say anything about not coming into work this morning?"

It took great effort to keep his tone civil, but it seemed to have worked when Pam pushed up the glasses she used for computer work and gave him an absentminded smile. "Erm... yes. He emailed me. He has a doctor's appointment and won't be in until later this morning. He's sent you all the updated quotes for the accessories you asked for, along with the additional costs for the changes required for the design on the handbags."

"Right." Booker went into his office and, instead of sitting behind his desk, he grabbed his car keys where he'd plonked them and headed right back out of the office.

Pam looked up. "You need something?"

"I've gotta... meeting. I'll be back in an hour."

Her brows met. "I saw nothing on your calendar this morning?"

It took genuine effort not to shrink under her gaze as he told an outright lie. "I put the meeting on my phone and forgot to slip it in the calendar." Booker didn't hang around and hustled to get to his car, acting like he'd not seen her pointed look.

He'd hate himself later, but for now, his worry for Frey took precedence over everything else.

Stalking...

Dear gods, this was an all-time low.

Could he stop himself?

He indicated to take the street he needed to go down, driving fast and safe to stop getting a speeding ticket.

It seemed not!

Chapter Twenty-Two

Frey

Dr. Hockings tapped at the figures on the screen, which made no sense to Frey. "This level here should be triple, if not quadruple, after a heat."

He'd blamed the drugs—possibly—remaining in his system for how the previous weekend had gone. Any hope he'd had fled as those words sank in. He really had broken himself.

Frey had gone to get his blood taken after a call with Dr. Hockings the previous Monday.

There was no way to describe what had happened the week before between him and Booker. Frey had outright flirted with danger, he could see that now with a week to reflect and listen to gossip from those who'd seen Booker being all growly bear, tearing through the building.

He felt awful... kind of.

Had that all been because of me?

Was the anger staff mentioned—and not in a good way—his fault? His tummy, which had twisted into a million tiny knots throughout the entire week of Booker evading him, made him queasy.

"—so you see, this is positive after your bodily reaction."

Blinking several times, he stared at Dr. Hockings, working to get his train of thought where it should be.

"What's positive?" he asked when nothing came to him when he glanced at the screen, which had different figures on it than before.

When did he change it?

Dr. Hockings tapped Frey's knee. "I know it's a lot to take in right now." He shifted in his seat and Frey was none the clearer to what he'd evidently missed. "I'll print out all the results, the correct levels, too. Then I've several information sheets on all their meanings, so it will give you a better understanding of what's happening for the next heat."

Giving up and pretending he had a clue what was going on, Frey asked instead, "What's going on with me? My heat wasn't normal? How will the next be any different when I didn't lose control and beg," Frey blushed but continued on, "for sex? Or really show any interest at all. I didn't even produce any... slick."

Dr. Hockings sat back in his seat and templed his fingers together, looking over them as he stared at Frey thoughtfully. "Yes, you mentioned that last week when we spoke. But you also explained that your body felt something—had a reaction—to a specific alpha, isn't that correct?"

One bushy eyebrow rose, and Frey resisted squirming in his seat, recalling exactly what he'd said after his encounter with Booker. "I... yes... Booker... you see... I... tingling... urges..." Oh gods, just spit it out!

"I'm attracted to Booker. Maybe it's all my fox," Frey stated, feeling the need to justify it for no apparent reason other than he needed to blame someone for how he'd behaved towards Booker, which Dr. Hockings knew nothing about.

Provoking him like that, what had possessed him? "He's getting pesky with his feelings over this whole situation."

That got Dr. Hockings' attention for sure, by the way he sat forward, looking enthusiastic. "Excellent. So you and your Fox are in tune. That would go with what I can see in your blood results."

"It does?" Huh? "How so?" Frey's gut, already in turmoil, decided to do the loop-de-loop to add to his woes at just how happy the doctor looked.

None of this made any sense to Frey. If he was defective, how could his fox's reaction change that?

"You explained how your fox side chose to shut you out when Ziggy arrived. That's the case, right?"

"It is. He got the hump with me." Frey couldn't decide if he was still miffed about that when he suspected that was part of the reason he sailed into work as normal last week, totally forgetting himself. Which, in effect, had caused Booker's reaction and the subsequent conversation he'd had with Hollis.

Seven whole days since Booker hightailed it out of his office faster than a cheetah chasing a meal. Then Booker had played hide and seek with him. It left Frey over analyzing everything and clueless about how to actually discover if, in fact, Booker was interested in him. His behavior could mean anything. Frey's real lack of experience with alphas really wasn't helpful.

He likes you. Stop being a dork over this and listen to me.

Can't you see I'm busy having a freak out here?

"There have been medical cases where the animal half of a shifter has taken charge to protect their human side. Your blood results would suggest this is the case. The spike of hormones here,"—he pointed at the screen—"reveals that this happened on Monday last week and was not part of your overall heat reaction. In fact, your blood work would suggest that you didn't have a heat at all, as I said, but this other blood work is all positive."

It was all as clear as damn mud. "But I used your predictor thingy and my temperature climbed to the levels you said it would for a normal heat."

The doctor nodded. "It could explain a predicted response, one you knew to expect was going to happen."

"You mean I made my temperature rise because I expected it to happen?"

"No, not quite like that." He chuckled, stroking his beard. "Yes, you expected your temperature to rise. However, did you get yourself worked up when it changed by a small margin from where it started? Were you worried? Think about it a lot. Obsessing?"

Frey sagged in the seat, knowing he'd done all of that. "A little," he confessed. "It was hard not to. Doing the sex stuff with a friend is... could have been stressful, if it had actually happened."

Dr. Hockings tapped Frey's knee once more. "It's only to be expected and could explain your reaction. But consider this, you get to ease into a heat without all the wacky hormones. You've had a small taste of what it feels like to be attracted to someone through a part of your heat. I'd suggest your fox is protecting you."

Frey snorted. "He wants to hunt down the bear and..." back to blushing, Frey ran an unsteady hand through his hair, shoving it back off his sweaty forehead, "and do stuff."

Dr. Hockings' lips twitched, his eyes sparkled with amusement. "Why yes, I'm sure he does after all this time being chemically restrained."

"I didn't think about it like that," Frey confessed, feeling stupid when they were two halves of one whole. "I'm worried about what he might do."

What we *might do.*

It was easier to focus on the doctor than on his snarky animal side.

"His feelings are inherently yours, Frey," he replied softly, getting a gleeful snort from Frey's fox. "Maybe you need to consider that."

It was hard not to with his fox.

After more discussion—with him actually listening—ten minutes later, Frey left, clutching the papers he'd gotten to read. He stopped on the curbside, knowing he wasn't quite ready to head back to work. Never one to skip out on his responsibilities, Frey trudged back to his car.

Inside, he placed the pile of papers on the seat next to him and drove out of the lot. Before he realized it, he was driving to the lake. He didn't question it. He could make up the time later. It wasn't like he had plans for his evening. Or any evening, for that matter, unless it was with the other PAs.

His lips trembled, and he sniffed at the glaringly obvious lack of social life.

Parked up, he got out of the car, dragging his thicker jacket from the back seat and slipping it on. There was a chilly breeze and his suit jacket didn't protect him from it. Leaving everything sat on the front seat, too lost in his thoughts to worry about anyone seeing them, he wandered the familiar pathways that lead him through the park, to the lake.

A bench closest to the water's edge was where he headed. He sat down and hugged the jacket closer to him as he eyed the heavy gray sky that suggested it wouldn't be long before it rained. The sounds of the water lapping and the occasional cry of a gull were the only things that broke the silence.

Why can't life be simple?

You're making it more complicated than it needs to be.

You mention Booker once more and I'm gonna scream.

Stop being silly, the bear is ours if you'll just admit it.

I warned you! Frey opened his mouth and screamed loudly.

A roar followed and the sound of shoes slapping on the ground, setting Frey's pulse to leap hard enough that he couldn't catch his breath. He spun around on the bench and watched open-mouthed as Booker charged out of the trees.

"What happened? Who touched you," demanded a furious, snarling Booker. his claws out ready to... *defend me.*

Oh my, look at him.

Frey could do nothing but look at him as Booker reached them. The spectacular bear came to a halt, the enormous claws looking lethal, sending shivers down Frey's spine.

Was that fear he felt at the aggressive alphas?

Heck no, Frey felt tingly again.

Booker, ready to fight for him, left Frey feeling... warm and sticky in places he'd not been sticky for years.

His mouth snapped shut when Booker lifted Frey off the wooden bench he'd found him sat on. Dangling for a second while Booker took his place on the bench and placed him into his lap, cuddling him. *What the heck was this?*

Booker's nose went into Frey's hair, breathing him in. Only then did Frey notice Booker shook so hard beneath him, except Frey was at a loss to why.

He didn't know if it was his fox or his own instincts kicking in, but he snuggled right in when Booker actually snuffled. The bear's heart pounding directly under Frey's ear, adjusted slowly as Frey gently stroked the part of Booker's chest he could get to without moving.

Was this all because he'd screamed? "I'm sorry, I was just venting my frustration. I didn't know anyone was around," he whispered, just in case he was the reason.

After a noticeable hesitation, Booker's arms tightened around him, and a sigh followed as his heart beat calmed. "Why were you venting?" Booker's gravelly voice rumbled up his chest.

The scent filling Frey's nose tempted him to bury his face in the shirt he remained pressed against. Should he be honest? He considered what the doctor had told him.

Then something else struck.

He pulled back, forcing Booker to lift his head. "What are you doing here?" He frowned as pieces slotted together in a picture that said this was more than coincidence. "Are you stalking me?" he squeaked.

Booker's gaze didn't quite meet his.

"I didn't give your secretary the doctor's address, and as I wasn't planning to come to the lake, there is no way you could randomly be here," he said quickly, realizing he was supposed to be at work and not nicking off for some personal reasons.

"I had a doctor's appointment, and then I needed a minute or two," he continued when his anxiety mixed with confusion, and Booker's silence, wouldn't let him stop.

Booker's cheeks were a ruddy color that Frey had only ever seen on a farmer who'd spent years outside. "I... yes."

"Yes, what?" Frey asked in confusion. His morning had been full of struggles to keep up and he was getting annoyed.

If it was possible, Booker's cheeks got a darker shade of red when his gaze dropped somewhere about Frey's nose. "I was stalking you."

"You were?" he shrieked, his glee and anxiety clashing spectacularly.

Chapter Twenty-Three

Booker

Booker's ears rang from the shriek and his bear decided to take cover, the coward he was. Now that they had the fox in their arms he wasn't sticking around for the next bit.

Coward.

Whatever.

"Yes," he admitted, working on trying not to sound defensive. The tiny fox had scared twenty years off his life, screaming like he was being attacked. Any thoughts of just watching had evaporated completely.

If he wanted to pretend this little fox hadn't captured his heart, then his actions pretty much made a mockery of that. Not that Booker wouldn't have rushed to help anyone who screamed. It was just pointless to pretend when that urge to defend also came with the overriding need to hold the man who was currently stroking his tiny hand over his chest. He hadn't even stopped when he'd made that alarming squeaky shriek.

"What... why? I don't understand. You spent all last week avoiding me and now this?" Frey released a heavy sigh, his hand coming up to touch Booker's bristly jaw. "What's going on?"

Those three simple words were a battering ram to his heart, which was hammering against the small hand touching him. "I... it's like this. I... we... us..."

"Yes?" Frey encouraged, wearing an expectant look that wasn't helping.

Despite the urge to get up and pace, which is what he'd normally do to release his frustration, Booker kept his ass planted on the bench, refusing to let go of Frey. It was totally irrational, but then he'd not been thinking straight for months when it came to the flirty fox.

"I like you," Booker muttered, like an absolute idiot.

"You do?" Back was the shrieky voice and Booker resisted rubbing at his ears when he couldn't decide if what Frey displayed was terror or jubilation.

"Didn't I just say it," he growled back grumpily, feeling seven shades of embarrassed and hating every minute of it.

Frey's eyes sparkled like diamonds glittering in the sunlight.

Panic came in a big dollop on top of everything else. "No... don't you dare. I swear I'll dump your ass in the lake if you so much as let one tear drop." His terror was real, he hated when folks cried. It did stupid things to him.

Frey sniffed and gave him this look that was both adorable and annoyed at the same time. "There's no need to shout at me."

Doomed, he was fucking doomed. A mantra he was getting used to.

"I didn't mean to shout," he replied, doing his best to keep his voice low. "Just don't cry, okay?"

He patted Frey on the shoulder like someone would to soothe a baby. If Frey noticed, he didn't say anything, but Booker's bear side was ass wiggling around his brain, enjoying himself way too much.

After another sniff, Frey wiped a hand at his nose as he watched Booker closely. "Do you like me, like me?"

"Huh?" What did that mean?

"You know, like me, not just a person you work with, but like a... boyfriend type liking? There's a difference and I need to be clear, 'cause everything is confusing me, and I don't want to make a fool of myself," Frey finished, flushed and breathless, eyes bigger than saucers.

They ate up his entire face, the color more gray than green, something that happened when the little fox was emotional. Booker hadn't had such a conversation like this in his whole dating life, so he nodded, hoping that was the right response when he felt more than a little tongue tied about using the word 'boyfriend'.

"So that's a yes, you wanna be my boyfriend?" Frey persisted, his cheeks glowing.

"Yes," Booker mumbled. Could this be any more mortifying? He was a grown bear, it shouldn't be this hard.

The big sigh that followed was not what Booker expected, or the tears back filling Frey's eyes.

Oh fuck, what now?

"I have to say something before... you decide if you really want to date me."

Date him?

Who mentioned dating?

Dear lord, he was going to have to come up with something to do. Wait... what did he mean? "Tell me what?"

"I'm not really a flirty fox."

Booker frowned, unsure what this had to do with anything, but he waited when Frey paused, licked his lips and glanced towards the water.

"I use it as a barrier. Flirting, I mean. It gives me confidence. Fake, yes, but it helps me deal with big alphas when I feel threatened by them... all the time." His breathing was choppy as he glanced back at Booker, never looking more vulnerable and punching at Booker's control.

"But... you're different. I don't feel scared around you," he whispered, looking shyly up at him from under his long eyelashes.

Booker's heart was back to thundering at the confession.

I told you so.

Give the fuck over right now!

"Who made you frightened?" It came out gruff and hurt his throat with how upset he was at the many reasons why someone would fear all alphas.

Except us!

He ignored his bear for now, watching Frey carefully and seeing the moment he decided to answer.

"In my skulk, there were more alphas than omegas and betas put together. My family liked the idea that I could have my pick of the more powerful alphas. Except..." He shivered once more, his gaze returning to the water.

"Except?" Booker nudged gently, needing to see what he was battling. Who he'd battle to protect the shivering fox.

"Except the leading alpha of the skulk decided I was his, no discussion, no asking if it was what I wanted. Then I got my first heat." His eyes grew distant. "He understood what was happening to me way before I could figure it out and he cornered me... was going to rape me... I wasn't ready, not even close. It wasn't consensual. I didn't want him to touch me..."

Booker's back molars took a beating as they ground against each other in an effort to keep his bear contained and his anger in check at trying to imagine how scary that would have been for Frey. Popi had explained once that the first heat was difficult for an omega. "Did he... did he..."

Fuck, he couldn't even say it. His blood ran cold even with the fury burning his innards with its wild heat.

"No... he didn't. In his rutting state, he was out of his mind and not thinking about anything other than..." When Frey returned his attention to Booker, his chest hurt from the pain Frey didn't conceal. "Fucking me. He sliced me up some, bruised me, tore my clothes and terrorized me out of the skulk, away from my family. I was lucky." At how he worked to inject some positivity into his voice, broke Booker.

He buried his face in Frey's neck, rocking them both in his need to soothe. "I'm so sorry," he murmured repeatedly. "So fucking sorry that he didn't seek your permission."

Frey's tiny hands crept around his neck, fingers sliding into his hair and clinging on. He said nothing, just held on as Booker worked to get his emotions under control.

Things slotted together. The conversation with Ziggy, why he would want an omega to help with his heat. He'd gotten attacked, that was enough to make all alphas off limits. What a fucking mess.

They sat like that for the longest time; the sky getting grayer and Booker not once stopping the rocking motion, regardless of the occasional passerby. He wasn't embarrassed, his sole thought was how he could make things right for the man who'd been brave enough to confess his deepest secret. To share with him... an alpha.

"That isn't all of it... but I... not today... is that okay?" he asked, not looking at Booker, which made his stomach take a nosedive.

What more could there be? He wasn't pushy... alright he was, but he got now was not the time.

"Would you mind if I took the rest of the day off? I'm hungry and tired. I'm not sure I'd be much use to you."

He sounded so unlike the Frey Booker knew, his throat felt raw when he swallowed, giving himself time to collect himself. "Of course. I'll order us takeout and I could run you a hot bath if you like..."

"Ohhh... like with bubbles?"

Booker's guts took another hit at the delicateness of Frey's hopeful look. "What's a bath without bubbles?"

He gave him a cheeky wink, mostly for effect, because he wasn't feeling cheeky at all. "And if you're good, I might even order a cake delivery and share it with you."

Frey's eyes widened. "You'd share your cake with me?"

Booker chuckled at the shocked awe. "Yep," he edged forward carefully, to stand with ease, not attempting to put Frey down. He settled him more comfortably in his arms as he headed towards where he'd parked his car.

"Erm... I can walk."

Coming to a stop, Booker met Frey's stare. "Do you want to walk?"

"If I said yes... would you put me down?"

Booker and his bear wanted to hunt the fucker down that put the doubt in Frey's tone. In his eyes. "Yes. Immediately."

His smile held a bit more of the flirty fox Booker was used to. "Then no, I don't wanna walk."

He nestled his head into the crook of Booker's neck. There was a slight pause before he brushed a kiss over Booker's pulse. "Thank you," he whispered, loud enough for Booker to hear.

Booker gave no thought to his next words as they slipped out. "*My little fox*, you're welcome."

He'd berate himself for his sappy behavior later, when he called Pam to rearrange his day. Whatever happened next, he wasn't leaving Frey alone when he was this emotional.

If that excuse works for you, go with that.

Fuck off!

Chapter Twenty-Four

Frey

However he'd expected this day to end up, it wasn't with him skipping out on work for a full day, having Booker run him a bubble bath, or ordering all his favorite take out. Which he'd consumed while sitting on Booker's lap at the kitchen table. No, not what he'd planned at all! Booker, Frey felt, had encouraged him in all kinds of ways he'd never have expected. Why else, when Frey had appeared in his onesie after his bath, had Booker asked which seat Frey wanted to take to eat? To Frey, that meant Booker was offering to let him sit any place he wanted, and that included Booker's lap. When he'd eyed it as Booker sat at the overladen table and had lifted his arm, that was all the encouragement Frey had needed.

Who lifted their arms like that if they didn't want some-one to sit on them?

His bear hadn't complained, not one teeny-tiny bit when he'd shyly crawled onto his lap. That was over an hour ago. Now Frey didn't want to move, but considered it was proba-bly over stepping to stay put, especially when his fox wanted to shift right where they were and have a snooze. Emotional rollercoasters always made his fox antsy and want to come out.

"Are you okay?" Booker asked gently, or as gently as his voice allowed when it had a great rumbly base.

Frey glanced over his shoulder, then put down the spoon he'd been twiddling between his fingers. "I... my fox... we... shift," he answered, explaining absolutely nothing.

"You want to shift?"

Frey wriggled around on Booker's lap and noticed some-thing happening under his bottom. He gulped and did his best to keep still. "Yes... I can wait if you're gonna go now?"

Don't go.

Please don't go.

"Oh... do you want me to leave? I wasn't planning on it... not yet anyway and..."

He paused for so long and his skin darkened over the bridge of his nose, Frey started to wriggle once more. "And?" he prompted, squeaking at how his own body got tingly.

"My bear wants to introduce himself to your fox." Booker spoke so fast that Frey had to take a second to run through what he'd said.

Yes.

Before Frey could utter a word, his shift was on him, and he peered up from the folds of the onesie at an... *amused* looking Booker, a second later.

"I knew you'd be cute. Your ears are adorable." His hand came up and hesitated right by one of Frey's ears. "You're such a pretty fox, aren't you?"

Making a sound of encouragement, Frey's fox butted its head at Booker's fingers in invitation, absolutely loving the compliments.

In his fox form, the noise was like he was humming a tune.

"Is that a yes to stroking your ears?" Booker clarified, and Frey's animal nearly rolled over to expose his belly.

They nodded and Frey gave an internal groan at how gentle Booker was when stroking his ears. "So soft and silky, my pretty little fox."

The way Booker spoke, it was as if he was talking more to himself as he grinned at them. His fox made more humming sounds until Booker scooped them up in the onesie and went to place them on the sofa. They watched as Booker stripped down to his boxer briefs, then Frey got his fox side to close his eyes to stop staring.

Only his fox had other ideas and opened them.

Don't stare, it's rude.

We need to know for later...

The bear that emerged was huge. Standing well over seven feet, they craned their head back to look at the magnificence that was Booker. Fur, a deep brown that in places looked almost black, covered him. Its silky texture shone under the lights as he lumbered into the middle of the room and lay down on the rug that Frey had. The bear curled up, but there was a space right in the middle that looked perfect for a fox to snuggle into.

Frey's animal was not like Frey. He was brave and wriggled out of the fleecy onesie to dart off the sofa. He swept his brush in the air to show off as he roamed around Booker's enormous body, sniffing.

The bear smelled so good.

His fox gave Booker's bottom a little cheeky nip, getting a rumble that sounded playful, so he did it again. The bear's head lifted, and he looked back at the fox. Something about his eyes touched the human part that remained in Frey's shifted form. He, while a fox, always let the animal side lead.

So they waited.

The bear lifted an enormous paw and ever so carefully stroked their pointy ears, once more making a rumbly noise in the back of his throat. His fox leaned into the touch and rubbed against the leathery pads. His fox explored some more, getting more gentle touches, the last to his brush. He stopped at the big head and eyed Booker before he swiped his tongue over the furry cheek, making Frey's human half blush at how forward his animal was. Then, before he could consider protesting, they curled up close to the bear's belly and rested their head on the bear's front leg.

His fox vocalized several more times before he closed his eyes. A peace he'd never thought he'd experience again seeped into his soul. A peace that came with a sense of knowing he was truly safe for the first time since he'd run away from his skulk.

Oh wow…

I'm in lo—

Don't think about that now. He's our bear, let that be enough for the time being.

He wanted to argue, but everything felt so good, Frey let the worry slip away and took his animal's advice. There'd been enough emotional upheavals today. There would be time for that—*tomorrow*—another day.

Another day seemed like a great idea because at some point they'd need to talk about the other stuff and Frey really wasn't ready for that, not by a long shot. If ever, in fact, with the possibility that Booker could reject him.

Our bear won't reject us. Now stop thinking, one of us is trying to sleep!

A phone ringing somewhere in the apartment roused Frey, only something was wholly different from when he'd fallen asleep. He lifted his arm, his bare arm, and jerked up to sit on something soft, squishy, and furry.

Ohhhhh.

Naked.

I'm naked on top of Booker's bear!

How could you do that to me?

How? Frey squealed, doing his best not to move too much while desperately trying not to freak out completely. He'd not been naked in front of anyone in forever. Unless under examination by his doctor, and that definitely didn't count.

How is it my fault you shifted back into your human form to rub yourself all over the bear? Look here, you're as responsible as me. So stop being all freaky and screechy. See, he rolled onto his back so you could spread out all over him. Isn't that nice? I mean, he wasn't like that when I curled up to go to sleep. So it really goes without saying, this is kinda your fault.

His fox's logic was not helping his freakout. In fact, it was making it worse because he was the one lying naked on an alpha...

Was the room moving?

Oh dear, he was going to faint.

His eyes snapped to the furry body moving under his ass and Frey stared right into the bear's warm chocolate eyes.

If it was at all possible, the bear gave him a cheesy grin. "Don't you go giving me that look. Close your eyes, now. I'm naked," he snapped, more out of fright than anger, because he'd bet he had drool on the side of his face and his hair was a frightful mess. He did not want the bear seeing him not looking his best for their first official meeting.

It just isn't right.

The bear closed his eyes but only, Frey noted, after they had roamed down his now flushing body. The moment they closed fully, he wriggled his butt off the bear, keeping the groan of delight at the feel of the silky fur on his bottom to himself. He darted for the sofa and grabbed his onesie and wriggled into it quickly.

He spun around at the groan... *the very human groan.*

Booker stood staring at where his naked butt had been a moment ago. Every inch of Booker was on display.

Lots and lots of inches...

Wow! Who knew it came in that size?

Will you behave?

You're the one staring at it.

Bottom!

He was, and now Frey discovered he couldn't shift his gaze. Knowing he should and doing it were two completely different things. He'd never gotten a proper look at a naked alpha before. Well, not up close and personally. Especially with one who remained perfectly still.

Lost in his desire to have a closer look, Frey took a step closer to Booker and the cock he was staring at twitched.

His head tilted to the side, his eyes narrowing in on its target. *Am I making it do that?*

Tongue between his teeth, Frey moved another inch closer. This time, the twitch came with a definite increase in size.

He's getting hard!

Holy fox's he's getting hard!

A part of his brain was screaming 'step away from the cock' while the other silly, non-compliant part was 'ooh, look, it likes us'. Frey wasn't actually sure if he had somehow woken up in an alternative universe where looking so intently at an alpha's cock was deemed as an everyday occurrence. Either way, he was staring, and he wasn't actually freaking out. That had to be good, right?

He licked at his drying lips, and the noise that came out of Booker got him looking upwards. His expression was fierce, yet not in an 'I'm about to attack' way. They stared at each other, and Frey wasn't exactly sure what Booker was thinking.

The one thing Frey would bet his life on, Booker would do nothing to him that Frey didn't want. It was there in the depths of those big, soulful brown eyes. "Is it alright to... look?"

"Yes," Booker rasped in a croaky voice. The hands at his sides clenched and unclenched as Frey inched yet a little closer.

"I've never seen a naked man before. Well, besides myself," Frey confessed, itching to reach out to see if the silky hair on Booker's chest was as soft as the bear's was. "But I look nothing like you. I don't have hair on my body." Frey also wasn't built like a linebacker.

Booker's upper torso was wide over the shoulders and back. He had a broad chest, but it tapered down to a slim waist and lean hips. His thighs were thick and solid, covered in as much hair as his chest and arms. A large cock, which originally had sat nestled in dark curls, now protruded from his body as the seconds slipped by.

"Does that normally happen when someone looks at you?" Frey asked tentatively, unsure he should voice such questions but seemingly unable to stop now he'd started this—whatever this was.

"No..." Frey glanced up. "It's all you."

Heat flooded Frey's cheeks as something very unusual happened to his ass. His hand flew to his bottom as the scent of his slick became prominent in the room. Alarm was his first reaction as his eyes locked with Booker's. His fear hurtled right back to the front of his mind, reminding him exactly what had happened to him.

"I'll never do anything to you that you don't specifically ask for."

Those rumbly words were a soothing balm, one Frey didn't understand but accepted as a new reality. One that he'd have to explore alone. Frey only understood one thing; Booker spoke the truth.

Booker

Booker sat staring into space, something he'd been doing more and more since...

He rubbed at his face, the sound of his beard rasping the only noise as he inhaled Frey's scent.

How have I gotten myself into this situation?

Our fox is not a situation.

Fuck you! You aren't the one suffering here!

Outside Booker's office, there was a noise before someone knocked and he called out for them to come in, needing a distraction because he was going out of his mind.

Taylin stepped in looking as fresh as a damn daisy, all pressed and glowing with happiness. He glanced at the seats in front of Booker's desk, his nose twitching.

"Who you looking for?" Booker questioned, sitting back in his seat, making it creak as he worked on acting calm and collected. He was neither of those fucking things, with his cock rock hard after his flirty fox had left mere minutes ago.

"You," Taylin replied, shutting the door behind him. "Although it smells like Frey in here."

"He works alongside me and what the heck do you think you're doing sniffing at him?" Booker reacted, defending why he'd had Frey in his office. That he'd had the little fox practically living in there was no one's business and definitely not Taylin's. His irrational brain was not computing why Taylin would notice Frey's beautiful smell, so he glared at his brother.

Taylin chuckled and held up his hands. "I don't sniff him. It's just impossible to ignore him when he smells of chocolate and spice, isn't it?" he asked, giving Booker an innocent look that didn't fool him.

Yet, that didn't stop him rising, his protective urges towards Frey triggered, his eyes boring angry holes into Taylin.

"You've got the hots for Frey," Taylin accused.

"Give the fuck over. 'The hots'? What the hell kind of adult thing is that to say?" Booker put on the act of not giving a fuck, shrugging despite his guts being twisted into a mess. He did not want Taylin letting on to his brothers that he'd fallen hard enough to break bones over the little fox.

Weeks had passed since the day he'd found Frey by the lake. Since the day in his apartment when...

Breathe. Breathe and don't fucking think about...

"The only kind that fits with your over the top reaction," Taylin replied, dragging him back into the conversation he would sell his left testicle to avoid.

Booker took his seat, working to contain his frustrated growl. "What do you want?" he asked testily, picking up a pen for something to do with his hands and tapped it on the arm of the chair.

"The trip back to the hellhole, is it necessary?"

Not really what Booker wanted to talk about after how upset Frey had gotten earlier over the incoming information from Minnesota where the head of security had stayed. Their legal team was there, working to keep the divergent omegas safe. Something that was proving harder with the supporters kicking off and putting cash behind the fuckers who'd imprisoned them.

Those shitheads were free, which was why Booker had spent an hour of his morning with Frey on his lap, rocking the inconsolable fox. He had such a big heart. Something else to add to the ever-growing list of reasons for Booker's attraction.

"Unfortunately, yes. They want us back there to go over our statements in person. Amatus' lawyer is requesting in-person meetings with me, you, and Rue." He threw the pen on the desk in disgust at how they were trying to manipulate them, reaching to pick up a sheath of papers and wave them at Taylin angrily, temper flashing in his eyes at what had come via email to him.

"We don't have to go," Taylin pointed out. "Legally they can't make us."

"No, they can't, or not yet. But..."

"It's the right thing to do," Taylin finished for him.

"I'm arranging for the jet to fly us tomorrow morning, as we have this family thing tonight."

Taylin frowned. "Family thing?" he questioned, "I wouldn't call dropping off some baked goods that Hollis made for Popi tonight, a family thing. Hollis could do that himself, without me."

Booker burst out laughing. In fact, he laughed so hard his chair creaked alarmingly, but he couldn't stop when he was nowhere near fooled by Popi's reasoning for inviting Hollis's parents around for dinner without letting Taylin know.

"What am I missing?" Taylin asked, deep furrows appearing as he stared at Booker, looking wholly unamused.

"Popi invited Hollis's parents over for dinner to get to know them and to talk about how cute you two are together," he choked out, continuing to roar with uncontrollable laughter.

Taylin flew out of the office and Booker had to take several deep breaths, wiping his eyes twice before he got himself under control.

It won't be so funny when it happens to you, his bear pointed out smugly.

What... no! Popi can't invite Frey's parents over, he has no contact with them.

Yet. He's safe now. He's ours, we'll protect him so he can go see his family.

All humor disappeared at how his bear projected something else. Revenge. As in ripping the alpha who harmed their fox a new asshole and shoving his head up there.

You really should learn some control.

Are you saying you don't want to do the same?

Of course he did. Frey was nothing like what Booker imagined. He was an alpha virgin. And that alone kept all the urges that ran through Booker tightly reined in. There was no way he wanted to scare Frey. He'd rather stab his own heart first. And it was feelings like that which had him absolutely terrified of what came next.

He's ours.

Additional time with Frey outside of work—*dating, we're dating*—meant that every day, Booker had no place to hide. His bear's insistence matched his own feelings, he couldn't lie.

He looked for his pen, for a distraction. Seeing it on the floor, he scowled, reached for it and went back to the long list of things he needed to organize for the trip back to Drinkwater, Minnesota, tomorrow. Frey was coming with them. He'd debated for all of five seconds before he'd reasoned that Frey needed to see the improvements they were making to the omegas' lives.

His little fox never stopped mentioning them.

Booker sighed and reached for the list.

Pissed because his bear remained annoyed at him for not inviting Frey to dinner tonight, Booker looked for a distraction when his dads' and Hollis's parents left the room at the sounds of a car outside.

"What's the betting Taylin has done something rash?"

"Rash," Laken asked from his lounged position on the other side of the room.

"Yep, rash," Booker said, listening out with half an ear to the conversation coming through the open doors.

Silas rose, tugging at the sweater he wore. "What do you know that we don't?"

Booker chuckled gleefully. "I kind of let slip that Popi had invited Hollis's parents for dinner tonight."

"Sneaky." Jupiter laughed, looking impressed. "I like it."

"Trust you," Kodi muttered, also getting up. "Let's go rag on Taylin. We don't get many opportunities now he's living with Hollis."

Up and following, Silas leading the charge, with Kodi, Laken, and Booker right behind. They heard Hollis's mom announce, loud enough the next town would hear, "Oh Hubert, look! He's engaged!"

They all gasped and made a dash for the door. Booker hadn't thought Taylin would go that far—or had he?

Would he?

A ball of anxiety formed in his gut as he went rushing out with his brothers. They barely stopped plowing into each other as they vied to get closer to see if it was true. One of them had finally taken the big plunge into *coupledom* bliss.

Taylin stood next to Derick, grinning foolishly at every-one. "You need to thank Booker"—he looked directly at him—"for spilling the beans about tonight."

"Jackass," Booker grumbled, working to control the heat wanting to climb into his cheeks at being called out in front of his dads. He knew he was in trouble when Popi spun towards him, tutting and wagging his finger.

"Were you trying to cause trouble, young man?"

Oh damn. He was gonna kick Taylin's ass for this.

"He always does," Kodi supplied, laughing, his eyes dancing with mischief.

"Shut up." Booker cast a warning look at Kodi, only Popi stepped between them and hooked his arm through Booker's.

"For that naughtiness, you can help me bring in what Hollis made, which you won't be getting any of." When Popi made a threat, he meant it wholeheartedly.

"What?" spluttered Booker, while doing exactly what Popi wanted.

On his way into the house, Booker muttered crossly at thoughts of missing out on the divine smells coming from the boxes. "Isn't it supposed to be a celebration? I mean, maybe I pushed Taylin to pop the question, isn't that what you've been angling for?" he groused, feeling hard done by.

Popi gave him a smile no one else saw before he nudged him towards the kitchen. "They make a lovely couple. Imagine how cute their babies will be. Although I imagine you'd make cute babies, too."

Booker gawped in shock, and nearly dropped the boxes he held as he stared openmouthed at Popi, who walked off.

"No Popi. No, I wouldn't," he said in a strangled whisper, for fear his brothers were there to listen to this nonsense.

He's right. Cute little foxes with pointy ears.

Don't even start with me. We haven't got to the naked stage yet.

We have. And he loved what he saw.

His internals were at boiling point for many different reasons. Booker felt the steam getting ready to come out of his ears as he stomped into the kitchen, slammed the boxes on the counter, and glared at everyone for good measure.

Bessie smiled at him from the stove as she'd done a thousand times before. Their family housekeeper was as much a part of their family as Booker. "Whose upset, my big boy?"

"He's been naughty and isn't getting dessert," Popi stated, all innocence.

"Popi!" he coughed in outrage.

"What? It's true."

Bessie waved the spoon she picked up at him, her eyes gleaming with delight. "So when do we get to meet your beau? Don't think I haven't noticed you skipping out of here all smiles."

Booker shoved the boxes to the side and dropped his forehead on the counter when Popi arched a brow at him. His hands rubbed at the sides of his hairy cheeks and shut out the two laughing hyenas.

"Never," Booker muttered. "I ain't bringing anyone home, you hear me?"

Who the fuck was I kidding?

Chapter Twenty-Six
Alphaholes

Booker: *That's another fine mess you got me into Taylin!*

Laken: *Be truthful, it was you that got you into that mess, Booker. You had to spill your guts while winding up Tay. No wonder Popi cut off your dessert supply.*

Taylin: *I'm choosing not to get annoyed with you, Booker, as Hollis is my fiancé.*

Kodi: *How many times did he get that into the conversation tonight?*

Taylin: *Not nearly enough!*

Kari: *You are that happy, Tay?*

Booker: *Couldn't you see the love hearts firing out of his ass?*

Rue: *Cute Booker, real cute.*

Booker: *It's a gift!*

Laken: *If you say so... where you at Silas? You normally have plenty to say.*

Rue: *All I'm getting is crickets.*

Kodi: *Me too... what are we missing? Booker?*

Booker: *Why you fucking askin' me? He can see this conversation!*

Jupiter: *When hasn't he got his panties in a twist? In fact, maybe that's why Tay drove off the deep end into the wedding pool of oblivion… it was nice knowing you, bro.*

Taylin: *Jealous… you're just jealous because you're all single, lonely fuckers. Well, not all of you…*

Laken: *Why did you have to swing that bat in all our directions? And who are you aiming that last hit at?*

Kodi: *He never did have a good aim…*

Kari: *Fuck, I've got the scar to prove it.*

Taylin: *Once more, you stepped into the path of the baseball. It's not my fault you can't catch for shit.*

Kari: You keep telling yourself that! Just don't ever play ball with Hollis if he takes off his glasses. The dude has even less chance of seeing you aiming for him.

Taylin: The type of ball I play with Hollis, he doesn't need his glasses... although...

Kari: Nope! No! Nada! Don't you dare...

Jupiter: Toy, now you get with the programme.

Kari: Don't you dare encourage this shit of over sharing, Jup, or I'll come down the hallway and spank your ass.

Jupiter: Promises, promises...

Booker: No words! Fucking none!

Jupiter: The things you typed with your big sausage fingers... they be words big bro!

Booker: *Whatever!*

Booker closed the app and released a grateful sigh that no one continued on down the low blow Taylin lobbed at him. He'd be having a fucking word with him in the morning—well away from Frey—for damn sure.

Chapter Twenty-Seven

Frey

Booker offering to pick him up this morning went a ways to make up for the fact Frey knew fine well that Hollis had gotten an invitation to dinner at Lane and Derick's with all the family the evening before. It was why Booker had declined Frey's offer to cook for him and how he'd discovered his plans.

Why hadn't he invited us?

Was Booker embarrassed to be seen with him?

Had it got something to do with Frey's past?

The secret he kept?

Stop over dramatizing.

I can if I want.

You're giving me a headache.

I'm giving you a headache? Yeah right. You don't have to live with all these unanswered questions.

What the heck do you think I'm doing right now?

Frey sighed his frustration, running a hand through the hair he'd carefully styled not ten minutes ago to prepare for Booker's arrival.

Things between them were... weird.

If Frey was honest, it was nothing like he expected from dating an alpha. Not that he expected anything, because he'd never really thought he'd be dating an alpha, never mind one who was his boss. He didn't feel so bad about that now that Hollis was engaged to Taylin. Only the logical side of his brain said that this was different. Hollis was on a level playing field with Taylin, as in, he had rights to make decisions in the company whereas Frey had no such authority.

It was all so confusing.

It's not. Get naked and see what our bear does. Simple.

Frey ground his teeth together and stomped back to the bathroom mirror to fix his hair. It was that or scream and the last time he'd done that...

He grinned at his reflection. It hadn't turned out badly at all. Although, that didn't stop him from being miffed at not being included in dinner plans with Booker's family.

Will you just stop?

Frey didn't get time to answer when the buzzer for the front door sounded. He grabbed his brush and quickly smoothed back his hair. When happy, he placed it back on the counter and speed walked to the door.

He stopped in front of it to take two deep breaths before unlocking it to offer a bright smile at the man towering in the doorway.

"Hi," he said breathlessly, which had nothing to do with rushing and everything to do with the handsome bear, smelling all kinds of delicious, dressed in a fitted suit that showed off his enormous, powerful body.

The bodily reactions Frey had were becoming more commonplace that they didn't freak him out so much now. But it remained a little disconcerting when his ass reacted and his scent changed. He looked up under his eyelashes at Booker, seeing if he noticed.

The bear was very hard to read at times and right then, he didn't so much as give a nose twitch.

"You ready?" Booker asked.

Resisting releasing yet another sigh, he nodded.

Frey turned to where he'd placed his suitcase an hour ago. "I am, let me just grab my suitcase."

Before he could lift it, Booker reached around him and picked it up. He staggered, his eyes going to the heavy bag he hefted up. "Hell, what you got in here, rocks?"

Frey's blush made it obvious he wasn't prepared to have to answer questions about his packing habits, but when Booker glanced from what he held, to Frey, it seemed he'd no option but to reply.

"I bought some things for the omegas, alright? I know they'll not have a lot of stuff because of those nasty alphas, so I went shopping." Frey shrugged off how uncomfortable explaining his behavior made him. "I got a little carried away."

Booker returned his attention to the massive suitcase. "A little carried away! How much of the stuff in here is for the actual trip?"

Frey reached for the small overnight bag Booker hadn't noticed. "This,"—he waved it about easily—"is my things for the few days we're away."

"Just the teeny-tiny bag?" Booker didn't sound convinced as he eyed Frey with skepticism.

"What are you implying? I'm not a high maintenance fox, you know!" Frey stomped past Booker, nose in the air, leaving the bear to lock up after him.

Yes, he was slightly overreacting. However, first he'd not got a dinner invite and now Booker was implying Frey couldn't manage with a small overnight bag for a trip away. Frey sniffed indignantly. He was *not* high maintenance.

Booker followed him down to the car at a snail's pace.

The driver stood at the side of the car, moving to open the door. "Can I take your bag for you, Sir?"

"Thank you," Frey murmured, handing it over, then getting into the back seat, not once looking at Booker.

He kept his gaze on the window next to him when he felt the seat depress right before the door closed and he got a full hit of Booker's scent. Breathing through his mouth was becoming a habit when in confined spaces. It was the only way Frey could stop his senses becoming clouded and his wayward thoughts from taking control.

"I'm sorry," Booker mumbled.

Frey sniffed once more.

"I am. Please, I don't know why I'm getting the feeling you're mad at me about something else. But it feels like I've pissed you off."

Really!

Frey shifted to turn his body so he could face Booker and give him an arched look. "Are we dating?" That was not the first thing he'd expected himself to ask, and it appeared Booker hadn't anticipated it either when he made a jerky movement with his hand in the air.

"I... erm... yes," he finished, his gaze traveling to the glass partition between them and the driver.

Frey sagged against the seat at how concerned Booker appeared at anyone knowing what was going on between them. He'd never dated and talking to Ziggy had allayed none of his actual fears that he'd mess up or worse, have a freak out. Ziggy told him to be honest.

He met Booker's worried stare. "Why didn't you ask me to come to your home to meet your family, like Taylin did with Hollis?" There, he'd said it.

Booker winced. Frey could see it, clear as day, and his heart sank. Booker evidently didn't like him that much.

Give over.

You give over.

He squealed as he found himself plucked off the seat and placed in Booker's large lap.

His lips trembled as he looked up at Booker, who growled, "No tears."

"Do you like me, like me?"

"Not this again." Booker reached up and yanked at the hair on the side of his head, causing Frey's eyes to widen. "I like you... *a lot*... a lot more than liking indicates... okay!"

Frey's lips curved up at the edges and he snuggled right into Booker's large chest, his hand moving so he could wriggle his fingers in between the buttons of his crisp white shirt to stroke Booker's hairy chest.

Dressed, Frey had no qualms about touching Booker.

You have no qualms touching him naked either!

Pleaseeeee, what kind of fox do you take me for!

His animal howled in his head, the laughter jarring, yet still Frey's lips quivered with the desire to giggle.

Muscular arms wrapped around Frey. They gave him a sense of warmth that touched the icy pocket of his past that he'd buried deep to survive.

"Is the crisis over now?" Booker's words rumbled through his chest as lips brushed over his hair.

Frey carefully tilted his head back to avoid clouting Booker on the nose. His smile, soft and warm, revealing the effect the other man had on him.

The catch in Booker's breath was evident. "You captivate me," he murmured, his head coming close enough Frey's eyes blurred.

Is he going to kiss me?

Seconds ticked off as he stared at Booker, willing him to follow through on the promise he could see in his eyes. They'd come close once or twice in the past week where he thought it could happen, but didn't.

I want those lips on mine.

"Can I kiss you?"

The softly spoken question sent a ripple of desire through Frey that left him shaken to his core. He'd never received a lover's kiss in his whole life. What would it be like? Would he be any good at kissing?

Oh drat!

"Can I?" Booker prompted, bringing him back to what was about to happen.

His need overcame his fear, and he whispered softly, "Yes."

The gentle brush of lips against his came with an exhale from Frey. His fingers curled in the silky chest hair as his lips pressed a little more firmly against Booker's, in an invitation to deepen the kiss.

A soft sigh, he heard it, but wasn't aware which one of them had made the sound. Frey had one focus, the lips touching his. They moved like a gentle summer breeze, caressing his skin. Touching, but not demanding. Caressing, but not forcing. They coaxed a breathy moan out of him when Booker teased the tip of his tongue over the seam of his lips. He parted them gladly.

Whirling sensations danced up and down his spine, his skin thrummed in ways it never had. It felt as if someone was brushing all the fine hairs covering his body to make them stand up so they could catch every vibration of air.

His arousal came in small waves of pleasure, washing through him like water lapping gently at the edge of a sandy beach. He never wanted it to stop. He wanted to live in this place of brightness, where everything made him feel alive—loved.

His heart stuttered in his chest, making his breath catch and causing him to struggle.

Booker lifted his head, his brows pinching together. "Was it too much?"

Concern, he'd need to be blind not to see it, and deaf not to hear it.

His fingers tightened on Booker's shirt. "No... I feel..." *Oh fiddlesticks.* His free hand reached up to touch his tingling lips.

"It's okay if you don't want to explain." Booker brushed his lips over Frey's forehead, moving back his hair.

At touching his plump, tingling lips, Frey really wanted to ask for another kiss, but with how emotional he was feeling, he wasn't sure it was a good idea. *Love.*

How could he not love Booker when he was so perfect for him? The urge to confess his feelings became a solid weight in the center of his chest. It pressed against his heart while Booker held him like he was precious.

Booker was slowly erasing everything about Frey's one and only encounter with an alpha. Replacing it with new and wonderful experiences that gave Frey hope.

He inhaled shakily, moving his fingers from his lips and murmured, "I'm falling for you." He said it like anyone would when they wanted to deliver bad news. Fast and to the point. Almost the point. Saying the L word aloud? He wasn't quite ready to have Booker run screaming from the car.

Try him, you'll see.

I mean it, behave.

Or else?

Shut up.

Chapter Twenty-Eight

Booker

His bear was doing a full on swing dance, booty pop-ping and giving out all the happy vibes at Frey's confession. Booker reeled from those four words. 'I'm falling for you', but what did that actually mean? Frey had blurted it out, almost as if afraid to speak them aloud.

Was Frey happy to have feelings for him?

The way he'd touched his lips after the kiss, he'd looked...

Gods, how he looked knocked Booker six ways to heaven. His heart stopped, then got shocked with force when Frey had run the tips of his fingers over his lips with an air of such wonder.

Was this his first kiss?

It had to be?

The fucker who'd attacked him was after fucking, not taking care of Frey. Anger that came with thoughts of anyone violating their little fox ran through him, heating his blood. Booker kept his breathing steady and even, but despite that, his heart thudded hard with the urge to hunt down the shithead.

He had no time to get further in his head when the glass partition between them and their driver whirred as it lowered.

"Sir," the driver looked at them in the rearview mirror, his expression giving nothing away, "we need to buckle up before I can leave."

Booker resisted snapping back at thoughts of placing Frey back in his seat. He glanced at the seatbelt and, with no hesitation, pulled the strap across the pair of them and buckled up. "There," he replied, not sure he could believe his own behavior.

Frey's mouth formed a perfect O before he placed his head in the crock of Booker's shoulder, not looking at anyone, but he didn't protest.

If the guy's lips twitched at such a move, Booker acted like he'd not noticed. "Thank you, Sir." The glass partition closed, and Booker didn't know how to go back to the conversation.

Frey remained silent, his fingers staying curled around Booker's shirt, an occasional finger played with his chest hair. Those little touches played havoc with him, and he had to keep his thoughts from straying with Frey sitting on his lap.

As the silence lengthened, nothing about it suggested Frey wanted Booker to break it, so he didn't. The weight of Frey against him, the sweetness and spiciness of his scent on every inhale, was perfect. He'd not had many moments like this in his life and Booker found his own enjoyment at the simple pleasure, which didn't evoke panic. When that reality punctuated through his thoughts, he actually grinned at himself right until the car stopped. Before he could release the seat belt, the door opened, and Taylin appeared.

One glance inside the car and Taylin gave Booker a sly smile he knew well.

Fuck, here it comes!

"Well, what's going on here, bro?" His voice was full of amusement that he didn't even try to disguise.

Frey stiffened in his arms and Booker gave Taylin a warning glare that told him to 'shut the fuck up'. "Nothing. Now be good and help with the suitcases." His smile was all threatening teeth as he kept his voice devoid of emotion.

Did Taylin take the hint? Did he fuck.

"I knew your ass was big, but I wasn't aware it meant poor Frey would have to sit on your lap." Taylin didn't hold back his hilarity.

"His ass is perfect," Frey exclaimed snappily, clicking the seatbelt release catch. He didn't give Booker time to help and shimmied off his lap with more dignity than Booker would have thought possible. Frey waved his hand at Taylin to get him to move. "You're just jealous," he continued.

Taylin stepped back, laughing. "Of his ugly ass? I don't think so."

Frey, now out of the car, wore a look Booker had never seen before and his body reacted forcibly. One leg out of the car, he hesitated to watch the show and get his body to behave.

Frey's hands went to his hips, his nose rising in the air as he gave Taylin a once over. It showed exactly what he thought of him and, to Booker's utter delight, it wasn't pleasant. "There is nothing ugly about *my bear*. Now you take that back and apologize to him for being mean!"

My bear.

His other side was back to booty popping.

Taylin never lost his amusement, but he attempted to look contrite, much to Booker's amusement. "Sorry," he murmured.

"So you should be." Frey cast Taylin one last look of displeasure before he stalked off to the waiting jet.

"That told you." Booker couldn't help but rub in his satisfaction at Taylin getting dressed down by his feisty fox as he got out of the car.

A scowl appeared, then disappeared as Taylin eyed him. "Yeah, well, let's see how you fare when I tell the guys what's going on."

Booker, who was on his way to the trunk to retrieve their suitcases, halted and glanced back. "You better keep your mouth shut!"

"What? And ruin a great opportunity to deflect from my engagement to Hollis? You gotta be kidding me." A second later, he held his phone. "Now, how to start the conversation?"

Booker made a dash for Taylin, reaching for his hand, only for his brother to skip back, laughing, slapping his hand away. "No you don't. You couldn't stop with the digs yesterday. Let's see how you like it."

"Don't you dare!" He scowled at the unrepentant look Taylin cast in his direction, his digits flying over the phone screen as Booker charged at him again.

"Too late!" Taylin exclaimed, shoving Booker back with one hand while his phone went into his suit jacket pocket. Taylin was strong enough to stop Booker's forward motion. "Revenge is always best served with a helping of 'serves you right'." He didn't lose the smirk even after stepping away from Booker and grunting when he picked up Frey's large suitcase.

Booker's phone buzzed frantically in his pocket. "I'll get you back for this!" he muttered crossly, resisting the urge to see exactly what Taylin had put in their group chat as he stalked after his asshole brother.

After arriving at the same hotel they'd stayed at during their previous visit and dropping off their bags, everyone headed right back out to visit the scumbags' lawyers. Booker was pleased to see they had the same suite, only nothing was the same this time round. The sexual tension between him and Frey when they'd dropped off their bags was different.

Intense. It messed with Booker because acting on it was not his decision, it was Frey's.

In need of something to distract him, his brothers seemed like the best option after they'd decided to have fun at his expense on the flight. Rue, Taylin, and Kodi had spent hours winding him up. Their PAs had sat huddled together with Hollis, at the opposite end of the jet to work, or so it seemed.

Whereas his brothers thought it would be more amusing to rag on his ass than work. He'd pulled out his laptop ten minutes into the flight and pretended to ignore their jibes, while the whole time his awareness was on their fox. Any signs of distress and his brothers would have gotten their ass's kicked.

Frey had to have heard the conversation, yet he'd not looked in their direction. Why was that?

"Pay attention," Rue muttered under his breath, nudging his shoulder just enough to gain Booker's attention, but not so much that any of the others in the fancy lawyer's office noticed.

Booker glanced sideways, then back at the elegant shark in front of them. The assholes' lawyers had ambushed them when they'd arrived, and the brothers' own lawyers had muttered some nonsense about being respectful. So now they were sitting listening to this shark trying to explain how they'd gotten it all wrong about their clients. Booker would have words with their suits once this shit show was over. It hurt him to look at Frey, who was at the opposite end of the table to him, looking pale and glassy eyed.

At the bullshit whitewash, Booker's frustration grew until he'd had enough. He didn't need to know exactly what they were saying. It was the same rhetoric they'd gotten before, he was sure. The assholes thought they could do whatever they wanted to divergent omegas with no comeback.

They were wrong.

He came forward in his seat, making his presence felt as the biggest man at the table, his gaze connecting directly with Amatus, the smug faced fucker.

"How did we get it wrong? Men were chained in squalor. Held against their will. Had their pittance of a wage taken from them, leaving them destitute if they'd had the actual choice of leaving."

Booker gave each and every man sat opposite him a steely eyed look that Silas had once told him could make a person piss themselves in fright. "Tell me again how we got that wrong? Because I'm at a loss how you think we'd change our statements, be stupid enough to believe the utter bollocks coming from your lips."

"There is no need for that," the shark stated in a snobby tone that grated on all of Booker's nerves.

Booker glanced at his brothers, and as a collective, they stood, their PAs following suit. "This shit is over." He waved in the direction of the assholes. "Prison is too good for them. They'll get three meals a day and be able to have a fucking wash." Back was the seething anger and Taylin placed a hand on his arm, which visibly shook with his rage.

"You needed us here to verify our statements, not have a discussion about the truth of our discoveries. That is for court. Now gentlemen,"—the way Taylin said it inferred they were anything but—"our time is precious. So we bid you good day."

Booker heard sharp, exclaimed words as they left the room, their own lawyers running to keep up with them. In the corridor Booker cast their lawyers a scathing look. "Why didn't you stop that bullshit? It was upsetting on so many fucking levels and totally unnecessary. Why do we pay you fucking big bucks if we have to wipe your damn asses?"

Taylin chuckled, whereas Rue made a choking sound that came out like he was struggling to breathe. The suit's lips flapping uselessly about just pissed Booker off further when Frey looked so upset. He continued down the passageway, only slowing to reach out and take Frey's icy cold hand and whisper in his ear, "I got you, my little fox."

Chapter Twenty-Nine

Frey

It was hard for Frey to sit in a room with an alpha such as Amatus when Frey's own experience of dealing with a nasty pig wanted to surface. He'd spent some time going over the omegas' transcripts and what he'd gone through was hardly comparable. He'd escaped, battered and bruised, but he'd gotten away. These men had no such luck, and it incensed Frey.

During the trip to the hotel where the omegas were staying, silence filled the car. No one seemed prepared to talk, almost like speaking about the awfulness made it worse. The trunk of the car had more than Frey's suitcase in it. It seemed they'd all had similar ideas about supplying things for the omegas. Frey couldn't have worked with better people.

When the car came to a stop, he was the first to get out, a nervousness coming at the memory of leaving the omegas behind to continue to suffer.

Hollis placed his hand on Frey's arm. "You have to stop thinking about the 'what ifs'."

"It's hard." He released a shuddery breath. "The suffering..."

"They're safe now," Monty said with utter conviction as he came to him. "That's what counts, and we all helped free them." The otter had a look about him that suggested no one should argue with him. Otters were known to be cute, but they were also vicious when it was called for.

Frey nodded as Lennon took hold of his hand. "We are helping now. The brothers are helping. Monty's right, it does count."

On the street, looking at his friends, Frey had a sudden realization he'd made his own family with the PAs. He had upset his family by not accepting the lead alpha, and why he had not gone back. The PAs all had each other's backs. He sniffed and his lips clamped together to contain the urge to blubber. *Stupid hormones.*

Distracted, Frey hadn't noticed the second car pull up until Booker was charging towards them. "What is it? Who upset you, Frey?" he demanded, shocking everyone around them.

Booker's furious stare went to the other PAs. Lennon started so hard he shook Frey's arm, then immediately let go of his hand and took a step back.

Frey wasn't quite sure how to take this change of events with such a public display when Booker's brothers were watching with avid interest. As were the PAs when he glanced sideways, trying to work out how to respond to the bear towering over him.

"Frey, what is it?" Booker asked, this time in a softer tone, his gaze fixed on him. His fingers flexed and curled into fists by his sides.

Did Booker want to touch him? Intrigued, Frey peeked up through his damp eyelashes, giving Booker a sad smile. He had no time to brace as Booker swept him off his feet, like a damsel in distress in one of the old movies.

How romantic.

Leave it out.

Frey didn't want to agree with his other half, but he was right. So he didn't bother to stop himself snuggling right into the massive chest. Booker's heart thundered hard against his ear. "I just got upset worrying about what the omegas suffered. I can't seem to stop it." That was the truth.

Booker jiggled him about a little and he came to rest on his hip, a large hand cupping his backside. The ease with which Booker moved and held him was a distraction all by itself. Frey blew out a breath, feeling heat warming parts of him that were wholly inappropriate right then. He really was going to have to ask his doctor for something to fix his hormones!

"What's this all about?" Kodi questioned, loud enough to be heard.

"Looks like big brother has been keeping secrets," answered Rue around choked laughter.

Booker didn't so much as acknowledge their ribbing, his attention was on Frey. "We can't change what came before, I wish we could. But we can focus on the now." His thumb hooked under Frey's chin, so they were staring at each other. "Things like what you've got in that large suitcase will help, so let's start there."

Taylin and the others were making noises, and again Booker paid them no mind, giving the increasing feeling of warmth inside Frey a tremendous boost until he felt like he might combust.

"Okay," he murmured and came forward with one thing on his mind. A kiss. He'd wanted a second one in the car and no one was going to stop him, not even himself. He pressed his lips to Booker's in a chaste kiss, feeling his whiskers rub against his skin, making it tingle. He wasn't sure he could offer more with an audience, but he was the one to initiate the kiss, so it was a total win for him.

When Frey eased away, Booker wore an expression that made him giggle. Stunned, looked good on *his bear*.

Our bear.

Frey wiggled, feeling smug satisfaction that everyone could see the bear was his. Booker carefully placed him down on the ground, his cheeks pink beneath his beard.

"Are we ready now?" asked Rue mockingly, as he eyed Booker in a way that suggested he would have lots to say in private.

With a confidence that came solely from Booker's re-action, Frey sauntered to where the driver had placed his suitcase. "Yes."

It took fifteen minutes to get through security and up to the floors where the omegas were staying. The plush hotel had clearly had instructions on how to keep the omegas safe, but Frey had to wonder if they'd left one prison for another, regardless of how nice it was. He tucked that thought away as the head of security, Oak-land, met them at the elevator.

"Oakland, can we have a status update," asked Rue, who stepped out first. Broad shouldered, he was a little shorter than Booker, but matched him physically other-wise. The rhino was the youngest Starling brother, and the one Frey had the least interaction with. The way he spoke suggested he'd been in the forces.

"We've a hotel suite for the base of operation, let's go there and I'll give y'all an update," said Oakland, spinning around to stride off down the corridor, the thick carpet muffling the sound of his heavy boots. Dressed wholly in black, tall, lean and built, he made a striking figure.

"Can't we go visit with the omegas?" asked Hollis be-fore Frey could.

Oakland halted and glanced back at them. "Of course. We have men stationed on the four floors at all the exits. They are aware you're coming."

"Which floor is Aven on?" asked Taylin, who had fol-lowed Oakland.

Oakland wore an expression that Frey couldn't read. "This one. He has the last room on the right at the end of the passageway."

"I'd like to go say hi to him," explained Taylin.

Hollis hurried after Taylin. "I'd like to meet him officially, too."

After a brief discussion, Frey headed up to the top floor alone, Booker having gone with his other brothers for whatever update they needed. As he exited the elevator, two things struck him. All but one of the hotel room doors were open in the long corridor, and yet there was hardly any noise coming from any of the rooms.

A large alpha, whose name Frey couldn't recall, stepped in front of him, the weapon holstered at his waist causing his tummy to heave unpleasantly. It didn't matter that it was to protect the omegas.

"I'm a-allowed to be h-here."

"Frey, right?"

He held out his hand, "Yes. And you are?"

"Brier." He glanced at the suitcase, nothing about his expression changed. "You planning on staying?"

Frey blushed at the natural assumption. "I brought a few things for the omegas."

A bright blond head poked out of a room as Brier moved aside. Frey couldn't get over how the omega he'd first noticed looked so different. He gave him a shy smile. "Hi, I'm Frey."

The slight omega came fully out into the corridor. Jeans and a T-shirt, both clean and well fitted, replaced the tatty, dirty clothes, making the guy look totally different.

"Hi." He took a step closer. "My name is Bo."

At the sound of his voice, other heads popped out of rooms and Frey's nose burned at seeing them look scared, but not terrified. Was that a win?

He blinked back tears, sniffing and lugging his case past Brier, unsure. "Hey all, I'm Frey, and I did a little shopping and bought some things for you guys, if you're interested."

Some came straight out of their rooms and others hung in their doorways, but it was the closed door that held Frey's attention. He shook off the worry for the time being, huffing and puffing while he lifted and laid the suitcase flat on the ground. Then he sat down on the carpet in the middle of the wide passageway, despite his work clothes, and crossed his legs.

He grinned at those now crowding closer, their scent clean. "So, who wants to see what I got?"

Three of them crouched down, including Bo, whose smile made his blue eyes twinkle.

A lump formed in Frey's throat at how he'd gotten taken advantage of. Life truly sucked sometimes.

"Yeah," answered Bo, looking at the omega next to him, whose arms were heavily scarred. "We do, don't we Harry?"

Harry nodded, then plonked himself down on the carpet. The others slowly followed when Frey unzipped the case. When he flicked back the lid, he got gasps, oohs, and several giggles. They were to be expected with the eclectic mix of things inside.

He lifted his arms wide. "Take what you want." There was a very obvious hesitation by them all. "Seriously, take what you want. I bought it to share with you guys, though if someone opens a bar of chocolate, could I have a piece?" he teased, wanting them to see him as non-threatening.

Bo seemed the bravest, and he was the first to reach in and pull out two books, then reached back to take one of the massive kilo chocolate bars. He wiggled back and leaned against the wall, grinning at what he held.

The others looked from Bo to the suitcase, and that was all it took to break the ice. Giggles, the best sound in the world, erupted as they pulled out the things Frey had thought to pack.

Frey couldn't remember a time when he'd had so much fun watching others enjoy the simple pleasures of life. As he witnessed their interaction with each other, he could see that they'd formed a bond. That their experiences had made them... *family*.

His gaze drifted to the closed door.

Who was in there?

Why wasn't he with the others?

He wasn't sure how long he sat on the floor with them before he heard Booker's voice behind him, talking to Brier. He looked over his shoulder and grinned at seeing Booker's hands full of shopping bags bearing the Starling logo.

A stillness came from those surrounding Frey, and he rushed to reassure. "It's Booker, you've seen him before. He was the one who helped you. He'd never harm an omega, ever."

Booker moved slowly as he gave Frey a smile that warmed his toes.

"You liked the work we did," said an omega who barely looked to be twenty years old.

Booker got down on the floor, placing the bags inside the still half full suitcase. "You do exceptional work." He glanced at them all. "You *all* do."

"Will we be going back to work soon?" asked Bo, wearing a serious expression.

"That will be up to you to decide. Those contracts you were all given mean that you get to control what happens next. If you wish to work with Starling Enterprise to create the leather pieces, then we'd be more than happy for you to do that."

"How will that work?" This came from an omega who bore a scar down the left side of his neck. His eyes were wary.

"The factory belongs to you guys. We can get lawyers to come in and assist you in getting new contracts with other companies. Or you can work solely with us and our designers. The choice is yours."

At the following silence, Frey's ears picked up the sound of a muffled cry. His gaze snapped to the closed door. Compelled to get to his feet, his heart thudded against his ribs. "Who's in the room with the door shut?"

"That's Toby's room," someone answered, but no one looked down the corridor, making Frey anxious for reasons he couldn't quite place.

He picked his way through the men on the floor and was running before he could figure out why. The sound of a scream made his blood run cold, and he knocked on Toby's door, but didn't wait for an answer. He burst in, his head swinging side to side. He smelled blood, but the room was empty.

"Toby," he called out as he went to the closed bathroom door, "are you okay?"

The next cry nearly brought Frey to his knees as he imagined the worst and, without thought to his own safety, he thrust open the door.

He gulped, his throat clicking at the sight of the small omega on his knees in the large tub, blood smearing his thighs as the head of a baby hung from him.

"Booker," he shouted at the top of his lungs as he crouched at the side of the bath, his hands hovering over the gray-looking omega, covered in scars.

Green eyes, huge and desperate, stared at him as he clutched at the edges of the tub. "Help me," he pleaded in a thready voice, "my baby."

Sounds came from behind Frey. "We need medics, a hospital," he stated as calmly as he could, though he didn't feel calm at all. "You need to push."

He could see by the color of the baby's skin—not that he'd seen a baby being born—it wasn't right. Blue, no baby should be blue.

Toby rested his forehead on an arm, visibly shaking. "Don't have the energy," he mumbled.

Those words made Frey fight his tears. "I'm gonna help you." How, he had no idea. He could hear voices coming from the other room, but he focused on Toby.

Frey stripped off his jacket, rolled up his shirt sleeves and climbed into the tub behind Toby, reaching for the baby's head.

"Do you feel your body wanting to push?" he asked shakily, doing his best not to think about the blood and slimy stuff he was kneeling in or covering the baby's head.

"Not sure."

"Okay. Okay." He blew out a gusty breath. "Can you push for me? Brace on the tub, use that to keep you up and push." Was he saying the right things?

A large medic bag landed on the floor next to the tub with a thud. Brier was there, looking much more confident than Frey, he was sure.

He glanced in Frey's direction. "You're doing great. Toby, we need to get the baby out."

Frey didn't fire back the sarcastic comment that sprang to mind. Toby was well aware that he had a baby trying to fight its way out of his body. Toby didn't lift his head, only making a mewling sound as his body writhed with pain.

"Push, I know you can do it," Frey encouraged.

Toby hissed through clenched teeth, looking back at Frey. He could see the head of the baby moving and Frey did something he'd never have thought himself capable of and put his fingers into the omega, driven by pure instinct. The muscles were flexing against his fingers as he wriggled them around the neck of the child.

"Push," he muttered as he slid his hand around a shoulder and worked to move it when it felt like it was stuck. Sweat slicked his skin, but Frey didn't feel it, his instincts guiding him.

He heard nothing but his own labored breathing as he worked with Toby, encouraging him as his hand manipulated the baby with each weak push. Then the baby was there in his lap, squealing loudly at the injustice of what had just happened.

It was the best sound in the world as the tiny thing looked up at Frey and Brier did something that separated the child from Toby.

"Get him out of the tub," demanded Brier, seconds later, in a tone that sent fear through Frey.

Before he could register who Brier was talking to or what was happening, he and the baby left the tub. He cuddled the child to his chest as Booker plonked them on a bed. He had a moment to consider what covered his pants before the baby let out a loud squeal, just as there was a thud in the bathroom and several curse words.

Chaos surrounded him, but Frey didn't take his eyes off the baby that clung to his finger, bringing it to their hungry mouth. Eyes so innocent stared at him while his finger was sucked on, quieting the cries.

Frey stifled a sob, feeling the loss hit him. The grief was overwhelming at the knowledge he'd most likely never experience this. Have this tender moment with a baby of his own.

He brought the infant closer to him, cradling it, ignoring the blood and goo to rub his cheek over the child's head. "I've got you." *If only for a moment.*

Booker

Running on adrenaline, Booker had done as Brier wanted, lifting Frey and the child he clutched and taking them to the bed before going back to help.

Laid on towels on the floor, the omega looked emaciated, gray and lifeless, except for the blood pouring out of him. "I need you to put your hand inside him," Brier stated, like it was an everyday occurrence. "We need to stem the bleeding."

Booker went to go to the sink, but Brier shook his head. "We don't have time for that."

It was then, looking at the unflappable alpha and his grim expression, that it hit Booker what kind of urgency was required. Down on the floor, disregarding the mess, Booker took a breath and pushed his hand into the blood covered, gaping ass.

He couldn't catch his breath at the warm fluid coating his fist and making a squelching noise. That could not be good. He watched Brier quickly and efficiently insert a line into the motionless omega, then set up an IV, hooking a bag of fluids to a door handle. He wrapped a blood pressure cuff around a limp arm, then attached pads to the omega's chest.

When Brier switched on the machine, he swore. "Move your hand."

He did as he was told and with it came a rush of blood. There was the sound of voices surrounding them, but Booker never took his gaze off the omega.

"I'm going to shock him. Get back." Brier took one second to scan the ground and hit the button on the machine next to his thigh.

More curses. "Shocking again."

They worked together, sweat trickling down Booker's spine as he did everything Brier asked him to without question, but still it wasn't enough. Booker didn't need Brier to tell him that the omega was dead. The amount of blood on the floor, soaking his pants, and the lifelessness in the man on the floor after the seven shocks and five rounds of CPR said it all.

Yet he didn't want to believe it as he stared at his bloody hands.

"Fuck it all!" grunted Brier, getting up and leaving Booker kneeling on the floor.

How had no one known he was pregnant? How?

His bear growled and Booker rose slowly, anger being the only thing to help quell his devastation. He couldn't bring himself to look at anyone as he washed his hands and heard the cries and sobs, along with Oakland's commanding voice.

At the lack of towels, Booker went to wipe his hands on his legs and stopped short, realizing he'd only make matters worse. As he stepped out of the bathroom, a paramedic came into the bedroom.

He took one look at Booker and came to him. "It's not mine."

A thin thread held his emotions in check and, as if sensing that, the man nodded, going into the bathroom.

Booker went to where Frey sat in the middle of an unmade bed, his own clothes in no better shape than Booker's. Only that wasn't what held his attention. It was his fox holding the baby cradled in his arms, crooning to it while it suckled on his dirty finger.

Another paramedic walked around Booker. "I'll need to take the baby," she said matter-of-factly, reaching towards Frey.

Frey clutched the baby tighter to his chest, his watery gaze meeting Booker's, pleading with him.

Don't let them take the baby from me.

His bear was adamant that shouldn't happen. His stomach twisted painfully hard.

"Why?" Booker demanded, his anger needing a target.

The dark-haired woman in her forties gave him a returning stare that suggested he was stupid. "All newborn babies need to be checked over. And with the circumstances of the birth, it's important that it happens sooner rather than later."

He could hear in her tone what she thought of him. Going around the other side of the bed, careful not to touch anything, he bent to get closer to Frey. "We need to let her check on the baby, love." He spoke softly and kept his voice low, so it was for Frey's ears only. "I'll make sure to watch her."

Frey edged off the bed to where the woman stood, leaving a blood trail over the white cover. "Don't do anything to h-hurt her," he mumbled, giving the baby to the woman, who showed no flicker of emotion.

A girl. It was a girl.

Booker stepped around the bed, going to Frey to wrap an arm around him as they stood together, staring at the child. His thoughts went to what would happen next. On who the heck the father was. Could it be one of the fucking awful alphas?

His blood ran cold at that. At the idea that the baby would have to be handed over to those monsters.

Frey clutched at him, tears dripping off his chin as he sniffed. "What's gonna happen to her?"

Four days of red tape. Of answering questions from the authorities about Toby's death and the birth of his little girl. A girl who remained nameless as they tried to figure out what came next. Taylin and Kodi had left to go back to Hazardville with their PAs the day before, leaving Rue, Monty, and Frey with Booker.

Frey was hollow-eyed, having not slept. Booker knew because the fox had spent most of his down time curled up with his bear. When he wasn't, Frey struggled to keep his tears in check at the worry over the baby they'd taken to the hospital and where she remained for the time being. It was soul destroying.

They'd discovered Toby had chosen not to let the doctors near him, that in fact he'd kept pretty much to himself. He had no family that Dad could find that were interested and as the baby was fatherless—none of the alphas admitting to touching the omega for fear of having rape added to their charges—they were flying by the seat of their pants to figure out what came next for her. There was also the funeral for Toby to organize after the autopsy revealed he'd died because of a uterine hemorrhage. Although that was not a surprise after what they'd witnessed.

Booker clenched his fists, working to shake off the feelings that came at what he'd done.

"—you sign the form and then we can sort a foster family."

Booker blinked his lawyer's face into focus, realizing he'd zoned out of the meeting he'd arranged while Frey was at the hospital. "Sorry, foster family?"

Randle Morris gave him a sympathetic smile. "As a Starling representative and having taken legal responsibility for all the omegas, I've checked. It includes the baby."

He opened his mouth, then shut it as he recalled Frey's devastation at being parted from the child. "I need to talk to Frey," he answered, his thoughts running away from him.

We could take the child. Be a family with our little fox.

Wait a minute—

No, it's what you envisioned, don't pretend. Our fox wants that baby girl.

How do you know that when we haven't asked him?

I know.

There was an utter conviction that made Booker's innards tremble. He got up from the table, unable to sit still. "Listen, hold on to the paperwork... no..." He rubbed at his temples. "Could you draw up adoption paperwork?"

"Adoption paperwork?" Randle croaked out, eyes wide with alarm. "For who?"

"Leave the names blank for now, just do it." Booker didn't wait for a reply. He headed out of the meeting room they'd commandeered in the hotel and stomped down the hallway, heading for the elevator. His hand reaching into his pocket, he didn't give himself time to think as he hit dial after searching his contacts.

"My darling boy, is everything okay?"

Popi's voice grounded him. They'd spoken daily, keeping them updated on the disaster. "Popi..." he came to a stop and pinched the bridge of his nose, working to get a hold of himself, uncaring people were walking past him.

"What is it, darling?" asked Popi in a soothing voice that he had often used when Booker had a nightmare.

"I... oh fuck. I think I'm about to adopt a baby girl." Saying it aloud made the surreal feel very real.

A loud sniff came before a hiccupped sob. "Oh... I'm gonna be a grandpopi."

Booker turned and laid his forehead against the wallpaper, shutting his eyes at the ball of emotion that burst in the center of his chest at the simple acceptance of a decision he'd not known he needed. "You are," he murmured.

Chapter Thirty-One

Frey

The scent of the hospital never failed to irritate Frey's fox. The antiseptic, blood and other stuff he didn't want to think too closely about, they were constant reminders of exactly where they were. Even in the maternity wing, they couldn't escape. Frey buried his nose in the neck of the little girl who cooed up at him. She smelled of talcum powder and soap.

If anyone asked him, he would say they were the best smells in the world coming off his little girl.

No, not mine, he reminded himself, for the fortieth time since he'd arrived that day. It was getting impossible to believe it, because it really didn't matter how many times he said it, his heart wasn't listening to his brain.

When he'd understood Toby had died, in his mind he'd become the little girl's popi. He'd helped bring her into the world. Been the first thing she'd seen. *She was his.*

Ours. His fox was in full agreement.

They wanted her. Wanted to be a father to the bundle who never failed to make his heart brim with joy when she opened her green eyes and stared at him intently, like she was trying to figure him out.

Frey released a heartfelt sigh. He just didn't know how to say that to Booker. To the others. They would probably think him silly, but Frey just needed to fathom out how to make them see that it was the right decision.

A little fist waved in the air and fingers grabbed onto his cheek. "I'm right here, Emmy," he murmured, not moving so as not to dislodge the tiny hand that also laid claim to his heart.

"Emmy?"

Frey froze in the seat and counted to ten to get his breathing under control as he peeked up, noting Booker dressed in a fitted black suit. He stood leaning against the doorframe of the parent room the staff let Frey use. How long had he been there?

There was something about his expression that gave Frey's belly a little hitch. "Don't you think she looks like an Emmy? I mean, we couldn't keep calling her baby, could we?" he asked, unable to keep the hope from his voice.

The staff had said naming her wasn't a good thing when they'd be leaving. Something about transference. He hated the idea of spending one minute away from her; he didn't care about transference.

Booker didn't move his gaze from them as Emmy started to fuss.

Frey lifted her and smelled her bottom, knowing it had only been an hour since he'd fed her, and she couldn't be hungry. He'd learned a lot over the last four days from staff in the hospital and the internet, while Emmy slept. The ripe scent made his nose wrinkle as he rose, grinning. "Someone needs a diaper change. Should Popi do it..." *oh no!*

His gaze flew to Booker to see if he'd caught the slip up.

"Do you want some help?" asked Booker instead, not revealing if indeed he'd heard what Frey had said aloud.

"Help?" he squeaked, when it sunk in what Booker had actually suggested. His heart skipped all over the place with what it would be like to watch Booker with the little girl.

He eyed the bear, who walked towards them, holding out his arms. "Do you know how to change a diaper?"

"You can teach me."

"I can?" Back was the squeakiness that made him want to slap himself upside the head.

Booker took the little girl from his arms, not waiting for a real answer. He dwarfed her and Frey's feelings expanded inside his chest until he couldn't breathe with how much he wanted this to be his reality. The three of them. A family.

The little pink bundle stopped fussing the second she lay in his arms and he gently swayed on the spot.

"Shall we get that bottom clean, sweetheart?" Booker walked to the changing bench tucked in the room's corner, continuing on. "I'm a novice at this sort of thing, so you need to cut me some slack, okay?"

Her response was to reach a hand up. Frey watched the world narrow to just the girl and Booker, who, when his face got close enough to the little girl, grinned widely. Emmy grabbed at his beard and clutched it with her chubby fingers, making Booker chuckle. "Look at you showing how strong you are."

Frey wanted to offer all the love he held inside him to the man and child who had more than staked a claim. They'd set up house inside him and he never wanted them to leave.

In fascination at this side of Booker, Frey stepped closer when he finally placed the little girl down and looked at him. "What's next?"

Frey blinked and, for a moment, could not find his tongue with how charmed he was.

Booker arched a brow at him.

"Erm... we need to undo those poppers between her legs."

Booker nodded and eyed the all-in-one-suit like it was a complicated work problem, giving it his total concentration. His fingers looked massive against tiny legs as they kicked up. Booker spoke to her the entire time, as he did as Frey instructed ever so carefully. "That's it, let's get this off so we can get you all cleaned up."

Frey bit his lip at the cute baby voice Booker was rocking as he grinned at him once more. "What's next?"

Lower lip firmly clamped between his teeth to hold back his giggles, Frey showed him how to tuck the baby all-in-one out of the way. Frey had learned that lesson the hard way. No one wanted poop everywhere with a wiggly baby who could make even the most careful person poop covered.

Frey grabbed the wet wipes and the fresh diaper, laying them on the padded bench. He pointed at the sticky tabs.

"Peel those back, then hold both legs in one hand when you pull the diaper between her legs."

He did that and Frey prepared himself for the ungodly poopy smell that a baby could make. Did he warn Booker? Why no, he didn't.

When Booker peeled it from between her legs—the gloopy greenish-brownish poop covering her lower half and right up her front—the sound of a loud retching noise quickly followed.

Frey creased over with laughter at the alarmed look Booker threw at him.

Pale faced, his nose wrinkling and his lips curling, Booker looked about ready to throw up. "What the hell are they feeding Emmy?"

He couldn't answer as he clutched his sides at the next round of retching from Booker as he moved his upper body as far away from the smell as he could get. Frey didn't tell him it was pointless, that he'd tried it. The smell a tiny person could create, there was no escaping once it was unleashed in a diaper.

Next, Booker's entire face scrunched up, just increasing Frey's amusement. "Pass me a baby wipe, for fu...sh...damn sake," he finished, looking helpless and making matters worse for Frey when he tried to avoid swearing. He was just too adorable.

The problem, though, was that Frey had not laughed in days, and now he had no control. His hands shook as he pulled out the wipes, handing them over and gave Booker a break by taking the diaper and putting it in the pail that sat next to the bench.

"Thanks," Booker choked out, his eyes watering as he swiped haphazardly at the poo, smearing it everywhere as another retch followed. "How the heck did Popi do this?" he gasped, his face going a deep shade of red.

"Do you want me to take over?" Frey asked innocently once he'd gotten himself under control... kind of.

Booker scowled at him while Emmy wiggled and made cheerful noises, unconcerned that she was inflicting torment on Booker.

"I can do it," he ground out through clenched teeth. "If I can manage a business and millions of dollars, then I can manage a diaper change."

Frey clamped his lips together to prevent more laughter from escaping at how Booker looked, clearly working hard to keep the next retch from escaping. Or when Booker inadvertently smeared poo over the cuff of his suit jacket. A very expensive jacket that they'd be hard pushed to get the stain out of. Frey should know, he had ruined two shirts.

When Booker had finished and Emmy was clean and dressed, Frey gave in and mentioned the jacket. "You got a little poop on your sleeve," he said, all innocence.

"Argh... eck..." Another round of retching, but to Frey's surprise Booker never let the little girl go as he slipped his arm out of the offending sleeve before letting it fall down his other arm and drop to the floor, where he booted it away.

Twenty-five minutes later and Emmy had a clean diaper on, something Frey didn't mention was a five-minute job.

Booker was redder than a fire engine when he sat down in the nursing seat with Emmy in his arms, looking utterly exhausted.

Emmy's lips parted, and she searched, her pretty face screwing up, her lips trembling.

"What's wrong with her?" asked Booker in an alarmed tone.

Frey knew what she wanted and sat on the arm of the big, padded chair, putting his finger next to Emmy's lips. "This. She doesn't like the pacifiers," he murmured. "Do you Emmy, you prefer Po—Frey's finger."

Blushing, he didn't dare look at Booker at his second slip up while Emmy sucked on his finger, making happy noises.

Not even a second later, her eyes drifted shut. He met Booker's grin with one of his own. They stared at each other, and Frey's heart picked up speed.

"She's mine," said Frey, compelled to speak his truth. He wasn't going to be able to leave her.

Then Booker spoke and Frey's life became perfect. "She's ours."

Frey burst into tears, but still mindful even as he deflated faster than a balloon not to jostle Emmy, he rested his head on Booker's broad shoulder, the relief immense.

"S-she i-is," he sobbed. "W-what do we do n-now?"

Chapter Thirty-Two
Alphaholes

Silas: In what universe does my brother go on a work trip and come back with a baby? Tell me.

Rue: An alternative one. Especially as he's bringing that little girl home to our place! What the fuck is that all about?

Kodi: He's lost his mind. That's what that is about. First, he picks Frey up and cradles him like a damn baby outside the hotel. I mean, when the fuck did those *two even get together? Wasn't he the one adamant that he wasn't for getting caught? Now he's adopting a baby with Frey!!!!! Mind fucking blown.*

Laken: *Looks like he's been keeping his cards close to his chest. That the case Silas? Even you appear shocked by the news when Popi mentioned it to us. If Booker was gonna tell anyone about all this, it would be you.*

Silas: *He doesn't tell me everything...*

Jupiter: *Holy crap. I knew something was wrong. He used to tell you every-thing, fuck, even when he farted. What the hell happened? You two have a fall-out and haven't been able to kiss and make out?*

Silas: *Fuck, why do you always have to make this about sex? We ain't interested in each other, not now, never have been and stop being a wind up merchant. 'Cause Jup. you do not get to spout that crap in front of Frey. Those two are gonna have enough to contend with.*

Jupiter: *Rue, you owe me fifty bucks. I told you something was wrong. And what's the betting we'll all get roped into helping? I need to find a place, because I don't wanna be babysitting, no damn way.*

Rue: *Way to fucking dump me in it, Jup. Who said anything about us babysitting? Booker is the one who decided to adopt that little girl.*

Kari: *Haven't you learned yet Rue, Jup would spill faster than a broken jug? And when was it decided the little girl was moving in with us? No one mentioned that to me. Babysitting duties might not be so bad…*

Kodi: *Don't you dare start offering, or we'll all have to because you know what Popi's like once he gets something into his head. And nobody told you Kari, because you're away in New York and not answering your damn phone. Your PA not able to figure out how to take a call?*

Kari: *Stop that shit right now!*

Kodi: ....

Kari: *I'm warning you.*

Taylin: *Behave you two. What is it with you guys lately? But let's get fucking real here. Rue, Kodi, you saw what went down in that hotel room. That little girl needs us. We signed up for this when we decided to step the fuck up and be a part of something that has far-reaching implications for many.*

Dad: *Well put Tay. There are going to be changes, and if any of you upset your Pop, with this bullshit, then you'll have me to answer to. That little girl is family. Our family, got it?*

Jupiter: *Sorry Dad, I'm sure I speak for everyone, we were just shocked and mouthing off.*

Kodi: *Yeah, we'll be there and support Booker, Frey and Emmy any way we can.*

Dad: *Good, because there's a family meeting to discuss just that tomorrow evening. I'll expect you all there. That includes you, Kari.*

Kari: *I'll be there.*

Chapter Thirty-Three

Delicious & Vicious

Bowie: Did I overhear right, Frey is adopting a baby with Booker?

Monty: Overhear? Yep. She's so cute.

Bowie: Who is she? Yeah, someone was talking about Booker.

Lennon: *The baby, Emmy. Isn't that the cutest name? Frey picked it and it really suits her. Those deep green eyes of hers. She looks like an old soul when she stares at you. And don't pull that one Bowie, we all know you're in New York with Kari, so it has to be him you overheard.*

Bowie: *It is, but I'm lost. How did they go on a work trip and find a baby girl?*

Hollis: *I'm not sure this is the appropriate place to discuss this.*

Frey: *It's fine Hollis. I helped an omega, Toby, give birth to his daughter. He died after the birth.*

Bowie: *Oh no, how awful!*

Frey: *It's so sad, we had the funeral for him yesterday. All the other omegas from the factory came. They are all like a family. Like us.*

Bowie: Doesn't the little girl have a family... a daddy?

Frey: They've found no one, or no one who wants her. And they can't figure out who her daddy is... so me and Booker, we've signed the adoption paperwork this afternoon. She's ours now.

Lennon: Does that mean that you and Booker... are a couple? I know he got real protective over you when he thought we'd upset you. But isn't this all a bit quick, if you don't mind me saying?

Frey: Confession time, we've kind of been dating for a little while. You know, figuring stuff out. But this... we both wanted.

Bowie: Wow, that's news. Only what happens to Emmy if you don't stay together? Figure it out? Who will get that little girl?

Frey: She's mine! I was the first person she saw when she came into this world. I won't ever let her go. The paperwork we signed says she's mine.

Monty: *Good for you Frey. She deserves someone like you in her corner after how her life started. Toby... he asked you for help and you're giving it to his daughter, that counts.*

Frey: *Thank you. That's not my biggest worry anyway, to be honest. It's moving into Booker's parents' home with all the other alphas. What was I thinking when I said yes?*

Isley: *You weren't 'cause how would anyone agree to do that? Eight alphas all in one place!*

Hollis: *Taylin lives with me, so that's seven.*

Lennon: *No Isley was right, eight, with Derick Starling.*

Hollis: *Oh heck yes, I forgot about him.*

Monty: *I don't know how. A silver fox like that, who could ever forget him?*

Hollis: *Lane can see the chat Monty!*

Monty: *Oops… it was a compliment, Lane.*

Lane: *He is a silver fox and hot in the sack. Frey, you'll be fine, just be you and they'll all fall in line.*

Hollis: *Please… nooooo he's going to be my father-in-law, Lane.*

Lane: *That doesn't change anything, he is hot and great in the sack. LOLOLOLOLOL*

Hollis: *Noooooooooooo*

Frey: *Let's hope so, or else you might feel like you've come back to work when they all start bickering.*

Lane: *I can handle those boys, don't you worry. The reason I popped in as I have a family meeting planned tomorrow night and I would like you all to come. I'd like to create a rota to assist Frey and Booker with Emmy, if you're interested?*

Frey: *Oh Lane, you're making me cry.*

Bowie: *Hormones… can you get that from adopting a baby?*

Lane: *Absolutely.*

Chapter Thirty-Four

Booker

"Sir, we are preparing to land, you need to buckle up."

Bleary-eyed and feeling like he had the worst hangover, Booker blinked the air steward into focus, or at least tried. When had he fallen asleep? Last thing he remembered was working on his computer.

He grunted, rubbing at his tired eyes as his brain tried to work out which way was up. The last couple of weeks had been a blur juggling work, legalities, and Emmy's needs. He reached clumsily for the seatbelt and snapped it into place, automatically looking at Frey and Emmy when they entered his thoughts. Which was—if he was honest—all the time, making it impossible to get through all the work he needed to do. Late nights had become his new norm.

Did he care?

One look at Frey and Emmy, and he found nothing else mattered, his heart had become invested with Frey... now he couldn't imagine a life without either the little girl or Frey in it.

His gaze softened on the pair sat on the seat next to him. Emmy was swaddled in a blanket and held close to Frey's chest, one of his fingers between her lips. The sight made him want to sigh at how much of his heart belonged to them. Emmy was theirs. Fuck, it made him ache seeing them like this, knowing his luck came from Toby's tragedy.

He shut out thoughts of things he couldn't change and focused on what he could do now, for a little girl who didn't like a pacifier. The chuckle felt good recalling how many shops he'd gone to hunting for the perfect pacifier. No matter how many Booker tried, all Emmy wanted was his or Frey's finger.

The dark circles that looked like bruises under Frey's eyes were testimony to this. Right now, his hair was a complete mess, with strands stuck up all over the place and he had baby spit-up on his shirt. He'd never looked more beautiful to Booker, but he got they needed a solution to the finger issue. He sighed half-heartedly at how much he loved it when she fell asleep sucking his finger, which came with a wallop of life-changing feelings whacking his chest. He was getting used to the intensity of them, mostly. Could he remember ever being this emotional about anyone or anything? No, and it scared him more than he would admit.

He's our mate, with our cub.

Don't start with me.

I'm just saying—

You're just saying nothing. We signed paperwork to make things legal with Emmy.

Booker snapped his teeth together and straightened up, doing what he could to stop staring at the picture Frey and Emmy made, snuggled as they were. He found he could stare at them for hours, which wasn't productive at all. His gaze lingered on Frey's unmarked neck, his gums aching with thoughts of...

Get out of my head.

Impossible, and paperwork means nothing to an unclaimed mate.

A growl rumbled up from his chest when it was getting impossible not to agree with what his bear wanted. To claim Frey as theirs and make them a genuine family. His bear had started nagging. This was all part of it, getting into his thoughts and changing their direction.

This wasn't me. It was you.

The arguing was a daily thing. Booker rolled his eyes and didn't bother answering. This behavior usually came when he was on his knees, tired. Late nights with a baby who needed feeding, when they were all sleeping in the same bed together. It was driving him to distraction.

They had a legal agreement. It was enough for now...

Keep dreaming.

The jet hit an air pocket and Frey started awake. His gaze went straight to the bundle he held before he glanced at Booker. "Is everything okay?" he asked groggily.

"We're coming into land." He wanted to fuss, to get up and check they were both secure. To check the baby seatbelt they'd had to special order for the plane to attach to Frey's or Booker's. He'd checked it twice while Frey was asleep, it still wasn't enough for his protective urges. Emmy had had an awful, fussy night and as neither he nor Frey could place Emmy in her crib and leave her there crying, she'd stayed in the bed with them. It broke both their hearts to hear her crying. He'd read up on the do's and don'ts, and both he and Frey were failing on so many. Babies in bed were a definite no.

They let Emmy rule their lives.

Was it wrong?

Possibly?

Did they care?

No.

His life was now in two parts, before Emmy and after. Everything in his world now revolved around the two people in the seat next to him and he didn't want to change a thing.

"Are you sure it's going to be alright with me moving *temporarily* into your home?"

Booker could easily see Frey's concerns, with his puckered brow and wary stare. They'd discussed it. His place wasn't going to be big enough for all the things a baby would need. Then there was childcare while they figured out Emmy's daily routine, or that's what the book he'd bought said.

"We're going to have a house meeting and discuss everything this evening when we get there. It will all be fine, you'll see." Booker fucking hoped so after he'd read the alphahole chat at two this morning. His brothers would stand by his decision one hundred percent. Helping him... that was still debatable.

Frey got a look that suggested he knew about the family gathering. "Lane invited all the PAs as well, to do a rota to look after Emmy."

"He said that? When?"

Frey blushed prettily. "In our group chat yesterday."

"Oh." Booker had spoken with Popi, and he and Dad had offered for them all to move into the house because it had the space they'd need for now. There were also folks there to help with things like the... *dirty diapers*. Booker continued to retch every time he did one. It was lowering when Frey managed without a problem. So he was going to inflict that torment on his brothers.

He chuckled at the very idea.

"You're planning something," Frey said, shifting as the plane thumped onto the tarmac and taxied down the runway.

Booker grinned, all teeth. "I don't know what you mean."

Frey shook his head, smiling. "You do, but it's fine. I'm too tired to argue."

His concern for Frey removed the humor all too quickly. "Popi has offered to have her tonight so we can get some uninterrupted sleep.'

Frey's frown returned. "I..." Frey glanced at Emmy. "We'll see."

Booker got it; he did. The need to have Emmy close. Did a parent ever lose that feeling? Booker had no answer, like most of the time. This was all so new, yet on the other hand, it was like he'd never been without Frey or Emmy by his side.

He remained quiet, packing up his things, ready to disembark the jet.

In the waiting car, the driver had strapped the car seat they'd purchased into the back. Emmy didn't stir as Frey got her into the seat and settled right next to it, finally freeing his chapped finger.

The silence between them continued and Booker chewed the inside of his cheek, debating with himself whether to talk about the bedroom situation. On the top floor of his parents' home were two conjoined rooms, usually reserved for guests. In the hotel, they'd had no option but to sleep in the same bed, with everything so new with Emmy. Would it be different now they would have help?

He hated the idea of not having Frey snuggling in bed with him. Sex was there, in the back of his thoughts, but he needed Frey to make the move, to show he was ready after what he'd been through. Also, having an infant in your bed was the most tiring thing in the world.

When the car drove up the drive to the house, Booker stared out the window at all the cars in the driveway. Shit, Frey wasn't kidding, all the PAs were there.

Emmy chose then to wake up. Not having Frey's finger in her mouth, she immediately started to cry. She was happy to reveal her lungs were in great working order with her piercing cries. They stopped the second she caught sight of Frey as he popped his head over the car seat.

"Popi's here, Emmy." At the sound of his voice, the tears stopped, and she gave him a gummy smile. It wasn't wind, not at all.

"Did you see that? She smiled at me!"

"You're a miracle worker." Booker released his seatbelt and Frey's, who seemed to forget he also had a seatbelt on while he struggled to get close enough to lift Emmy out so he could carry her into the house. He didn't even consider leaving her in the car's travel seat. His preferred method was in his arms. Online, Booker had found a wraparound baby sling with a rainbow pattern on it, and had it delivered to Popi while they were away. He wanted to surprise Frey with it. He could then do stuff with Emmy strapped to him... like peeing.

The car door burst open and Popi's head peered in. "Oh my," he hiccup-sobbed. "Please, let me have a hold of my grandbaby."

"Erm..."

Popi looked expectantly at them both, his hands fluttering at his sides.

"I'm sure Frey would like to be the first one to carry our sweet girl into the house. Like an introductory kind of thing," Booker murmured softly, not wanting to upset Popi but also understanding that Frey was a little anxious about letting Emmy go, right this second.

Frey's body sagged against the seat, almost appearing conflicted.

"Of course."

Popi didn't get a chance to move back to give them room before Frey spoke, "You could hold her while I get out of the car, if you like?"

Popi beamed as though Frey had offered him the world, and smoothly transferred the baby into his arms with such effortless ease.

Booker's jaw hung open at the fluid move that he and Frey had yet to manage.

"Aren't you just the most adorable, beautiful girl?" Popi nuzzled Emmy's cheek, making her squeal in delight.

Frey fidgeted on the seat, looking a little forlorn. Booker rubbed a hand over Frey's shoulder, squeezing gently. "It's hard, I know, but you made Popi's day. Heck, his month, possibly his year. He'll love her as much as us," he murmured quietly, knowing it to be the truth. He'd experienced that love and it changed a person for the good.

A loud sniff and a quick dash with the back of his hand over his eyes, and Frey looked at him. "I know... it's... just..."

"She's our baby girl and sharing the joy is hard when it's so new?" Booker finished for him, getting it.

Another sniff and Frey came closer and pressed his forehead against Booker's chest and released a shuddery breath, his arms going around Booker's middle in an awkward hug. "She's just so precious."

He kissed the top of Frey's talcum powder scented hair. "It's gonna be fine. I swear it."

"Are you two coming in or just gonna sit there all day?" asked Silas, his gaze meeting Booker's over the top of Frey's head as he took Popi's place.

Booker could easily see the silent question in Silas' eyes, asking if they were okay without saying it out loud. The night they'd gone for a beer, they'd avoided talking about Ziggy, so things at times were still awkward. Booker kind of expected it after so long of not speaking openly about what had gone on between them.

He nodded and gave him a cheeky grin. "You gonna be the first to offer to babysit, bro?"

"Fuck off, I'd rather—"

"Silas." The way Dad spoke his name stopped whatever else Silas was about to say, and Booker's smile widened.

Frey wiggled out of Booker's arms and climbed past the car seat. He stood looking up at Dad with a somber expression. It was so different from what Booker was used to, he scrambled to get out of the car.

Frey offered his hand. "I want to thank you for the offer to let us stay until we get something else sorted."

Booker watched Dad ignore Frey's hand and pull him in for a hug, getting a startled squeal from the man he held. "Welcome to the family."

It was hard to dislodge the lump in his throat, and Booker had to look away for a second to collect himself. Silas slapped him on the back hard enough to make Booker stagger forward. He side eyed his brother. "What you do that for?"

"Stop you going all teary-eyed. One sap in the family is enough."

"Huh... Taylin?"

"Who did you think I meant?" Silas questioned, frowning at him.

Booker shrugged, feeling a little too warm for comfort when he spotted Kari standing in the doorway with Bowie. "I'm sleep deprived. I don't know what I mean anymore."

Silas's eyes narrowed, then he grinned. "That's what happens with a baby." He glanced at Kari and pointed a finger. "I remember when he and Kodi tag teamed Dad and Popi, one crying, then one would stop and the other would start."

"Memorable moments that you treasure when they grow up," Dad murmured, letting go of Frey who looked a tad shellshocked. "And become a complete pain in your ass."

"Hey," Silas said in outrage.

Kari's brows drew together, and he stood a little straighter. "What, a pain in your ass? Never!"

Dad's lips twitched as he winked at Booker. "If the shoe fits..."

"He's joking." Not sounding convinced, Silas following Dad into the house after a disappearing Kari.

Bowie hung by the doorway, staring at Frey like he wanted to talk to him. Placing a hand on Frey's lower back, Booker guided him to the door. "I think someone wants to talk to you." He kissed the top of Frey's head and wandered inside, leaving Frey and Bowie alone.

He followed the sound of voices into the dining room. Only the table was gone and in its place were lots of chairs. By the wall at the far end was a flip chart on a stand.

Oh gods! His eyes widened.

Shit, Frey was right. Popi had indeed drawn up a rota for Emmy. He glanced back out the doorway, unsure whether to laugh or hide from Frey. It was a close call with an interfering Popi who always got his own way.

You'll get more time alone with Frey when you aren't tired, his bear pointed out gleefully.

Booker glanced back at the flip chart... *that was true!*

Chapter Thirty-Five

Frey

"What's up?" Frey asked, placing a reassuring hand on Bowie's arm when he didn't seem able to find his voice. He kicked at the floor with his sneakered foot.

The longer the seconds drew out, the more Frey had to fight the urge to traipse over to where Popi held court with Emmy, waiting with some of the other PA's. The lack of crying was a good sign. She was very vocal when something wasn't to her liking. Did that make him feel better?

"I... you see..." Bowie sighed and rubbed at his flushed face. "You won't give up that little girl if things don't work out for you and Booker, will you?"

It took a second to realize that Bowie wasn't being horrible. Frey recalled a little of what Bowie had shared about his past. What he'd mentioned before in the group chat must still have been on his mind. Frey could see the genuine concern Bowie had for Emmy and that it came from a place of understanding what it was like to be rejected by those who adopted him.

Blowing out a breath at the unexpected emotional hit, Frey dragged Bowie in for a hug, struggling a little to get his arms around his shoulders. In the end he gave up, slipping his arms around Bowie's waist, drawing him in to whisper in his ear, "I would cut off a limb before I'd give up my baby."

He meant every word. When he'd signed the paperwork Booker's lawyers had pushed through for them, he'd become Emmy's Popi for life.

He squeezed hard, then released Bowie to cup his cheeks, holding his stare so he could see Frey was deadly serious. "She's mine in every way. I helped bring that baby into this world, possibly even saved her life. Her daddy asked me to help, and I am going to honor his life by doing just that."

Bowie's eyes searched his. "What if you get pregnant a-and don't want her 'cause you h-have your own flesh and blood?"

Frey blinked back a sudden rush of tears. He hated his hormones, he really did. It took a moment for him to gather himself to admit his secret.

"I can't have children." Saying it hurt a little less with everything he'd become blessed with. "I took heat blockers for too long and they messed up my hormones. I don't have a heat the same way because of it."

Speaking the truth aloud felt freeing. He'd discovered he didn't need to give birth to feel like a parent, Emmy had taught him that.

"You what?"

The strain in Booker's voice got him releasing Bowie to swing around. They stared at each other as Bowie said something and scuttled off down the hallway. "I was going to tell you, I swear." Frey felt the panic climbing when he couldn't get a read off the motionless man.

After an eternity—two seconds—Booker removed the distance between them, his dark brows doing combat. "Was this what you meant about there being more to talk about that day at the lake?"

There was little about the question that helped Frey's nerves as he nodded.

"Why did you tell Bowie and not me?"

Hurt. It shone out of the deep brown eyes that had captured Frey's heart. He'd seen the gentleness beyond the bear's grumpy exterior.

His chest heaved as he released a shuddery breath, then inhaled, taking that last step that separated them, trusting his instincts. "Bowie is worrying I'll get pregnant and reject Emmy."

"What! You'll never do that, not in a million years," Booker blustered angrily.

Frey's lips curved into a sweet smile, and he slipped his arms around Booker's middle and snuggled right in, his heart brimming with love. "I love you."

Booker became a statue. Chest unmoving, like he'd lost the ability to breathe as it struck Frey what he'd let slip out. Oh no, he'd ruined everything by rushing things. Booker clearly wasn't ready for such a declaration.

"You d-do?" His whole body remained still.

Tell him again.

Frey ignored his fox and eased back, looking up. What he could see in Booker's eyes rammed his heart from the front to the back of his chest. Emotion's made the words slip out with full intention this time. "Yes. I love you. I'm not saying it because of Emmy. This is because of who you are. I know things are... different between us b-because of my p-past, but I want you, all of you, *in every way*." Saying it made it real, made everything real. But was this type of real too much for Booker?

Stop being daft, nothing is too much for our bear.

The two seconds that followed were the longest in Frey's life, despite the conviction of his animal spirit. Then Booker scooped him up off the floor and his feet dangled in the air while large hands held onto his bottom. Booker lifted him until they were eye level and kissed him. It wasn't the gentle exploration of their first kiss. This held passion the likes Frey had dreamed of but never thought he'd experience.

His lips parted and where once would have been fear, all Frey felt was raw need. It banished the fatigue, burned it clear away. He lifted his legs without thinking and wrapped them around Booker's waist. The snug fit made him gasp and mewl at the realization his body was wholly on board with this new situation, right along with his brain.

Heart thundering in his ears, his fingers sank into Booker's thick, silky hair and clung on. Booker deepened the kiss, his lips devouring Frey's, one hungry kiss after another.

Frey felt achy all over and his clothes felt too restrictive when Booker stopped. "We gotta stop... or I'm..."

"Or you'll what?" Jupiter asked from somewhere behind them.

It didn't quite dampen Frey's arousal, but it helped lessen the heat, if not that of his cheeks, which burned at being caught like this.

"Get lost." Booker didn't so much as look away from Frey.

"I would, but then Dad might come looking for you. I'm sure you don't want him to find you making out where everyone can see you both, outside and in, with the front door wide open?"

Frey wriggled and dropped his legs to dangle in Booker's arms, not wanting to be caught like this despite Derick's warm welcome. No, that would be too much on the first night in their house. Heck, any night in this house.

When Booker was slow to let him go, Jupiter laughed aloud

Frey frowned. "Let go," he murmured, his eyes begging the man who seemed less inclined and caused a level of conflict in Frey he'd not felt before. "Please."

Booker scowled over his shoulder and then placed him on the ground, whispering in his ear, "We'll finish this later." He rose and reached for Frey's hand, entwining their fingers, giving him a big grin. "Let's see what Popi has planned."

Frey registered that everyone had disappeared inside, including Popi and Emmy. He didn't sigh in complaint when he had been the one to kiss Booker and declare his feelings with an audience he'd forgotten about. He had no one to blame but himself for Popi taking their little girl inside while he had been... *otherwise occupied.*

"Yeah, let's," Jupiter replied, rolling his eyes at them. Dressed as casually as Frey had ever seen him, in slim fitting sweats and a Starling Enterprise hoodie, Jupiter still looked like he'd just stepped out of the pages of a fashion magazine.

"You can always say no," Frey felt compelled to say.

Jupiter aimed a sardonic grin at them. "You have met Popi, right?"

"We wouldn't force you to do anything that took time from your playthings," Booker muttered snappily.

Another eye roll and Jupiter shook his head. "They'll wait for me,"—he winked at Frey—"'cause they know I'm worth it."

Booker tucked Frey into his side, making it awkward to walk when they headed inside and off down the hallway in the direction of the sounds of voices, leaving Jupiter behind.

"I'm not interested in him," Frey pointed out in a quiet voice.

"I know." Booker glanced over his shoulder. "I just need someone else to know that."

Frey kept the laughter tickling the back of his throat to himself at the show of jealousy. He'd never have expected that from Booker.

They entered what Frey knew was the dining room, and he came to a sudden stop, jerking Booker to a halt. Whatever guilt that wanted to worm its way in at thoughts of what happened outside, didn't have time to take root. In Derick's arms nestled Emmy, looking right at home and it seemed loving the attention.

There were all the PAs standing around Lane, adding their names to—Frey strolled towards them, his gaze fixed—a large flip pad on a stand. There were three calendar months mapped out with the days broken down into three sections. "W-hat..." he swallowed, licking his dry lips and trying again. "What is this?"

"There you are. I hope you don't mind. I brought Emmy in," he coughed. "You looked a little busy."

Frey's blush burned his cheeks. His head bobbed and the furrow between Lane's brows disappeared as he grinned. "Come and sit, I've already started filling in the chart," Lane said excitedly.

"Popi," Booker said in a warning tone.

Derick looked at them, then at his husband. "Maybe you should explain yourself love, to prevent Frey freaking out and running for the door with our granddaughter."

"Oh... yes, sorry." Lane waved a hand at him, and Frey came to a halt in front of the chart wearing a bemused expression as his friends made room for him. "Booker said you wanted to keep working, and as I really struggled to leave my boys when they were babies, I thought maybe if I could help with a daycare rota for when you're in work with the other PAs, those you trust of course." He tapped at the boxes. "You can take Emmy to work, use the space I've set up for her, and the guys are going to take hourly slots around their workload. You'll be close at hand so if they have a problem, you'll be right there to deal with it."

Frey sniffed and felt his nose burn at the reality he could go to work, have Emmy close by and have help. It was so much more than he could have imagined. Having Emmy was a dream come true, but this? He was being offered everything he wanted and so much more.

"Then, see, I did one for when you're here, after work, so it's not so tiring. I've also factored in sleeping. Babies can make sleep a distant memory along with..." his gaze shifted to Booker and a cheeky grin appeared, "alone time."

"Popi's sorting your sexy time, big bro," Rue said through his laughter, before Derick landed his gaze on him. He instantly sobered and dropped his head. "Sorry."

Frey wasn't sure what to say as he sniffed louder than the last time and dashed a hand over his damp eyes. "It's..." he burst into tears, sobbing uncontrollably.

"Fuck."

"Oh, shit."

"Why does he have to do that?"

"Booker, do something," Silas snapped.

"I'm sorry," Frey sobbed. "It's just all so overwhelming."

Booker wrapped his arms around him and lifted him up to sit on his hip. "Please don't cry." The hitch in Booker's voice was unmistakable.

"This shit's catching," said one of the twins, but Frey couldn't tell which when Booker's wide shoulder blocked his view.

"Less of that, you're setting a poor example to Frey and the other PAs." Derick's command, though said in a low voice, which Frey appreciated when he was holding Emmy, held a wealth of alpha power.

"S-sorry." Frey worked to get himself back under control, not wanting anyone to get into trouble because of his choices. His body shuddered, as did that of the man holding him.

"It's not your fault I have dicks for brothers." There was a smattering of laughter at this.

Frey scrubbed his face and worked to get hold of himself, taking deep breaths. When he could finally look at the room of people, he gave them a watery smile. "Thank you. All of you, for this. I made a promise to Emmy's daddy, Toby, before he died to help. Only it's not about that now. I love her, she's my daughter." He met Booker's shimmering gaze. "She's our daughter."

"She is," Booker murmured softly before he kissed him gently, setting off flutters inside Frey at how he didn't care that they had an audience. "Part of our family." The latter, Booker said to the room.

"Of course she is," Lane said, slipping his arm around Derick and resting his head on his shoulder, looking directly at Emmy. Back was the urge to cry at what Lane was offering. Love was all Frey could see as Lane stared at their child. "She's our very first grandbaby."

Lane smiled at his sons and Frey's urge to cry turned into a wet giggle at the unmistakable look of alarm that five of the brothers wore.

"I wish you'd adopted me," Bowie said, loud enough for everyone to hear. He blushed when several heads turned in his direction. Including Kari, who wore a look that gave Frey pause as he stared between both men.

Jupiter laughed and distracted Frey. "I think that wouldn't work, for obvious reasons."

"Jup..." Derick walked to his son and, without warning, placed Emmy into his arms. "Here, let's give you something else to think about."

Frey, about to ask to be put down, parted his lips in surprise as Emmy made a noise that he'd describe as a giggle. Jupiter looked down at the little girl and Frey witnessed the moment of wonder that fleetingly crossed Jupiter's face. One he recognized from Booker. It was gone in a flash, replaced by a cheeky grin.

"See," he smirked, "even Emmy can see I'm adorable."

Groans filled the room.

"You are adorable." Lane's statement brought more good humored groans, with the exception of Wilder, who was watching Jupiter like a cat watched a mouse. Frey wasn't sure anyone else noticed. Being sat on Booker's hip, he was higher up and had a better view of the room.

"Urg... what's that smell?" Jupiter's nose wrinkled as he lifted Emmy closer to his face.

"She needs a diaper change, and it looks like you're up, bro." Booker's glee brought a head shake from Jupiter.

"Fu—no way. She's your daughter."

"And your niece," Popi said, guiding Jupiter to the door by his elbow. "I'll explain how to do it, don't worry."

They could all hear Jupiter's alarm as he left the room. "What! No, you can't be serious. Can't you smell that?"

As his voice trailed off, it took all of two seconds before the room erupted with laughter. Booker looked at Frey, his eyes dancing with mischief. "I think I better go check if he's okay."

"You mean watch him suffer?"

Booker placed Frey down and kissed him once more. "That too, but hey he's my brother." As if that explained it, Booker was off, hustling after Lane and Jupiter.

Derick came over to Frey before he could decide if he should follow. "You only have to say no if it's not what you want. I'll make Lane listen."

Frey hadn't missed Derick's name next to Lane's on the chart for taking Emmy overnight twice a week. "How does that usually work for you?" Derick's lips twitched, and Frey responded with a grin. "I thought so."

"It doesn't stop me from trying."

Chapter Thirty-Six

Booker

Two weeks later

A cry woke Booker, and he rolled off the bed, even before his eyes were fully open. His brain had become attuned to the sound of his daughter's distress. He'd not even taken two steps in the dim light coming through the open door leading into the nursery before he heard Frey moving behind him. "It's my turn, stay in bed."

Receiving a grunted response, Booker chuckled and headed through the open door. They were getting there with a routine as much as anyone could with a baby. At just five weeks old, she'd turned everyone's life upside down. Popi was in his absolute element. Booker was discovering a side to his dad he'd never seen before, a softness that gave all his brothers cause to pause occasionally.

The low light reflected rainbows over the crib, guiding him. Booker had purposely left Frey and Lane to the conversation about having Emmy in bed with them. Whatever Lane had said had persuaded Frey to set up the crib in the room that had a conjoining door. The door never got shut, but she was in her own room. Booker was still undecided how he felt about that. It had taken three days before Frey had seen it as beneficial, given it meant they weren't both awake all night. Frey's emotional outbursts had decreased now he was actually getting some sleep. It seemed he could be as cranky as Emmy, though Booker would never say that aloud. He liked his balls where they were.

His nose wrinkled at the smell as he reached the crib, knowing exactly why Emmy had woken only an hour after her last feed. The girl was a poop factory. So far, she'd managed to poop on everyone except Silas and Jupiter. They all had gone through retching over what his little girl could produce at some point, except Jupiter, who seemed to have some sort or superpower when it came to diapers and poop.

He bent over the crib and the low light showed Emmy's red and screwed-up face, fists waving in the air at the injustice of a poopy bottom. His heart thudded painfully as he picked her up and soothed her before heading to the changing bench that Lane had fitted for their return home.

"What's all this fussin' 'bout, hey? Daddy is here. You don't need to be getting all upset." He kissed her forehead before he laid her down, the cries now more sniffles as she reached up, trying to grab for his beard. It was her most favorite thing to do, and it melted Booker's heart every damn time. He was a total sucker for her.

With shallow breathing, he undid the poppers and released a relieved sigh at the lack of poop seepage past the diaper. Something else that Emmy was great at was spreading the love beyond the diaper. Only the day before, she'd gotten poop all the way up her back to her neck. He'd not noticed when he'd picked her up. A full body shudder followed the memory as he took one big deep breath and held it as he peeled back the diaper.

He worked fast; the practice was definitely helping. Three minutes later and with only one extra breath, he fastened the clean diaper, slipping her all-in-one back in place and doing up the poppers. "There, see? All done, and Daddy didn't retch once," he murmured softly, lifting her back into his arms.

Emmy's eyelids drooped, so he lifted her hand and helped to put her thumb into her mouth. Another trick Popi had shown them. No longer was Emmy unhappy at the lack of their fingers in her mouth when she could suck her own. She made suckling noises as he stood next to the crib, rocking her while he hummed softly.

Frey liked to sing to her, but Booker wouldn't torment his daughter with his voice. He'd never win any awards, whereas Frey had a sweet voice that Booker and his bear side loved to listen to.

He carried on humming long past the time Emmy fell asleep. He was coming to cherish these quiet moments with her, despite it being in the middle of the night. He enjoyed not having to compete with work and the general busyness of life or the others wanting some Emmy time. What made it perfect was when Frey was right there with him.

They were a unit, and things just worked. Their lives were much like Popi's rota split in three. Work, where they spent their day cramming in as much of the work stuff as they could, so they each were able to take an hour to spend time with Emmy. And alright, he'd admit that they both sometimes eked that out with quick visits they both made to check she was okay. They were making the necessity of parenting and being in the office, work.

When home, his brothers had all bitched about helping out, but ultimately, they'd all stepped up. Jupiter was the surprise, as he was the one who gravitated towards Emmy most frequently, especially at feeding times. It was bizarre to see when Jupiter had only ever been interested in fucking.

The nights remained a bone of contention between Popi and Frey. As yet, Frey wasn't ready to allow Emmy to even go one floor down and sleep in the space Popi had created in his suite for Emmy. It didn't matter how persistent Popi was with the offers or how beautiful the crib was. Booker got it on one level, but lying next to Frey in bed night after night, Booker was struggling to keep his hands to himself, since Frey had told him he was ready for more. There just had not been the right moment, despite Frey being a snuggler.

His fox to Booker's bear, they'd found their connection easily and the big furry rug Popi had placed in their bedroom was a perfect spot for that. But as yet, they'd not gotten further than kisses and once or twice, some rolling around on the bed playing before Emmy interrupted them.

It was torture. Booker was being reasonable. However, he was constantly reminding himself that no matter what he wanted, things would happen when the time was right. Booker's reaction to Frey was getting harder to conceal when he wandered about wearing only a towel around his slim hips. Twice this week Booker had darted out of the room before he did something. Fuck, they'd been close calls. Frey smelled so delicious, but of late, it was like salmon to his bear, far too tempting.

"Is she okay?" Frey murmured sleepily.

Booker glanced over at the disheveled man walking towards them, cracking an enormous yawn and pushing his bangs from out of his eyes.

"She's good, just needed a diaper change." He kept his voice low. "I was just making sure she was asleep before I popped her back in the crib."

Frey's smile was all knowing as he met his gaze. "She looks asleep to me."

He blushed and managed not to squirm before he lowered Emmy back into the crib, careful not to jostle her and dislodge the thumb from her mouth. He only let go of his breath when he rose back up. "She's so stinkin' cute."

Frey knocked Booker's arm. "Less of the stinking."

He resisted arguing and took Frey's hand to lead him back into their bedroom, only once looking back before heading for the bed. "It's three thirty," he tugged back the covers, waiting for Frey to slide in before he climbed in after him, feeling for where he was so as not to squash him, "we might be lucky, and she'll let us sleep till six."

Frey came to rest his head on Booker's chest, then he squirmed until he was all but plastered to Booker's side. A thigh came over his, close enough to his balls that Booker had to think about smelly poop to prevent a growing problem.

"Let's hope. We've got a full day. Lane is going to come collect Emmy late afternoon and take her home as we've that dinner with the buyers."

Booker groaned. "Fuck, I forgot about that."

Frey's fingers threaded through his chest hair as he sighed. "I almost did until Bowie reminded me. He and Kari are coming, too." The silence lengthened between them so much that Booker thought Frey had fallen back to sleep. Much like Emmy, he could drop off quickly. "I'm glad it's Friday… it's been a long week."

He searched for a moment to find the top of Frey's head to kiss it. Frey mumbled something with his hand clutching tighter at his chest hair.

"Sleep, my little fox." Booker hummed and stroked his fingers up Frey's naked back, feeling his body relaxing at the rhythmic motions.

"Frey, can you find me the file for Cross Leathers, I seem to have misplaced it?" Booker asked in frustration. His hands lifted and placed down what was close to him on his overly messy desk.

"Here." Frey held out a blue file, having reached to lift it from the pile to Booker's left he'd picked up and placed back down. "If you looked with your eyes, it might help."

The sass was there, along with Frey's amusement shining in bright eyes. The dark bruises from lack of sleep under his eyes had slowly faded with Emmy sleeping for longer periods through the night and them taking turns to get up. After the diaper change in the early hours, Emmy had let them sleep until six-thirty, so they'd both woken refreshed, if Booker discounted his boner.

"You know I'm the boss here?" Booker said, keeping his expression serious and doing his best to avert his thoughts. Frey's scent today was driving him a little batty for some reason—or more so than usual.

Frey gave him an exaggerated brow arch before he went back to looking at the iPad he'd been using to make notes for their upcoming dinner that evening. "Cross Leathers have confirmed they've got the perfect person to assist Aven with putting a new management structure in place. They will be able to commence the next phase of the business set-up for the new company."

Booker sat back in his chair and twirled a pen in his fingers as he considered this. "Get Oakland to do a background check on whoever Malcom has offered to help. I don't want any missteps. Aven, though strong willed, does not need another asshole to work with."

"I'll reach out to Oakland once I have the name. We have requested it be an omega," Frey reminded him.

"Yeah, but we still aren't taking any chances. Those men need to feel safe going back." Booker twirled the pen. "How far along are they with the remodel of the factory? Has there been any update on the basement?"

Frey tapped at his iPad and then offered it to him. "The remodel of the basement is complete." He sniffed and Booker, who had taken the pad, pointed the pen at Frey, his heart getting a bump it didn't like at the glistening eyes.

"No tears in the workplace." He sounded way more gruff than normal.

With one swipe at his eyes, Frey gave him a head shake. "It's my hormones."

"You can't keep blaming them," Booker groused as he eyed the pictures on the screen, placing his pen down in his excitement to see more. He scrolled through the pictures of the now brightly lit space. The extensive area had been sectioned off. Instead of the cramped cots and dark shabby walls, there were thick padded sofas and chairs in bold colors that invited one to sit down. Plush, pale gray carpet replaced the awful flooring. Three corners of the space had areas designated for eating, with small kitchenettes offering facilities to cook food.

If Booker hadn't recognized certain structural features, he'd say it was a different building altogether. The upgrade was almost unrecognizable.

Booker's smile widened when his attention returned to Frey. "They've done an amazing job. I'm excited to see the upper factory floor when it's finished."

Everything would get ripped out and replaced so it looked like a whole new building, or that was the hope.

"I spoke to Aven yesterday. He's as excited as you and says that most of the other omegas are, too."

Booker's smile dimmed. Three of the omegas were too unwell to return to work; two physically and one whose trauma left him struggling to adjust. They had set aside the funds to support all three men and were getting them the care they needed. Booker didn't want to think about Toby's funeral and how gut wrenching it had been seeing their distress first hand.

A hand stroking down the sleeve of his shirt brought his blurry gaze to the man now standing at his side, taking the iPad from his hand. Without saying a word, Frey slipped into his lap and snuggled right in.

"We're making it better. Talking to Aven, I can see we are. We have to focus on that." The edge of desperation in Frey's words showed he wasn't always able to listen to his own advice.

Booker, who'd automatically wrapped his arms around Frey, tightened them, kissing the top of his head before coming to rest his bearded chin on the silky strands. "I know."

It never ceased to surprise him how much he got from simply holding Frey, and although it was completely unprofessional to be sitting at his desk like this, Booker couldn't find it in him to care.

He inhaled, his nose burying in Frey's hair, and groaned. "You smell so good."

"Only when I'm not covered in baby puke."

Booker chuckled, getting that Frey was aiming to lighten the mood. "You even smell good then."

He didn't need to wait more than a fraction of a second for Frey to huff and pull back, giving him a narrow-eyed look that was cute and totally non-threatening. "No one smells good covered in baby spit-up. No one."

He wiggled and got off Booker's lap. Booker resisted keeping hold of Frey when his body pulsed with arousal from the scent and wiggling.

"You do," he said around his laughter when Frey scowled.

"Booker, you got five minutes to go over—"

One look at Laken stood in the open door and Booker grunted. "Knocking is what you do when a door is shut."

"I did, you were too busy playing 'let's sniff my PA'." Laken's expression was passive for a whole two seconds before he caved at Booker's hard stare and shook with laughter. "It's the truth," he spluttered.

"Oh, shut up. No one likes a smart ass!"

"I do," Frey muttered, winked and walked off with his iPad in hand.

"Where are you going?"

Frey stopped at the door, glancing back. "To finish attempting to work through this list after giving our daughter a kiss before Lane whisks her away."

Booker pouted at not getting to do that too when Laken took the seat Frey had been using.

"It suits you," Laken said, as the door closed behind Frey.

"What?" Booker asked in confusion, frowning at the man opposite him.

"Being in love. Being a daddy. It looks good on you," Laken explained.

Booker eyed his brother, trying to see if he was trying to get a rise out of him. They'd always been at cross purposes with each other, though Booker had never figured out why. Seeing nothing to suggest he was ragging on him, Booker's grin reappeared. "Thank you."

Laken shrugged, the cut of his suit jacket extenuating his broad shoulders. "It's just an observation." There was a moment of silence as they stared at each other before Laken continued. "The Becker contract, do you have five minutes to go over some of the finer details?"

Chapter Thirty-Seven

Frey

Heat poured from Frey as he rolled to get out of the bed, away from the radiator sleeping beside him. Sweat slicked his upper torso, and his cotton bottoms stuck to his lower half as he walked to the bathroom, thinking about any way to cool himself down.

Water. He needed icy cold water.

He closed the door softly, to avoid disturbing Booker or Emmy in the other room, before he switched on the light. White spots flashed in front of his eyes as they adjusted to the sudden brightness. He gave himself a chance to get his eyes working before walking to the sink. Dry mouthed, he placed his hands on the porcelain sink, enjoying the cold against his sweaty palms. When he glanced in the mirror, his lips parted and closed as everything registered at once. He counted back, staring at his appearance.

He couldn't be?

Could he?

Swallowing hard, he reached with shaking fingers for the glass on the countertop and filled it with cold water, drank it, then refilled it, all the time staring at himself in the mirror. Rather, gawked at his feverish eyes and flushed skin. Drinking the second glass, he placed it down to reach for his toiletry bag to find his thermometer.

Two minutes later, he couldn't look away from the reading that told him exactly why he felt so hot. Why Booker had mentioned his scent several times the day before. He was coming into his heat... *was in heat!*

His legs wobbled, and he dropped the thermometer. It clattered on the countertop unnoticed as Frey clutched at the unit. What was he going to do?

He inhaled and, at getting a good dose of Booker's scent, a fog of lust came in an unexpected wave. His nose wrinkled as he panted, willing the feelings away. No matter how hard he tried to insist to his lust-addled brain that this wasn't happening to him after the first epic fail with Ziggy, his body told him otherwise.

I need Booker.

I need Booker.

I need Booker.

It ran on a cycle through his mind, his cock hardening painfully as slick soaked his sleep pants. He panted harder, trying to fight his instincts, ones that this time came naturally.

The door behind him opened and in the mirror, he met Booker's gaze. He stood looking all kinds of gorgeous. Hair ruffled from sleep, his broad, hairy chest naked, his sleep pants hanging off his hip bones, revealing his cum gutters. Frey's ass dripped, and he got the insane urge to rip off Booker's pants and...

"Shit, you're in heat," Booker uttered in a voice that was all deep and guttural.

It was sexy as fuck.

Frey turned and took a step towards him.

Booker held up his hands. "We need Popi."

Frey's lust fogged brain took a second or two to catch up. "Emmy," he murmured past a dry throat.

"I'll take her to Popi. Stay here, I'll need to warn the others to keep away."

Frey didn't try to keep up with what Booker was talking about. His skin was alive with need at how Booker's aroused scent surrounded him. Swamped him. He needed his bear to fuck him.

"Need you," he demanded, ignoring Booker's request. "Touch me."

"Fuck! Please, Frey, stay here. Let me sort our daughter." Booker jumped away from him, and Frey grinned at the challenge, giving chase.

A door slammed in his face and he heard the snick of a key in the lock. "Booker," he cried out and hammered on the door, his thoughts chaotic as the violent urge to fuck took hold.

"I'll be back in five minutes, I swear it, my love," came the muffled response through the door.

Frey rested his head on the cool wood, his hands pressing hard against the doorframe. Breathing hard, he counted. His bear would come back and help him. He would.

Where was he?

He whined, his nose pressed to the wood, sniffing out their mate.

After what felt like forever, a sound came from beyond the door. Sweat stung his eyes as he lifted his head and mewled louder. "Booker?"

"I'm coming, love." The door pushed against him, and he stepped back as it opened, revealing his mate.

Whatever logic Frey had was gone, his heat taking all reason from him. He launched himself at his mate and large hands caught him and stroked over his skin. The contact made the need inside him burn hotter than the fires of hell. His hungry mouth sought Booker's and his hands were everywhere, touching the hairy body, growling at the rippling flesh. The kiss was full of desperation as his cock ached in his pants. He ground against his mate. When this wasn't enough, he rutted.

A strangled moan rumbled through Booker and into Frey's mouth.

"Fuck me," he exclaimed against Booker's parted lips, "now!"

Another groan came from Booker, and Frey found himself against the cool wood of the door. Booker held him up against it as he tugged his sleep pants down his legs. The air touching his sensitive skin was too much, yet not nearly enough.

"Touch me," he demanded, trying to swing his body closer to Booker's.

Booker pressed his hard body to Frey's, pinning him fully to the door. "Are you sure?" Booker asked, his lips teasingly close to Frey's, making him cry out once more.

"Kiss me, fuck me."

"Please, Frey. I need you to try to think about what you're asking of me."

Frey gasped in jagged breaths, working to understand, to fight past the clawing need to impale himself on Booker's cock pressed against his belly. Hot, pulsing and ready for him.

"Fuck me, you're mine." Sharp teeth dropped from his gums, and he surged forward and bit true. The coppery taste drove his desire. He swallowed, scenting cum as wetness splashed his belly. He rutted madly against Booker until his cock exploded over the one pulsing next to his.

His teeth released. "Bite me," he growled.

"Are you sure?" Booker gasped.

"Mine. Mine. Mine," he rasped, punctuating each word with a thrust of his hips. "Always mine."

The noise Booker made drove the desire beyond Frey's control. Lips trailed hotly down the side of his neck until Booker reached the base of his throat. Frey pushed up, offering himself.

"Be mine," Booker snarled, "forever," as teeth bit hard.

They both groaned loudly, shuddering in pleasure as more cum spread between them, aiding the glide of Frey's cock tunneling over Booker's slippery belly. Slick trickled out of Frey's ass, scenting the air. Frey's hands reached up blindly to take hold of Booker's head, keeping him right where he was as emotions, not all his own, surged through him. His cells buzzed as if he'd developed the worst case of pins and needles.

He embraced it. Felt liberated somehow. Not only because of the love he felt deep in his heart, but from the soul's connection. The unbreakable bond he shared with his precious bear.

"Mine," he moaned in approval.

Teeth released his skin, and he felt the loss before a tongue lapped at the wound. "Yours forever," Booker responded, then the head of his cock was there against Frey's slick skin.

Impatient, Frey bucked his hips forward, impaling himself on the head. His body was ready for this and all that came from the move was pleasure. Deep-seated, it coiled through him while he clasped the hard flesh, wanting it deeper when he understood it would help with the fire inside of him. He hung on to Booker and shimmed down the long shaft. His body responding to the need for this. Needing it to survive.

"Yes," he cried out. "Give it to me."

"Slow, my love, I don't want to hurt you."

"You won't! Please," he begged unashamedly, his damp palms sliding over Booker's shoulders, trying to convey his want.

"Hold on." Booker's teeth gritted together.

Frey did, his ankles crossing as he linked his hands around his bear's neck. The move shifted the cock deeper in his ass and Frey groaned anew at the flood of erotic gratification that followed. Inch by delicious inch filled him, the fullness strange, but there was no pain. His body wanted this. Needed this.

"More," he whined, pressing his sweaty forehead against Booker's, eyes locking.

A blaze burned intensely in his bear's gaze, one Frey wanted to unleash. "Give me everything," he demanded sassily, his ass squeezing the hard length pulsing inside him.

"Fuck," Booker roared, and Frey's body was once more pinned to the door, the shaft going deeper until Frey became consumed by the fierce driving passion. Nothing existed but this. The cock inside him touched him like no one ever had or would again—only Booker. It was liberating. On some level, he understood Booker was freeing him of his past. Replacing the terrible memories with new, brighter, bolder ones. Ones he could live in, forever.

They moved as one, slick and sweaty. Skin slapped against skin, the sound, its own music, driving Frey to want more. For it never to stop.

"More. More. More," he chanted around choked cries as their hips moved at a frantic pace.

The rasp of breathing came with wicked moans and groans, along with his harsh demands until Frey had no voice left. He used every fiber of his being to express his needs. Riding the waves of pleasure that were never ending. He surfed over them, fighting for the next one. Each time his cum sprayed Booker, his need drove him to do it again. To cover his mate in his scent.

Vaguely aware they moved from the door to the bed, his only thought was *'more'*. He needed more. He rose over the man on the bed and impaled himself on the hard shaft, groaning wildly as he rocked blindly. The change in position allowed Booker to go deeper, to allow Frey to feel the shaft throb inside his pulsing sheath as he clenched tight on each downward thrust.

Heaven!

"So beautiful. So perfect."

Words fluttered in the air like confetti. They touched him but left little trace as he sought to assuage the driving desire to fuck.

Chapter Thirty-Eight

Alphaholes

Laken: *I don't think there's a pair of sound canceling headphones made to block out the damn noise coming from the top floor. How much bloody longer is this gonna go on? I think I need to find a place to stay because I'm not sure I can cope with this every few months. What's it been? Four days?*

Silas: *Yep! There is no fucking place to hide, that smell, crikey it gets every-*

where. And Laken, you promised Popi not to move out, remember?

Laken: *Fuck!*

Rue: *I'm so glad I only had to listen to them for a day!*

Jupiter: *At least Tay had the courtesy not to do this shit on his own doorstep. Rue, at the rate they're going at it, they'll still be up there when you get back.*

Taylin: *Thanks, I think...*

Rue: *Fucking wonderful!*

Kodi: *Jup, I thought you like exhibitionists?*

Jupiter: *It's my brother getting his rocks off in spectacular style. No brother needs or wants to see or fucking hear that. I'm with Laken, this has been the longest four* days. They must be hitting some sort of record.

Silas: You got that right! I think he's traumatized me for life. I'm not sure I'll ever be able to look Frey in the eye again. But I seem to remember Tay spent several days with Hollis in a hotel room. So maybe we should get clarity from him?

Dad: Give over, the lot of you. A heat for an omega with their mate is a wonderful thing to experience.

Taylin: Thanks Dad. And I'm damn sure you guys have experiences of a partner going through a heat.

Jupiter: Nope. I don't do partners!

Taylin: Why doesn't that surprise me?

Jupiter: Takes a bow...

Laken: Whatever… that doesn't mean we have to endure it with Booker and Frey?

Dad: I didn't hear you complaining when you went off with Emmy for a couple of hours. Wasn't that you saying it was nice not to have Frey or Booker looking over your shoulder while you had Emmy all to yourself?

Laken: Dad… did you have to!

Dad: Of course, you're my son, and I like to keep it real. Now pipe down, no one wants to upset Booker, do they?

Chapter Thirty-Nine

Booker

Booker lay sprawled on his back, covered in cum, his eyes slitted against the light pouring through the open blinds. He had no clue what time it was, in fact, what day it was. Frey, for now, was asleep on top of him where he'd collapsed after the last bout of hot, sweaty, mind-fucking-blowing sex.

Booker had enjoyed sex and thought he had enough stamina to give his partner what they needed. It galled him that Frey might defeat him. Letting Frey down in that way... yeah, it didn't sit well with Booker, or his bear. The very idea that they'd need to invest in a dildo made him grumpy.

Was Frey's need because of his lack of a proper heat reaction? The drugs?

We're just irresistible.

Booker rolled his eyes heavenward at his bear's choice.
Granted, but what if we can't give our mate what he needs?

You did, couldn't you hear him scream our name repeatedly?

Booker blushed at just how loud Frey had gotten and the fact his family was one floor below. Fuck, he was sure to be ragged on by his brothers for this. He could still see Lane and Derick's amused expressions when he'd barged into the bedroom in a desperate hurry.

"Popi, Dad, please wake up," he hissed into the darkness, doing his best to keep his voice down with Emmy asleep in the crib. He'd lifted the entire thing, forgetting to separate it from the stand in his haste to get back to Frey.

Lane was the first to reply as a soft light illuminated his side of the bed, allowing Booker to glance down at Emmy to see if it had distributed her. He breathed a little easier, though his chest remained constricted with Frey's whimpering cries ringing in his ears after he'd locked him in the bedroom.

It was for his own safety.

"What is it? Is Emmy sick?" Lane kept his voice low as he got out of the bed, eyeing the crib as he came towards them.

"Popi, Frey's in heat. He needs me, can you take Emmy for us?" Although it was a request, it came out as more of a demand, because he was already lowering the crib to the floor. His body burning with desire to get back to Frey. It warred with his need to keep Emmy safe, too.

With the crib on the ground, Derick got out of bed and strode towards him, his nose wrinkling as his dark eyes gleamed like polished glass despite the lateness of the hour. "Smells like you need to get back upstairs." Booker heard the amusement, and it matched Lane's as they grinned at one another.

"Will you watch over Emmy and keep everyone away? Please?"
he begged, his own pheromones becoming more obvious as his bear
got more antsy to return to Frey.

Lane laid a hand on his arm, smiling softly. "Go take care of
your mate."

Booker gulped at the truth. Frey was his—forever. And trust
Popi to know this! The meddling ole coot.

Did he care? Not one iota. He affectionately kissed Popi's cheek
and then made a mad dash for the door, hearing them chuckling
when he tripped, hit the doorframe and bounced right into the
passageway, having to right himself before face planting the op-
posite wall.

Booker let out a soft chuckle. His parents were the best,
they'd kept everyone away and left them trays of food so
Booker could feed Frey and himself to keep their strength
up. It eased Booker's conscience a fraction when he thought
about how Frey had cried when he'd left him alone. Although
a valid reason, it still hurt him when Frey wasn't in his right
mind to understand. Booker hoped when Frey was fully out
of his heat, there'd be no guilt at not thinking about Emmy's
needs. Booker had enough of those with how he barely had
the wherewithal himself to ensure she was taken care of
before leaving her.

Being a parent was fucking hard!

Frey moaned as he shifted, as if to get more comfortable,
one hand running over Booker's pec and landing on his nipple. All thoughts scattered like leaves on the wind. The pad
of a fingertip sat atop the budded flesh and remained still for
a few seconds, then it twirled over the sensitive bud.

Booker bit back a curse. His whole body ached and every sensitive nerve ending felt connected to Frey's touch. *Mates.*

Lane was right, they were mates—soul mates. His to treasure for all eternity and wasn't that just fucking perfect!

"Booker." Frey's sleep rasp was sexy as all hell. The edge of neediness wasn't as prominent now, but Booker didn't miss the desire.

He rolled them over and met Frey's heavy-lidded gaze. The lust blown pupils juiced up Booker's tired body and blood surged to his cock once again. It firmed as he rocked his pelvis against Frey's. "What do you need, foxy love?"

Gentle fingers ran over Booker's scalp, down to the base of his nape, where they dug in. Frey's attention on Booker was as stimulating as his touch. "A kiss..." His lips puckered.

"Just a kiss?" he teased, lowering his mouth until it was barely an inch from Frey's lush, kissable lips.

"For starters," Frey murmured as he claimed Booker's mouth. The bold little fox was all it took to bring Booker's body fully back online. The kiss this time was a sexy, slow dance of plump lips sliding playfully over Booker's. His taste was intoxicating. Their tongues danced to their tune of divine love.

A sigh escaped Frey as the kiss turned from one to two, until they were breathless, both of them aroused, but there was no sense of urgency. Just a slow build that made Booker's heart beat hard against his ribs as he cupped Frey's whisker roughened cheeks and held his stare, searching to see if there was any regret. Any fear.

"I'm fine." Frey lifted to kiss him. "In fact, I'm more than fine, although my ass might not like me or you for a few days after,"—he blushed a deep pink but never looked away—"what we did."

Booker's chuckle held a wealth of relief. "Does that mean you don't want..." he nibbled on Frey's lower lip, "to do anything about the little situation that we got going on?"

Raucous laughter shook Frey's body, making Booker moan at the cock rub he got. "There is nothing little about your *'situation'*. My ass can attest to that!"

"Cheeky imp!" Booker held in his amusement and de-light for about a second before he couldn't help himself.

"I'm telling the truth." Frey moved his legs, and they clasped around Booker's hips, pushing their groins to-gether along with another part of him that was more than happy to go with what Frey was doing. "But maybe we need to test the theory, just to make sure I'm not lying," he cheeked, smiling like an angel. Booker noted the devilish light sparkling in his eyes like a neon sign.

"Is that right, foxy love?" The kiss he gave Frey was hot and potent. Tongues sliding against each other, their lips clashed in a battle. Aware of his size, Booker was careful not to put all his weight on Frey as he rolled his hips, the head of his cock sliding over Frey's wet hole. His slick aided Booker as he pushed against the rim, feeling it give before the head of his cock slipped inside. Incredible heat, the shock of it, without Frey's urgency, sent Booker into a tailspin of desire. He eased in another inch before reversing, getting a thrill with each thrust as he repeated the move, until he was fully seated inside his lover.

His little fox's breath came in short pants as wide-eyed wonder came with a heady look of lust. The combination was Booker's undoing.

"I love you," he moaned, kissing Frey once more, moving his hips in a sexy slow roll. Booker drank in the whimpers and cries Frey released as he made love to him. Cherished him.

When Frey pushed at his shoulders, Booker eased out of Frey and rolled them over. Frey didn't wait a beat before straddling Booker and in a sexy ass move put a hand around—nearly—his cock as he angled it at his ass, then teased Booker by sliding the head against his slick. It dripped over and down his cock, covering them both while the little devil on top of him aroused them both.

"You're playing with fire, foxy love."

A low groan came as Frey pushed down, just the flared head of Booker's cock sat in the incredible heat. Then Frey gave a slow roll of his hips, his ass muscles clenching and releasing.

"I like fire. Oh-hh... feels so good," he rasped breathlessly, keeping up the motion, driving Booker to distraction.

"Show me," he demanded, despite the growing need to thrust. To feel Frey clasp his throbbing shaft deeper inside.

"Like this." He wiggled but only another inch down, biting his lower lip. The flirty side of Frey had captured Booker's attention, but the shy smile he wore now was what kidnapped his heart.

Booker hadn't failed to notice that Frey had gravitated to being on top during sex. Booker had no issue with that, not when he got to see Frey lose control all over him. Only, in the back of his mind, he worried it was because of what had happened to Frey before. He locked away the concern for now and clasped his hands around Frey's waist as he rose, holding him in the same position, and leaving it up to Frey to move if he chose. Booker remained mindful of any change in Frey that indicated he wasn't happy with the situation, as he had done every time they'd touched so intimately.

His nose touching Frey's, he grinned sexily. "You are such a tormenter."

Frey fluttered his eyelashes, and all the while, his ass squeezed the head of Booker's cock until he thought his balls might rupture with the violent need to come.

"Who, me?" Frey went for innocence and would have succeeded had he not chosen then to move his pelvis in a slow rotation going down Booker's cock.

"Mother fucker," Booker ground out and had no chance to catch his breath as Frey slid the rest of the way down, not releasing his ass muscles. "Don't move," he gasped, slamming his eyes shut to avoid looking at the visual delight in front of him. Problem was, that made all his other senses come to full alert. The crazy tingles in the base of his spine said that if Frey so much as moved a hair, Booker would come embarrassingly fast. Last thing he wanted was to disappoint his mate.

He frantically searched for something to think about, anything other than what was happening. Frey, it seemed, had other ideas. Booker released a shuddery exhale, then chugged in a breath, but the air in his lungs stayed put as the imp relaxed. He lifted himself off, only to repeat the move, lowering himself fully on Booker's throbbing shaft, seating himself. It was too much when he squeezed once more. Booker arched, a silent scream caught in his throat, along with the air trying to escape his lungs. He hung between heaven and hell, his body warring as cum filled Frey while he shuddered violently. His vision blurred as his balls ached at the suddenness of the release.

"Yes," Frey moaned in delight, his hand working his cock, and moments later, he sprayed Booker's chest with milky splatters of cum.

Booker's lungs gave up trying to do anything as he collapsed backwards onto the bed, the aftershocks continuing to rock his world. His grip tightened on Frey, but not enough to prevent him following Booker and lying on his heaving chest. Warm breath danced over his sweaty skin when Frey breathed like a freight train pulling out of a station.

Cum and sweat slicked them both and Booker had a thought to clean them, then he remembered nothing, exhaustion knocking him straight into sleep.

Legs weaker than a newborn kitten, Booker limped to the bedroom door. He wasn't too proud to admit that Frey had

more staying power in his heat than Booker had ever en-
countered. That last round, though not as energetic as the
others, had wiped him out. Frey was definitely making up for
lost time. To think he'd thought himself defective when his
last heat hadn't gone to plan. Booker was eternally grateful
to be able to support Frey the way he had. Whatever came
next, he would make sure to be more prepared.

The urge to kick himself for not planning for this eventual-
ity re-emerged at how frantic Frey had gotten at him leaving.
Fuck, why hadn't he understood, with Frey's scent change,
that he was coming into his heat? Emmy had taken a good
chunk of their time and energy, though he would not blame
their little girl, hell no. It was all on him.

He reached the door and took a breath, his hand resting
on the door handle, preparing for what was going to come
his way from his brothers. Booker rolled his shoulders at the
stiffness in them and dragged his ass out the door.

When did they last eat?

It felt like days to Booker. Utterly spent, he needed fuel.
After having debated for a minute on whether to shower
before seeking food, he'd had the quickest wash to get rid
of the cum crusting his skin. Now, dressed in old sweats
and a T-shirt, his hunger drove him on. He was starving to
the point his stomach was cramping painfully. He'd eaten
everything on the trays Lane had left outside their room with
notes updating them on Emmy, who had remained fine.

The last had been days before—or so he believed. It was
hard to tell; they had lost track. Although his belly rumbles
had gotten him out of bed and into the shower, Frey re-

mained asleep. He'd looked so peaceful, Booker didn't have the heart to waken him. His scent, softer, warmer than the sexy spicy undertone that had increased during his heat, made it a simple choice to leave him.

With thoughts of bringing up another tray of food and getting some Emmy cuddles, Booker continued down the stairs. A scent wafting from below had him increase his pace from a snail to more of a tortoise. Hurrying wasn't an option with how he ached everywhere, despite smelling Bessie's homemade meatloaf.

Booker groaned at how his body protested on the last flight of stairs. Whether Frey's behavior during his heat was because of the lack of a proper one in the past, Booker wasn't sure. It was a comfort, with how fast everything had turned on its head, that what had happened between them was in a place where he could keep Frey safe.

"Oh, lover boy has decided to make an appearance."

Booker grunted in Rue's direction, finally noticing the other man standing by the door, a computer case sitting next to a suitcase.

"You going away?" he asked as he came to a halt at the bottom of the stairs, working to keep control of the heat of his embarrassment.

Rue laughed as he shrugged off his suit jacket and, like they all had a habit of doing, hung it on the bannister post at the bottom of the stairs. "I've been and come back in the time you've been—"

"Don't say it," he threatened, seeing Rue's expression, one that suggested he would not hold back. "I don't wanna have to ram your teeth down your throat again."

"You loosened one tooth, and it was an accident."

Booker gave Rue a toothy grin. "Was it?"

Rue's eyes narrowed on him. "It was."

"Whatever you say." Booker swung in the kitchen's direction, his nose twitching as his mouth watered.

"Where you going?"

"I need food," Booker answered, but didn't stop walking.

"Not fucking surprising from what I saw in the group chat. Your fox sure knows how to get his freak on."

A growl roughed up Booker's throat as he swung around and jabbed a finger at Rue. "Do not talk about my mate like that, you hear me!"

"What's all this," Lane demanded, from behind Booker.

"Ask him," Rue muttered, stomping towards Booker. "It's not like the whole fucking house didn't hear or smell them! Now I'm not allowed to talk about the bear in the room."

Lane stepped between them as Booker went to get into Rue's face. "Now, we'll have less of that. I have just gotten Emmy down for a nap, and you two will not make a racket and wake her up." He looked at both men. "Am I understood?"

Lane might be a lot smaller than both of them, but Booker noted Rue wasn't unaffected by the 'don't mess with me' tone Lane could rock.

Rue nodded and threw Booker a look that suggested he wasn't going to let it drop.

"I saw that, Rue,' Lane smacked at his chest. "Behave."

Booker's lips twitched, and he suppressed the urge to smile, knowing better. "Is Emmy okay?"

"Now he asks," Rue muttered, stomping off.

"She's absolutely darling." Lane slipped his arm through Booker's and gave him a knowing smile. "So, how are you feeling?"

Never really a squirmer, Booker had to resist doing so now as Lane's gaze moved to the neck of his T-shirt. His nose wrinkled and his smile spread to his eyes.

"Oh..." he sniffed, and Booker groaned internally at seeing Lane get all damp eyed.

"Please, don't," he begged unashamedly, with no brothers around, "don't cry.'

"You found your mate," he sob-sniffed, eyes glistening bright as jewels.

He couldn't think of anything else to do, so he picked up Lane and hugged him. "I did," he sniffed, ignoring the sob that caught in his throat.

I'm not crying.

I'm not.

Chapter Forty
Delicious & Vicious

Ziggy: Has anyone heard from Frey?

Bowie: No, not for days. He went off Friday and we had plans for me to go with him and Emmy to the park and he never showed. I think he's fallen out with me 'cause he never answered my messages.

Ziggy: Don't be daft. It's got to be something else. Booker hasn't been at work either for the last few days. Just wondering if anyone knew if they were on a trip or something and I'd missed the memo.

Bowie: Oh, do you think it could have something to do with Emmy? She's not sick, is she?

Hollis: Nothing is wrong with Emmy and Frey would have contacted you if he could.

Bowie: What do you mean… if he could? Has something bad happened to him?

Hollis: No. Think about it, Bowie…

Ziggy: What Hollis is trying to avoid saying is that Frey became otherwise occupied with his alpha. Right, Hollis?

Hollis: Nicely put Ziggy and yes. It seems what happened was… a little unexpected.

Isley: *How can it be unexpected? It's a heat. We all know when they happen because they are as regular as clockwork or why else have a calendar for work so we can plan to be absent? What am I missing? I feel there is something amiss here, or why would we be having this conversation?*

Wilder: *Evidently something. Do you know anything Monty? Lennon? Now that I come to think about it, Frey never took the same amount of time as everyone else. Was he on blockers? Those things can be pretty nasty. Maybe now he's with Booker, he stopped them and got his heat unexpectedly?*

Ziggy: *Maybe we should just see what Frey has to say on the subject... if anything.*

Wilder: *You know something, don't you?*

Hollis: *Don't pester Ziggy.*

Wilder: *Hey, he was the first to ask if we'd heard or seen Frey, I'd like to point out.*

So it's only to be expected we'd ask questions!

Hollis: Point taken Wilder. But let's wait and see what Frey wants to share with us. And maybe, Wilder, you could make better use of your time and send me the report I asked for an hour ago?

Chapter Forty-One
Frey

Missing three days of work...

To Frey, it felt very naughty, especially as his heat had mostly ended by Tuesday evening. On Wednesday, he had spent time with Emmy at home, needing to reassure himself she was fine and that he wasn't a terrible parent for leaving her without a thought. Lane—no Popi as he said he should be called now Frey was family—had been open about his experiences of his heat when he first had Silas. It had helped, along with how Emmy was so happy to see him.

Lane had done an amazing job of looking after her, and Frey felt bad for denying him the overnight sleepover with their little sweetheart. Lane had insisted that he get her at least once a week overnight and Frey hadn't argued after recent events in the bedroom with Booker. They'd made love. They'd had beautiful, soul changing sex, and he'd loved every moment.

Everything about the entire experience was nothing like he'd imagined without the fear clouding his judgment. Without it there blocking him from making a physical connection, his thoughts lingered on how they could do it again without his heat driving it. For him, that meant they did indeed need a night to be free of other commitments because Frey wasn't sure he could let go with Emmy right in the next room, with the door open... no. The ease of accepting Lane's generous offer drew a little conflict about leaving Emmy, and he expected that. Did it make him a terrible parent when he grinned on the inside, already anticipating things he could try with Booker alone in the bedroom?

Lane said no, and he wanted to believe him with how his body reminded him of the four whole days of sex, mind-blowing—from what he could remember of the first couple of days—wonderful, exciting sex where he didn't freak out. Yeah, he wanted more. In his mind, he had years to make up for what he'd missed. And he planned on doing that with Booker...

"Frey, wait up," a voice called from behind, pulling him from where his thoughts had once again wandered without permission while he was at work! He came to a stop and turned to watch Ziggy lope down the carpeted hallway from the direction of the elevators. "I was hoping to catch you."

Frey grinned, his cheeks pinking at the messages in the group chat. "Hey, sorry, I meant to send a reply to you last night." He sighed. "Then I got a little distracted by Emmy, who was a little fussy when I put her to bed. It seems Popi prefers to hold her rather than put her in her crib."

Ziggy clutched the cashmere vest covering his shirt, belly laughing. "You're as bad. I've seen you," he spluttered.

Frey gave him an unrepentant look, shrugging. "She's my daughter, I'm allowed."

Nudging him with his shoulder, Ziggy nodded while continuing to chuckle. "You are. And she is a total sweetheart. But I see we have something else to talk about." He pointed at the small bit of scarring that peeked out from the top of Frey's button-down. "It went that well, your first proper heat?"

He'd kept his voice down, but still Frey checked the hallway before he nodded. "It was... amazing!"

"That good?" Ziggy's eyes lit up with enthusiasm.

"Let's go to the coffee lounge, I'm starving as I missed lunch." Frey, after seeing the chat, wished he'd been more considerate after how Ziggy had wanted to help. It was understandable he'd be concerned for Frey, they'd grown to be close friends. Frey wanted to share his success of getting through a heat and actually loving the bond he'd formed with Booker, only without the possibility of being overheard.

Frey closed the door behind him, but he got distracted by the offering of cakes on the counter. The amount of energy he'd expelled recently, he definitely deserved cake. All the cake.

He strolled to the counter and grabbed a couple of plates, not waiting for Ziggy. The chocolate and raspberry cake Frey knew Lennon had made that morning smelled heavenly. He cut two enormous pieces, plated them and lifted them to turn and offer one to Ziggy.

He eyed the plate Frey offered with a conflicted look, then took it and put it under his nose, sniffing.

"Fuck, that smells so good." Ziggy patted his stomach with his free hand. "I'm sure I've gained at least five kilos since I started work here. Maybe I should half the slice?"

Frey rolled his eyes at his friend. "Give over, there is nothing wrong with you and all I'm saying is Lennon makes the best chocolate and raspberry cake in the history of cakes."

The chuckle came with a wry smile as Ziggy took the fork Frey offered, before he collected one for himself and went to the comfy couch to sit down. When Ziggy stood staring at him, he arched his brow. "What?"

"Being mated... it suits you."

Blushing, Frey sighed happily. "It does. I've never felt more alive. Like everything is brighter, more colorful. Smells better." He dug into the cake and took a mouthful, groaning at the taste explosion on his tongue. "So good." He groaned and took another bite, barely giving himself time to savor it. "But honestly, I'm just down to the bone happy."

Ziggy came and perched on the sofa next to him, waited for a beat with the look of conflict reappearing, then dug into the cake with his fork.

Frey watched him.

"Good god, that's so fucking good," he groaned around a mouthful of cake.

"It really is."

The silence between them lasted until the plates were empty and both wore satisfied smiles. Ziggy took Frey's empty plate and got up to place them into the dishwasher.

"Want a coffee?" he asked as he grabbed the coffee pot that someone had recently filled, by the look of it.

"Please." Frey watched Ziggy, noticing that his usual easy smile was nowhere to be seen now the cake was gone. "You okay?" *Was this my fault?* Had not reaching out to him pissed him off?

Ziggy didn't reply immediately while he added cream and sugar to Frey's drink and brought the two mugs over. "I'm fine." The smile never reached his eyes.

"You're not," Frey accused as he took the cup and reached out with his other hand to keep hold of Ziggy's. "Whatsup? You were there for me. Can't I offer the same to you when it's obvious to me something is off?" Frey didn't think he was reading the situation wrong.

Ziggy sagged down onto the sofa next to Frey, forcing him to let go. He twisted on the seat, his knee knocking Ziggy's, who stared into his cup. "Please, you can trust me."

He heaved a sigh and took a sip of his black coffee, the silence lasting that long Frey was about to try a different tack when Ziggy aimed sad eyes in his direction. "You know the alpha I was sort of seeing?"

Frey nodded, trying to recall what Ziggy had said about the guy when he had raised concerns about Ziggy helping with his heat. "Yeah, it was a causal thing, 'cause that was what you wanted?"

"No, not strictly true." He ran a finger around the edge of his cup, gazing at it. "He didn't want anything more than a casual thing between us. I was fine with that…"

"But," Frey nudged when it looked like Ziggy wasn't going to say more

"Something changed between us." Ziggy placed the cup down on the table and got up, walking to the window. His steps were jerky, like he was having trouble holding it together.

The worry drove Frey to place his own cup down and follow. He gently stroked a hand down Ziggy's arm. "In a good way?" Frey didn't believe it was with how Ziggy was acting, but he couldn't be sure.

Ziggy fired him a quick look over his shoulder before looking back out the window. There, in the depth of his gaze, was utter misery. Frey recognized it from seeing it a time or two in the mirror. Frey's stomach twisted into knots. He slipped an arm around Ziggy's waist, giving him an awkward side hug. "Wanna talk about it?"

Ziggy's stiff posture radiated tension. "There isn't much to say. I want more, he doesn't. He's made that perfectly clear. I need to move on."

It sounded like it was the last thing he wanted to do, but Frey didn't know what to say to that, having never experienced this situation himself. He couldn't imagine Booker rejecting him. He didn't want to when it caused a shiver of fear to run through him.

We're mates, he'll never reject us.

I know. Frey did in principle, but it was still all so new.

"Listen, I'm not gonna drag you down with my shit—"

"You can stop that nonsense right now," Frey cut in. "You were there for me and I wanna be there for you. We're friends, aren't we?"

Ziggy took a step back and turned to face him, wearing a look that made Frey want to box whichever alpha's ears for making his friend sad. "I don't want to talk about him. It hurts too much right now. So if it's alright, let's talk about you and Booker?" He winked, but it held none of the usual fun, his eyes brimming with pain. "I'd rather hear about your sexcapades with the hunky bear."

"Is that why you didn't answer my messages?" Bowie asked quietly from behind them.

Ziggy and Frey both spun to see Bowie standing in the open doorway. Neither of them had heard him come in.

Had he overheard what they'd been talking about?

Frey glanced from Bowie to Ziggy, whose jaw ticked as he frowned.

"I'm sorry about that," Frey murmured, returning his attention to Bowie. He walked towards Bowie, purposefully blocking his view of Ziggy for a moment, to give his friend a chance to regroup. "I got my heat and, well, it was unexpected."

"Yeah? Was it bad?" Bowie gave him a sympathetic look.

"To be honest, it was my first proper heat," Frey confessed, working on deflecting any attention from Ziggy. "I was taking blockers."

Deep furrows appeared between Bowie's brows. "You mean you ain't had a heat before this one?"

He sounded confused and Frey got it. But now was not the time to relay the full story of his past, not at work. He checked his watch. He had a meeting in ten minutes' time. "It's a long story. Maybe we could do the park this weekend and I can explain it properly?"

Bowie lost the frown and beamed at him for all of two seconds before it disappeared. "I want to, but I kinda got plans this weekend."

Frey patted Bowie's arm with how conflicted he appeared, chewing his lower lip between his teeth. "It's fine. We can do it another weekend."

"We can?"

The smile was back, and Frey nodded. "Of course, just let me know when you've got a free day at the weekend, and we can plan something." Frey glanced back at Ziggy, giving him a 'this isn't over look' before explaining he had a meeting to go to.

Back in his office minutes later, grabbing his notepad and the two files he'd set aside for the meeting before he went to get cake, he was still thinking about Ziggy. Frey didn't really know any alphas except for the ones he worked with, and he chewed over whether he should ask Booker if he had any friends that might be interested in someone as great as Ziggy.

Back out of his office, he barely made it to the boardroom with a minute to spare. Booker had taken a seat next to Silas, their dark heads together, murmuring about what they were looking at. Two seats down, Wilder sat tapping away at his laptop. His slim fingers flew over the keyboard that he didn't once look at.

Frey wasn't that good and once had said to Wilder how he envied him. Wilder had groaned and complained that Frey wouldn't have enjoyed his teacher, who had covered the keys and hit his fingers with a ruler if he tried to cheat and cop a look.

When he sat down next to Wilder, he glanced up. "Have you got the information printed out I asked for?"

Frey nodded, taking the file he held and offering it over, his mind switching to the reason they were having this meeting. "I did, I added my comments about the logistics of getting all the merchandise to the shopping malls. The company we use for transport has upped their costs by 5% so I took the liberty of looking at other options."

"When did they change the costs?" Silas questioned, sounding pissed.

Booker glared at his brother and Frey bit the inside of his cheek to keep his amusement from spilling out at Booker's reaction. God, he was adorable. "I sent you an updated email about it last week."

Wilder made a noise in the back of his throat that Frey didn't get when he looked between the two men.

Silas looked fit to be tied as he reached for his iPad and tapped at the screen. "So you did," he gritted out.

"Apologize to Frey," Booker said in a tone that Frey knew all too well.

Oh dear! "He doesn't need to apologize," Frey quickly interjected.

Booker shook his head, ruffling the silky strands. "He does, he was being pissy with you for no reason."

If Silas had gotten annoyed before, now he was at the next level. His skin flushed red and his eyes were sending daggers at Booker.

Frey had the urge to push his seat back to get out of the line of fire.

"Why? When you two are the reason I missed it. You stunk up the house, making it impossible to concentrate on anything," Silas accused. "And let's not even talk about the noises."

Frey didn't dare look at Booker as he blushed, squirming in his seat at what exactly Silas and the others had heard. Smelled. Having avoided this confrontation in the house, it seemed he had brought it into work for him to deal with it in front of Wilder. *Great.*

"You could have come into the office." Booker's teeth actually snapped together on each word. Frey felt his own jaw ache in sympathy while he tried to come up with something to say that wouldn't aggravate the situation further.

"Is this really the place for this conversation?" Frey asked as Wilder watched them with avid interest. "I apologize for any inconvenience I caused. It was not intentional."

"How so?" Silas snapped.

"Silas!" Booker growled, his teeth dropping in his gums and gleaming in the overhead light.

Frey's ears started to buzz. *Oh no, was Booker gonna go all furry?*

"I apologize, too," Silas muttered, clearly not meaning it as he held Booker's gaze. "What other trucking companies did you look at?"

Frey shot Booker a warning look when his lips parted, like he was ready to continue the argument. "I have the list here."

Frey took the additional copies he'd printed off with the figures and companies he'd contacted, all but shoving them at both men. "As you can see..."

Chapter Forty-Two

Booker

Stomping down the hallway, Booker's head throbbed with a tension headache at holding back after Frey's warning stare. He'd kept it together for the rest of the meeting and the subsequent one he had after, but now all damn bets were off.

At Silas's office door, he didn't bother knocking and came to a complete standstill at the sight of Silas, sitting head in hands with his shoulders shaking.

"What the fuck?" Booker rasped through a throat that felt three sizes smaller, making it impossible to swallow while he tugged at his tie.

Silas's head shot up, puffy, blood-shot eyes filled with misery stared at Booker and he stepped into the room, quickly closing the door behind. "What's wrong?" he demanded gruffly, trying to remember the last time he'd seen Silas cry as he came to his desk. "Is there something wrong with Dad? Popi?"

Silas scrubbed his face and shook his head, sniffing loudly, making Booker's stomach quiver.

"Then what is it... is there something wrong with... *you*?" Booker's chest expanded from the deep inhale as he waited, watching Silas to gain a clue as to what the hell he was missing. Was he ill? Was the short temperedness because he was...

His legs weren't quite steady from where his thoughts wanted to wander without his fucking permission. He came around the desk to perch his ass on the corner, never once looking away from Silas as he searched for a clue. "I know we haven't been seeing eye to eye of late." *Fuck, I was a shit brother for not noticing something awful was going on with him!* "But you know I love you. Would do anything for you."

Silas pressed his fingers to his eyes, increasing Booker's fear something was majorly wrong, and he'd somehow missed it. "Talk to me, you fucker," he growled. "Are you sick?"

Silas's hands dropped away. "No, I'm not sick unless you call getting stuck on something and you can't unbridle!" he muttered mournfully.

What?

Stuck on something? What in damnation was that supposed to mean? "You've lost me. Are we talking about a horse?" Silas's second biggest love was his horses, family being first. He was mad for them, had been since he was a teenager.

Silas's messy, dark hair fell over his forehead as he shook his head. He sat back in the chair, lines etched into his forehead and around his mouth. He looked... grim. "My horses are fine, or they were the last time I checked in with Ethan."

He sounded so weary it made the anxious knots, having a field day with Booker's stomach, tighten. "Then what the fuck is it, you asshole, you're worrying me. I haven't seen you cry since..." Booker took a deep breath and willed away the images of the last time when it involved the awful night he'd gotten cast out by his actual parents.

"Since your dad went to hit Popi," Silas finished for him.

"Yeah, since then." That night, Booker had gained something precious and lost all respect for his family. Silas had cried for Booker. For the reality Booker had to face being cast out for helping Silas. For stepping in front of Lane when his father had gone to hit him. Those punches his father had landed knocked Booker on his ass and left him bloodied on the outside, but also on the inside. His heart had taken that battering too when he'd never allow his father to hurt Lane, who the fucker was aiming to punch.

His actions had created a shit storm which resulted in Derick teaching Booker's father a lesson that night, never ever threaten his family—that, it turned out, had included Booker. His life had changed and, in immeasurable ways. He gained a family who loved him wholeheartedly and who agreed with his belief that everyone should receive respect—*even divergents*. That brought about a reality his father hated when Booker was the one defending them.

The perceived betrayal caused the fight that had ensued after Booker had gotten knocked to the floor, and resulted in Derick intervening. His father had shifted into his bear form, ready to commit murder, but Derick's wolf was a powerhouse too.

The sounds, tearing flesh, howls, screams, crashing furniture, had haunted Booker's dreams for months after. Derick had gotten injured, but he'd held his own. Booker's biggest regret was not getting up to help. He had remained in shock, glued to the ground by the weight of it, even when the neighbors had called the police and they'd broken up the fight. His mother screamed abuse at Lane while his father had refused to shift, his fur matted with blood, not all his own. It was something that would stay with him forever. A reminder that the motto of Starling Enterprises 'love for all' was real to those men.

"That night changed everything," he said softly. "It made us brothers, and nothing has changed that... yet somehow I've managed to fuck you off enough to make you distance yourself from me." It was easier to focus on the now than what had been.

Silas pinched the bridge of his nose, sighing before he rose, coming face to face with Booker. "It's not you."

He focused on Silas, seeing nothing to indicate he was lying. "Then what is it? Talk to me."

Suddenly, after Silas opened up about what was bothering him, that fight they'd had all those weeks ago made sense. The problem was, Silas had all but handcuffed him with promises not to interfere, so he couldn't help to try to make it better.

Distracted as he approached the road leading up to the drive of the house, he set aside the worry he had for Silas. He decided to talk to Popi—alone—to see if he could figure out something to get Silas out of his current funk.

His headlights illuminated the front of the house and the door opened, light spilling out to reveal Frey holding Emmy. His lips tugged into a big ass grin at the picture they made together. Booker's heart wanted to burst out of his chest at how damn fucking lucky he was. Parked, he grabbed his work laptop case, not thinking too hard about the amount of emails he had to deal with later—much later—once he'd had some time with Frey and Emmy.

He got out of his car two hours later than he should have, trying hard not to think about that fact.

"Look who's home, Emmy," Frey cooed at their daughter, who made a gurgling noise—that no one would convince Booker wasn't a giggle.

"There's my girl." Booker had messaged Frey to let him know he'd be late. They had gone to work in separate cars for this very reason. That and the fact that Frey could easily operate Emmy's car seat brackets. Booker hated them, his big fingers struggled to find their way in the tiny gaps to release it or make it click safely into place.

He knocked the car door closed with the heel of his shoe, coming around the hood. "Has she had dinner?"

"We were a hungry girl this evening. It seems she's been awake a lot today." Frey nuzzled the top of the peach fuzz Emmy had for hair. "So I had to give her a bottle earlier than normal."

"Sh—crap I wanted to feed her."

"You can give her a bottle for her night feed." Frey gave him an innocent smile.

"I thought it was your turn," Booker replied before pressing a kiss to Emmy's head, then to Frey's soft lips, feeling them twitch under his.

"You were the one who missed dinner time," he pointed out, smirking just as a noise came from Emmy that was chased by a god awful stench.

Nose wrinkling, Booker gagged and took a step back as Frey offered Emmy to him. "I think Emmy wants her Daddy."

As if Frey had planned it, Emmy reached out her tiny fists to Booker, making his chest warm with love. "You did that on purpose," Booker complained halfheartedly, already placing what he held in the entryway to the house to take Emmy. "Your Popi thinks he's funny. He's not."

"You know I am," said Frey, giggling.

"Yeah, yeah, yeah," Booker muttered and when Frey stepped aside, he walked inside, doing his best not to breathe through his nose. "Let's go sort you out, then Daddy can have some snuggles."

As he walked to the stairs, he rubbed his nose over her hair, inhaling, then coughed at what came with her baby smell.

"How can a small person make such an awful smell?" came a muffled question from Laken, who was coming down the stairs, a hand covering his mouth.

"It's a talent, right Emmy?" Booker chuckled at his daughter, waving her fists in the air as if in agreement.

Laken stepped aside. "It's something, for sure."

"You just need more diaper changing practice to get used to it."

Laken eyed him like Booker had lost his mind. "I know your game. I'm not falling for that."

"Falling for what?" Jupiter asked as he bounded down the stairs right behind Laken, his hands already reaching for Emmy. "There's my sweet girl."

Booker struggled not to snatch back his daughter when Jupiter, with an ease that was so natural anyone would believe he had a whole hoard of kids he'd practiced with, took her. Instead, he gave Jupiter a toothy grin. "Looks like you copped diaper changing again."

"Uncle Jup is much better at it than Daddy, isn't he?" He didn't even hesitate and bounded back up the stairs, making Booker's baby girl coo.

Conflicted, Booker stared after them.

Laken's laughter made Booker scowl at his brother. Tears glistened in Laken's eyes at how hard he was laughing. "No one would believe it if we told them Jup was a big softie at heart who lived for a poopy diaper change."

Booker chuckled because Laken was right.

"I thought you wanted to spend some time with your daughter?" Frey pointed out, carrying the laptop bag to where Booker remained on the stairs.

Looking sheepish, he slipped an arm around Frey and lifted him. His feet dangled over the stairs as Booker held him secure and close enough to scent his cologne and baby powder. The smell was oddly erotic. "I enjoy spending time with my mate, too." He kissed Frey with the love that could still shock.

"Oh for fucksake. Please, no more," Laken complained, striding past as Booker turned to smirk.

"You're just jealous."

"Of course I am, who wouldn't want a cute little fox scream—"

"Don't you dare," he shouted after Laken, a scowl replacing the smirk.

"Why does everyone have to communicate through shouting?" Lane appeared at the bottom of the stairs, looking between them.

"Don't look at me," Laken said. "I think you'll find it was Booker." He strolled off after giving Booker a smug look.

"Brothers, who'd have them!"

Chapter Forty-Three

Frey

Frey pushed the stroller, listening to the sounds of the birds in the trees as he headed down the path towards the lake where he was meeting Bowie and Ziggy. Hollis had cried off an hour ago after Taylin had come home from a business trip a day earlier than planned. Frey got it. He would be the same. Booker had gone away for three days, having left two days before, taking Lennon with him because Frey didn't want to leave Emmy.

This had brought about a difficult discussion—one Frey had prepared for when he wanted to continue to work with Booker but didn't want to leave his baby girl. Lane had offered to have Emmy when they were required to go away. Only Frey didn't want that. Having a heat was different, that was a situation they couldn't control. Work they could, and he believed his daughter should come first.

Booker had spoken to Silas, and he had called a meeting for all the PAs and his brothers to talk about what possible changes could be implemented to help. A nursery set up at work was the first thing to happen for all staff. No one had an issue with that when it would improve and encourage folks to work for a company that could support omegas returning to work after having children.

With some reorganization of space, they'd found an area on the first floor, and it was currently being redesigned. Hollis had assigned himself to interview the staff for the new nursery, with Frey's assistance. He was excited about it and already had a long list of criteria they would need to meet to satisfy him about their ability to look after Emmy. However, that didn't stop the issue of traveling and how to cope with that.

Frey didn't want Emmy to come on work trips, it didn't feel right. He said as much at the meeting. Hollis had come up with the idea of a team of floating PAs to work alongside the ones assigned to the brothers to learn each area so they could fill in the gaps when needed. Frey had noted some reactions to this from both the brothers and the PAs. Some were most definitely not happy. The vote came down to Hollis when the brothers couldn't all agree, so he had the final say. It was a little tense in the room and Taylin hadn't looked happy with how Kodi, Laken, Rue and Kari had given Hollis a hard time.

It was the first time, it seemed, that Hollis had flexed his power to wield a deciding vote on anything. Frey wasn't worried and, until they had trained the new PAs, the others had offered to fill in for Frey on the trips away.

Frey felt the ball of emotion form once more at how lucky he was. He'd lost his skulk but had somehow gained a makeshift one in the form of his work friends.

"Are you deaf?" Bowie asked breathlessly, as he waved a hand in front of Frey's face, looking flushed and sweaty. "I've been shouting your name for the last five minutes. I had to run to catch you."

He offered Bowie and Ziggy, who strolled up to them at a slower pace, a sheepish smile. "Sorry. I was just thinking about how lucky I am to have a friend like you."

Ziggy slung an arm over Frey's shoulder. "What about me?"

Frey glanced sideways, grinning at Ziggy. "You, too... but you will have to learn to bake to gain full friendship status."

Ziggy groaned and rolled his eyes. "I'm telling you that if you tasted my cakes, you'd never want to be my friend because you'd possibly not survive the poisoning."

Frey barked out a laugh as they strolled on towards the concession stand that Frey knew made the best chocolate brownies.

"We haven't tried, so how can we judge?" Frey eyed the queue they were headed towards, counting the number of people waiting. "I hope we got here early enough to nab some brownies."

"You and your sweet tooth." Ziggy stepped up his pace to match Frey's, revealing just how keen he was too. Frey might have bragged a time or two about this place. The lakefront had several concession stands, but this one was Frey's favorite to visit. Ella made the best brownies Frey had ever eaten. They were better than Bowie's, not that Frey would be mean and say that.

"I have one, too," Bowie confessed. "I can't seem to stop baking or eating cake no matter how many times I get told off by Da—"

Frey glanced sideways at the sudden stop to see Bowie glow brighter than the one time he'd gotten sunburnt when they'd had a work picnic at the beach. "Are you dating?" Frey asked with interest, trying to recall if Bowie had mentioned having a boyfriend.

Bowie dropped his gaze and stared at the ground intently, like it held the answers to a complex scientific problem, his cheeks going a darker shade of red. "Nah... not dating..."

"Then who tells you off for eating cake?" Ziggy enquired in a gentle tone, like he didn't want to spook Bowie.

"I-I..." He groaned and ran his hands through his messy hair. "Can we change the subject?" he begged, still not looking at them.

Ziggy shrugged at Frey, dropping his arm from around Frey's shoulder when he gave Ziggy an enquiring look. Most of the PAs went to Ziggy with their problems, Frey had noticed. He got it. Ziggy was easy to talk to and a great person to rely on.

Ziggy laid a hand on the stroller and gave him a begging look. Laughing at him, Frey took a step to the side.

"You," an angry sounding guy growled, right before someone grabbed Frey's arm, almost wrenching it from the socket. Frey got violently spun around, his heart racing as he squealed in pain, "how the fuck did you con my son into adopting divergent scum?"

Ziggy hissed, but Frey didn't look away from the giant in front of him as he panted in pain. Murderous eyes so similar to Booker's, it was impossible to mistake the family resemblance when Frey's gaze swept over the man towering over him. Fingers dug painfully into his flesh, bruising, adding to the burn in his shoulder joint.

Booker had clearly gotten his height and size from the man in front of him, but not the nasty personality. Frey had always been fast on his feet, and it took little to figure out Booker's father was referring to the newspaper article from the week before.

The same asshat who had hounded Taylin and Hollis and wrote awful things about Taylin being divergent in the newspapers, had found out about Booker and Frey's recent adoption. Booker had gotten madder than a den of bears disturbed from hibernation at the invasion of their privacy. They all suspected it had been the lawyers for the previous factory owners trying to throw around some diversion tactics by not painting them in a particularly pleasant light.

Frey hadn't cared one iota what the press wrote, he knew the truth, and that was all that mattered. Emmy's daddy deserved respect and that meant not being goaded into a battle in the press that could harm their chances of winning against those scumbags.

As he stared at the glaring giant, attempting to pull his arm free, it seemed others cared, but not for the right reasons. "Don't you dare speak about *our* daughter in that way!" he snapped, all teeth.

Booker hadn't fully opened up about how he'd come to be ostracized by his family. Although now Frey was questioning whether he had been. Because why would this man refer to Booker as his son if they weren't in contact?

"I can say whatever the fuck I want," he spat. "That *thing* will never be welcome in our family!"

Frey grimaced in pain when he was shaken by his arm, almost losing his footing as he tugged harder to escape. He felt something pop in the joint, making his eyes burn.

The crowd at the concession stand were taking notice and Frey, who hated to make a scene, shouted out in panic, "Someone call the police, I'm being attacked."

"You let go of my friend," Bowie said, with absolutely no force in his quivering voice.

"Fuck off," the bear growled, "before I rip your divergent head off!"

Bowie cowered back just enough to get out of the reach of the guy. Ziggy pushed the stroller at Bowie. "Take Emmy," he demanded forcefully.

Ziggy waited but a beat for Bowie to do as he requested before he shifted and an enormous snake, one that made Frey's fox, who was struggling to escape, recede quickly.

Frey staggered at the speed at which the bear let go to step away from the rearing, hissing snake. Amazed at Ziggy's size, Frey stared in wonderment, his own concerns disappearing as he watched his friend slither through his torn clothes and chase the bear as it turned tail and ran off.

"Look at him go!"

Frey looked at Bowie giggling—possibly in hysteria—and nodded, clutching at his aching arm. "Who knew snakes could be that fast?"

Bowie had the wherewithal to call Kari before Ziggy had returned, just as the police arrived. It was a total mess and Frey had no idea how he was going to explain this to Booker when he got home the following day. Would Booker blame him?

He groaned in misery.

"Sorry," Derick murmured, misunderstanding what the issue was.

"You didn't hurt me," Frey responded quickly, through the rawness of his throat, his eyes pleading with Derick. "I just don't know how to explain this to Booker when he gets home tomorrow."

Frey, who had sat on the huge couch, became distracted by Emmy, who Lane held and rocked when she became fussy, as if sensing the tension in the room. Derick was kneeling in front of Frey, checking out his injuries, cursing through gritted teeth. Frey was finding it hard to hold back the tears, now the shock had worn off. He avoided looking at the ugly bruising that spread from his wrist to his elbow. The finger impressions were impossible to hide. Not that he could do that when the police had escorted him home after several people had explained what they'd witnessed.

Also, when the asshat had wrenched his arm, he'd torn the ligaments in his shoulder, making it very difficult, if not impossible right now, for Frey to hold Emmy safely. The police had taken him via the emergency room to get checked out before coming home.

He needed to shift to heal, but it didn't look like that was going to be possible for the foreseeable future, as Derick didn't stop fussing over him.

"He's coming home today." Derick's words penetrated through Frey's thoughts when he said it like it was inevitable, and Frey barely had a chance to consider that when Derick carried on. "I'll kill the bastard this time. I fucking swear it." Frey didn't doubt it with the deadly intent glinting in the eyes of the wolf. Only he didn't know what he meant by 'this time'?

It hurt to swallow with how tight Frey's chest was. Many times, Frey had considered that Derick was a force to be reckoned with, he'd just never suspected just how much until now. This man, who was sort of his father-in-law through mating, appeared ready to go and rip Booker's father's head off. It was there in the barely concealed—contained—fury.

How would Booker feel about that?

What have I done?

You've done nothing, and our bear isn't going to be mad at us.

Me. You mean me!

"You will do no such thing," Lane grumbled softly. "We will not lower ourselves to his level, not again. We have to consider the impact on our grandchild and Booker. He wouldn't want that."

The sound of a door crashing into a wall got Lane cursing softly, his gaze going to the doorway.

"We're about to find out," Derick replied, already moving away from Frey to stand next to Lane, placing a protective arm around his shoulder.

At the noise of shoes thudding on marble, Frey's pulse danced hard enough to make his ears buzz. The door burst open, bouncing off the wooden cabinet sat behind it when Booker charged in like a bear ready to attack. His hair was a mess and his clothes were in disarray, like he'd dressed in a hurry in the dark.

He flicked his bangs off his face while he searched the room with a crazed, wild-eyed look. When his gaze landed on Frey, it took all Frey's courage to hold his stare and offer him a wobbly smile, hoping to reassure his mate he was fine.

Booker's large body shook as he stared at Frey's exposed forearm. Large hands formed into enormous fists as Booker growled ominously, lifting the hairs on Frey's body. He came and dropped to his knees in front of Frey. "Who did this?"

The softness of his tone belied the same murderous look Derick had worn when he'd seen Frey's injuries. Frey found he couldn't get his tongue to unglue from the roof of his mouth.

"Your father," Derick seethed, shoving his hands into his slacks, his face a rigid mask of fury.

Booker's head swung towards Derick, his hands hovering over Frey's injured arm. "He came to the house?"

The rasped question made Frey shudder at the iciness.

"No, I was by the lake, meeting Bowie and Ziggy, when he must have seen me," Frey rushed to explain, wanting to reach out but unsure whether his touch would be welcome, having never seen the expression Booker wore. It revealed nothing. It was as if his face had been carved out of stone. Emotionless. Dead. Only his eyes betrayed him. "Ziggy chased him off in his snake form."

"He did!" Silas questioned in a strangled tone as he strode into the room.

Booker paid Silas no attention as he focused back on Frey. "I'm so sorry, foxy love."

Hearing the endearment eased a little of Frey's anxiety. He reached to touch Booker with his injured arm and hissed when the pain radiated right into his shoulder, reminding him it wasn't a wise move.

"I'm gonna fucking kill him. I fucking swear," Booker growled so loud, Emmy started to cry.

"Shush, it's alright Emmy." Lane rocked Emmy, his attention on Booker. "As I said to your dad, you'll do no such thing. We will deal with this like civilized people."

Frey didn't miss the exchange of looks between Booker and Derick. Lane did as he returned to fussing over Emmy.

Heart lodging in the back of his throat, Frey tried not to think about what it meant when a part of him wanted Booker to kick the asshat for scaring him and his daughter.

Chapter Forty-Four

Delicious & Vicious

Bowie: *You guys, we have the most wonderful person as our friend. We really do.*

Isley: *What's going on?*

Ziggy: *Bowie, please don't.*

Wilder: Bowie, what are you talking about?

Bowie: Ziggy, god, he was absolutely amazing today. So brave.

Ziggy: Pleaseeee…

Bowie: It's nothing to be embarrassed about. You saved Frey.

Hollis: What are you talking about? Saved Frey from what?

Lennon: This all sounds very dramatic. What did we miss on a Saturday outing while I was away working, only to find myself left behind because Booker high-tailed it home! Is this because of what happened with Ziggy?

Wilder: I feel like I'm in the middle of a TV drama. What's going on? Spill Bowie.

Ziggy: You guys… it was nothing.

Bowie: *It was everything. You chased off that nasty bear who was attacking Frey. Don't say it was nothing. You ended up naked and showing all your bits to everyone at the lake. And we didn't get the brownies.*

Wilder: *Ziggy, you dark horse…*

Bowie: *No, he's an enormous snake, not a horse, Wilder. So beautiful and his scales were warm!*

Lennon: *Bowie, did you touch Ziggy's snake?*

Bowie: *With his permission.*

Lennon: *I wasn't being funny. I bet it was so cool. I love snakes. Ziggy, will you show me your snake?*

Hollis: *Lennon, read back what you wrote… Ziggy, did you attack someone?*

Ziggy: *Bowie! No, I didn't attack anyone. I chased off a bear who was manhandling Frey, shouting at him about having a divergent child. I got the impression he was some relative of Booker's with how he looked and what he was spewing. Awful creature!*

Hollis: *Dear gods, is Frey alright?*

Bowie: *Sorry Ziggy. You were so amazing for defending him and Emmy from that monster. Why wouldn't you want the guys to know what a wonderful person you are? Frey went to the hospital with the police.*

Frey: *I'm fine, a little battered and bruised. Ziggy, you were epic, and I'll be eternally grateful for what you did for me today. I'm sorry I never got the chance to say it before I left. I hope you didn't get into trouble with the police.*

Ziggy: *They were cool, and I got a date with one of them... so it was a win for being naked in public lol...*

Bowie: *You did? Was it the cute, dark-haired one?*

Ziggy: *Yep and you're right, he is cute.*

Monty: *Ziggy, it seems a good deed will reap rewards. I'm not sure my otter would have gotten the same outcome.*

Bowie: *Your otter side is gorgeous and so playful.*

Monty: *Why thank you… when are we going to have another play date?*

Lennon: *Play date? When do you get play dates and why wasn't I invited?*

Bowie: *Erm… would you like to join us?*

Lennon: *Heck yeah. Do we get cake?*

Hollis: *How do we always end up back to cake?*

Ziggy: *Cause cake rules!*

Chapter Forty-Five

Booker

It had taken Frey's fox-half four sessions in his animal form to heal his injured shoulder, though there remained some residual bruising which burned Booker's ass every time he looked at it.

"Do you know if they moved?" Booker questioned, his eyes on the road as he sat in the passenger seat with Dad driving.

"They are still in the same house," Dad answered, not looking at Booker as he navigated the busy afternoon traffic.

Booker knew Dad had kept an eye on his old family to make sure they didn't cause him any problems. Booker suspected Dad had paid handsomely for his father to allow them to adopt him. It had all been too easy, something that—when it came to his father—never happened.

"What did you tell Popi?"

They'd had to be cunning to get away at the same time so as not to garner suspicion from Frey or Lane. They'd both been warned to stay away from Booker's father and let the lawyers handle it. Only, with the memory of the terror on Frey's face when he'd recounted to Booker exactly what happened, made it impossible to sit and do nothing. Dad, knowing him well, had rung him the day before to ask when he was going to pay a visit. Booker hadn't wanted Derick to come, but he wasn't for being dissuaded and it warmed Booker to his core. Dad had always been the person he measured himself against, and this was why.

"That I needed to find him an anniversary present."

"Shit, it's next week. Maybe we should reconsider—"

Dad raised his hand off the steering wheel, cutting Booker off. "Don't. We are doing this today. You are worrying about what he'll do next. We need to nip this in the bud, make him understand that we aren't going to tolerate him attacking our family."

The steel that ran through Dad's voice and the truth of his words were all it took for Booker to settle. "I'll take the blame if Popi finds out, okay?"

Dad's rich, deep laughter filled the confined space. "Like you could save me from Popi? He'll kick both our ass's into next week if he finds out we did this."

Booker chuckled at the concern Dad tried to hide. Popi might be an omega and divergent, but he would and could match Dad for sheer strength of will. "Yeah, what was I thinking?"

"You weren't, son, but don't worry. We aren't going to get caught."

Booker hoped so. He didn't want to upset Frey and cause him any more worry. But to do that, he needed to make it clear to the man who'd tossed him aside that if he so much as breathed on his mate, he'd end him. The police had given his father a warning to stay away, and although Frey had pressed charges for assault, which the hospital records supported, it wasn't enough.

"Looks like he's home," Dad murmured as he slowed to find a place to park.

Booker didn't question how Dad knew the BMW, shining like a new cent, was his fathers. Parked two houses down, Booker got out of the car and waited for Dad to join him.

Dad rested a hand on his sleeve. "Let me do the talking."

Booker shook his head. "Not this time, Dad. It's time I faced him and dealt with this shit once and for all."

Over the years, Booker had seen his father on the street with his mother a few times. They'd snubbed him every time, and that was fine. Then he'd left Hazardville, and he could almost believe that Derick and Lane had always been his family—if he ignored the nightmares.

Coming back had been difficult, and now Booker understood why. The memories of his childhood remained tied up with this town and they weren't all bad. He had a family of his own now and he didn't want his past to contaminate his present, especially in the form of the asshole who hated divergents.

He'd attempted to explain this to Frey when they'd gone to their bedroom for Frey to shift and heal after Booker had first gotten home. His bear had wanted to curl around their fox and wasn't for letting anything stop him. So the talking had gotten curtailed and since then, Frey hadn't brought it back up.

Stop blaming me, you avoided it.

I'm not blaming you.

"Shall we?" Dad enquired, one brow arched as he looked at Booker.

He took a deep breath and nodded. "Let's do this."

When they reached the door and knocked, Booker found it easy to push aside the flood of memories of times when he'd have walked into the house without an invitation.

The door opened and there loomed his father, larger than life, wearing an ugly sneer when he saw who was standing on his doorstep. "What the fuck do you think you're doing coming here? If you're after my forgiveness 'cause you adopted a *divergent*, you got another think coming," he snarled.

The way he referred to Emmy made Booker's blood boil, and he had to take a moment to stop himself from reaching up and throttling the fucker who shared the same DNA as him. Genetics didn't make a family, love did, and Booker clung to that as he stared his father down.

"Beg your forgiveness? What a crock of shit. I have done nothing that requires forgiveness." Booker jabbed a finger into the enormous chest in front of him.

"You, on the other hand, have," Booker spat out, as he poked a little harder. "You touched my mate. Laid hands on him in front of our daughter." As he spoke through clenched teeth, his fingers gripped the shirt he was touching and dragged his father, who he could easily match for size now, into his face.

He met his angry glare with one of his own. "You come near my family, any of them, again, and I will tear your fucking head right off your shoulders and shit in it."

Booker was too angry to look away when he heard Dad chuckle. He wanted to make sure the man in front of him got the point, because he meant every damn word. This was his family and there was nothing he wouldn't do to protect them. It was the first time he completely acknowledged what a gift Derick and Lane had given him. He had always appreciated them, but never truly gotten what they had done for him until Emmy.

"H-how d-dare you t-threaten me," his father gasped, going red as sweat popped out on his brow.

"I do dare." Booker used both hands to grip his arms in a painful hold and lifted him clear of the ground, his bear pushing him to make the point. "I dare very fucking much."

Booker shook his father hard enough to make his teeth rattle before he let go and, with satisfaction, saw his father sink to his knees, groaning.

He crouched down and grabbed the collar of his button-down and twisted his fingers in the material until it was cutting off the air supply. "Am I making myself clear?" he ground out.

Grunts and saliva dribbled from between lips that parted when Booker twisted a little harder, making him moan and gasp for air. To add further insult, Booker brought the toe of his shoe down between his father's legs and ground down hard. "Am. I. Making. Myself. Clear?" he enunciated each word.

His father's head bob was barely more than a flicker as his face scrunched up in pain, fear lodged in his teary eyes. It left Booker satisfied he'd made his point. He let go and watched the bully slump down, retching as he tried to drag in oxygen, his hands clutching at his balls.

Booker gave him one last look and swung around, stalking off.

He was done.

All the way fucking done!

At the gate, it took a moment to realize Dad wasn't right behind him. He glanced back to see Dad bent, murmuring something into his father's ear. What color he had leached away, leaving him pale and glass eyed before Dad stood and walked to Booker.

"Time to leave, son." He slipped a hand down Booker's back and encouraged him to walk.

"What did you say to him?" Booker questioned as he walked back towards the car.

"It doesn't matter what I said, just that I made my point the same as you." He slapped Booker's shoulder, grinning when they came to a stop. "'Rip his head off and shit in it'..." Dad's laughter helped ease the tension riding through Booker. "You do have a way with words, Booker."

Grinning widely as he got into the car, he did his seatbelt up as Dad started the car. "I learned from the best, Dad."

Booker didn't need a tarot card reading to predict his future when he got home that evening. Frey was waiting for him in their bedroom, his hands going straight to his narrow hips, his blond, damp hair shifting as he tilted his head, giving Booker a hard stare.

He must have been home a while if he'd showered and was now dressed in cotton lounge pants and a baggy T-shirt that made him appear younger than his years and as cute as a damn button.

"Where have you been this afternoon?"

Booker stripped off his suit jacket, trying to calculate just how much trouble he was in. "You know where I was."

He threw his jacket onto the back of the chair, then tugged at his tie, feeling like it was restricting his air intake. Taking it off, he placed it on top of his jacket as he watched Frey out of the corner of his eye.

"Do I?" Frey stepped closer, his bare feet moving soundlessly over the wood. "Really?" Blond brows arched up and Booker resisted squirming.

"I... it was... I thought... I-I..." Fuck, just spit it out. Only that seemed impossible when Frey reached up and knocked Booker's hands away from the shirt he was unbuttoning. His body heated at the simple touch and Booker's gaze went to the open door where Emmy slept.

"Emmy is with Jup." Frey answered his unspoken question as he pushed aside the cotton of Booker's shirt, trailing his fingers through the hair on his chest. The move, one Frey loved to do when they were lying in bed together, brought with it desire. "Now explain to me which part of 'stay away from your father' you didn't get? Hmmm?"

Those nimble fingers stroked Booker's treasure trail to his belt buckle. His concentration shot to hell, he couldn't remember what he was supposed to be saying. The story they'd come up with in the car if they'd somehow gotten caught disappeared with the sound of his buckle flicking open.

"What?" he croaked, as Frey slowly tugged down his zipper, allowing his fingers to graze the bulge beneath.

Frey's gray-green eyes sparkled with mischief and made Booker's throat become drier than the one time he'd gotten a mouthful of sand after face planting the beach.

"What. Is that any kind of answer?" Frey said in a teasing tone that made Booker's dick throb and thicken until his shaft pressed against his boxer briefs. It was the only thing that stopped it from touching the fingers than were parting his slacks.

Somewhere in the past few weeks, Frey's inhibitions about sex had disappeared and, although Booker had no issue whatsoever about that, it was hard to focus on any subject when Frey unleashed this new playful side.

"I don't know." He groaned when Frey sank to his knees, tugging on Booker's suit pants. The head of his dick, slick with pre-cum, poked out the top of the band of his underwear as Booker hyperventilated at the sight of Frey licking his lips.

He tsked at Booker, all the while he unlaced his shoes. "Didn't we talk about how communication was key to any relationship?" Booker lifted his foot when Frey tapped at it. "Isn't that what you said to me when we talked about your father? And when we talked about my family."

"Yes." Booker groaned in frustration, growling at how his body was on fire with need as Frey came up on his knees, his face just below the straining fabric trying to contain his erection. Hot breath hit the wet head as Frey breathed out gustily, tugging down Booker's boxer briefs. His cock bounced and slapped off his stomach, making Booker groan once more as he closed his eyes at the sight before him. Feeling at a distinct disadvantage, Booker wondered how the heck Frey had him wanting to beg. To cry mercy when it seemed Frey wasn't coming any closer with those pretty lips or wrapping them around the hard shaft right in front of him.

"Yes, what?" Frey asked cheekily, the giggle barely suppressed as Booker opened his eyes to meet those of his mate.

"You're planning on torturing me, aren't you?" he asked, resigned to his fate. One he'd not change for the world.

Frey teased his balls with the soft pads of his fingers, a glint in his eyes that answered Booker's question. "Did you go to see your father when I expressly asked you not to?"

Swallowing twice, Booker attempted to focus on answering despite how Frey took hold of balls and gently squeezed them. His shaft throbbed at the flood of sensation. More pre-cum made the head shine in the overhead lights.

Was he panting?

It fucking felt like it.

"What was the question?"

Coming closer, Frey licked once more at his plump lips, making them as shiny as the head of his cock, which was mere inches from those juicy lips.

"Did you go to see your father?" His breath wafted over the slick skin, causing his shaft to bob in time to his frantic pulse.

"Yes. *Fuck,* yes I did," Booker gasped, his hands forming into tight fists at his side to resist dragging Frey closer.

Chapter Forty-Six

Frey

It was a heady feeling to be in control like this. Lane had a hand in giving him the confidence, when Frey had come home an hour ago and been informed Booker had expressly gone against his wishes.

Lane, who had forty years of being with Derick, knew his tells when he told a lie. It seemed that when Derick had gotten home from his trip to see Booker's father, he had confessed to what they'd been up to. Lane had more than willingly shared the information with Frey, and that had given him the time to consider a course of action. One that Booker would not forget in a hurry.

There'd been no sign of Derick and by the smug look Lane had worn, Frey suspected Derick was possibly otherwise occupied up in the bedroom, where Lane headed after their talk. It had given Frey the idea, so he had asked Jupiter, who'd arrived after Lane had left, if he could take Emmy for a couple of hours. His eagerness to have Emmy continued to surprise Frey, but right now, that wasn't what was on his mind.

No, it was the man who he literally had by the balls. He squeezed them a little harder after rolling them in his palm, watching how Booker's nostrils flared and sweat gleamed on his skin.

"So... you lied to me?" he asked sweetly, licking his lips, inhaling the musky scent of his mate, which drove his desire to spike. His own neglected shaft wanted some attention with the way it pressed against the fabric of his cotton pants.

"I didn't mean to," he whined, making Frey's confidence skyrocket.

He didn't want to make this fierce man cower, no. What he wanted was for Booker to understand that he was making a point. There should be no lies between them. None. Frey would not tolerate that, despite how a part of him hoped Booker had given that big bully a solid kick to his balls.

"Is that so?" He held Booker's hooded gaze, his pupils engulfing the brown of his irises. Slashes of deep red covered Booker's cheekbones, which were noticeable above his beard. "So you were planning tonight to come home and tell me what you'd done?"

Frey noticed the hitch in Booker's breath as he glanced away before returning his attention to Frey when he gave a firm squeeze. "Did you?" Frey pushed, Booker's eyes not moving from Frey.

Booker's whole body shuddered, the open shirt he still wore revealing how his chest heaved when he shook his head. "I won't do it again," he said in a hoarse whisper. "I swear, I won't."

Frey came closer to the dripping cock, running the tip of his tongue over the slick head, one hand slipping around the root and moving up the sticky shaft. Hot and silky to touch, Frey angled the head so he could swipe his tongue over the whole surface. Booker's essence coated his tongue as he brought it back into his mouth and swallowed. He groaned at the slight bitterness that was all Booker.

He resisted doing more at hearing Booker's growl of approval. No, he wasn't quite ready to give in yet. "Are you sure?"

"I am," he moaned as Frey slid his tongue around the head, lapping at it.

Frey's body was burning up with need, driven by how Booker smelled and tasted. The front of his pants was stuck against his shaft, his bottom not much better as he leaked with excitement. "How do you plan to make it up to me?"

Another shuddery breath and those eyes pinned Frey in place with pure desire. "I'll do whatever you want. Give you whatever you desire."

Frey released Booker, doing his best to conceal how much those few words affected him. "Lie face down on the bed."

At the bridge of his nose, a wrinkle appeared as he looked at the bed and back to Frey. "Face down?" There was nothing about the question that said Booker was worried, yet...

"Yes," Frey answered, his lips quivering when Booker let out a heaved sigh and walked to the bed, slower than his usual pace. Frey didn't want to top, no. But he wanted to taste his bear's ass. Savor it.

It was a thing of beauty. High, tight and round like two halves of a peach. Frey wanted to sink his teeth into it. He wanted to lick it until Booker lost his mind. Once, he'd touched him intimately there and Booker had quickly stopped him. The noises he'd made prior revealed he'd not been averse to it, maybe just a little freaked out. At the time, Frey was too busy coming apart to pay too much attention to being stopped.

Today, while he'd showered and got ready for Booker's return home, he had thought about that reaction. Understood why his bear held back. He didn't need to do that anymore with the level of intimacy between them. Frey wasn't scared. He wanted Booker to let go, and this was how he wanted to achieve it. Show him he wasn't fragile any longer because Booker had changed everything.

Booker rested his head on the arms he folded when he removed his shirt and positioned himself in the center of the bed. His eyes tracked Frey as he went to the bedside drawers, where he'd placed some scented oil that he'd found in the bathroom. He made a show of opening the bottle and putting one knee on the bed and leaning over Booker. His back was a work of art. All golden skin covering firm flexing muscles. Booker's ass also flexed as Frey poured a liberal amount of oil just above it, at the hollow of Booker's back.

Frey took pleasure in how Booker had displayed himself, so placing down the bottle, he stripped off. Booker's eyes fired with lust as they wandered over his exposed skin, lingering on his erect shaft. Too eager to remain too long under the avid appraisal, Frey straddled Booker's legs. They both moaned at the touch of skin.

Wanting a better position, Frey wriggled down, feeling the hair on Booker's legs brush sensually against his until he sat on Booker's thighs.

"You aren't to move unless I say you can, understood?" he murmured as he dipped his fingers into the oil to coat them.

"I'll try."

The dry, rasped response made Frey's grin widen. "No," he squeezed his thighs against Booker's, provoking another moan. "You will not move unless I say you can."

Booker sighed heavily and glanced over his shoulder at Frey. "I've created a monster."

Frey couldn't have agreed more. "Then it should teach you to behave in the future." Without further discussion, Frey ran his oily fingers over the crease of Booker's ass, making him tense. It didn't stop the oil from seeping between his cheeks. The position only allowed for his fingers to tease. For now, that was fine.

Booker's ass squeezed and Frey spanked his cheek, leaving a red imprint and making his palm sting. This got another groan, this one more guttural. His cock bobbed and dripped onto Booker. "What did I say?"

Not a word came from Booker while he appeared to force himself to relax, judging by the way his large body shuddered under Frey. Once he had settled, Frey went to dip his fingers back into the oil, smearing it over the golden globes of flesh, making them glisten in the lights.

"So pretty," he murmured, more to himself as his teeth ached in his gums. His feisty fox was pushing for him to leave their mark right there on one of the firm cheeks, preferably the one with the handprint.

There was a constant stream of sexy noises coming from Booker, making Frey bolder as he lifted off carefully and demanded, "Spread your legs."

At the lack of hesitation, Frey smiled to himself. He crawled between the spread legs and groaned at the sight of Booker's glistening hole and heavy balls. He was hairy everywhere but his ass and balls. Frey hadn't considered it before, but with how smooth he was down there, his bear must wax. Eager to test his theory, Frey moved to stretch out his lower body until his feet dangled off the bed. Then he placed his nose against Booker's crease and ran it down. Oil coated his skin, the scent didn't mask Booker's smell and Frey groaned. "Smells so good."

Not thinking but working on instinct, he eased Booker's tight cheeks apart and swirled his tongue over the pink rosebud.

"Motherfucker!" Booker rasped but Frey was too busy focusing on the smooth and silky skin he lapped at, whimpering in delight.

Frey's fingers dug into Booker's flesh as he tasted all of his mate. His musk was intoxicating as Frey's tongue got frisky with the rosebud, feeling it twitch under his ministrations.

He wasn't sure how long it was before Booker's hips started to rock. Frey didn't want to let go of his treat, so he slapped

Booker's ass cheek once more. Only this time, Booker came up on all fours, dislodging him.

Booker's cock hung heavy between his spread thighs as he rocked back. "Fuck, touch me," he demanded breathlessly. His entire body moved, unable to keep still, as oil spilled down his sides.

Frey rose and followed, his teeth sinking into the reddened globe, and he bit true. Blood filled his mouth and his body reacted violently. His hips surged forward, his cock hitting the side of Booker's thigh. The hairs added to the sensation overload as he swallowed and sucked at the hard flesh.

"Argh... what... damnnnnn," Booker cried out loud enough to make Frey's already buzzing ears pound as he scented his mate's cum.

Frey reached blindly between Booker's legs, his teeth not letting go of their prize, and loosely held the throbbing shaft, relishing the knowledge that his mate was coming without one stroke to his cock. Frey growled into the flesh as his teeth retracted and he jerked his hips back and forth, using Booker's thigh for friction and coming moments later. His body bowed while he licked at his slick lips, taking in the lingering taste of Booker, giving his cock an added boost of sizzling pleasure.

Booker collapsed forward onto the covers a second after. Frey followed, barely having the wherewithal to move his hand as he splayed over Booker's oil and sweat coated body.

Booker chugged in air like a dying man and Frey rested his cheek against Booker's back, feeling the beat of his heart as he rose and fell repeatedly, lulling him as his eyelids drooped. Who knew being a top was so much hard work?

Chapter Forty-Seven

Booker

Coming into the sunroom two hours later, after having a snooze with Frey, who had remained on his back, Booker's ass twinged from the bite. His bear had lost the plot to feel their fox mark them like that. It was such a dominant move, and his bear loved their fox for it.

Booker rubbed at his ass cheek, unsure how he felt about this new dynamic and, when he had five minutes alone, he was going to ask Derick about it. Because from what Frey had inferred before he'd come down to leave him to shower, he wasn't the only one to get into trouble for lying.

He sighed, running a hand through his damp hair at how conflicted he continued to feel about the dressing down he'd gotten, in such a non-dressing down way. Frey had him by the balls for sure.

"What's with you?" Silas asked, his gaze going to Frey, who had the seat next to Popi. Popi was pushing the swing crib where Emmy was sleeping. Booker shrugged, doing his best to not blush.

All the family were there and Booker did not want an audience when he was feeling a little out of sorts. Frey had shown him who was boss and by doing so, he'd made him come in a way Booker hadn't done since he'd had wet dreams as a teenager. It was... fucked if he knew, when his groin tightened in anticipation of it happening again.

"Have you had something to eat?" Popi asked as he rose gracefully from the couch. The look he cast at Booker told him he was still in trouble for what he'd gone and done with Derick.

Can't I just catch a break?

His stomach gurgled and, clearly not wanting to get into any more strife, he went with honesty. "No."

"Follow me," Popi said, and Booker swallowed the groan when his brothers all glanced at him. He didn't miss their smug smirks or how Dad bit his bottom lip as if holding back a chuckle. Seeing he would not get any help there, Booker, like a man trying to find if he had the ability to walk on water, swung around and unfortunately caught Jupiter's eye.

"Someone's in trouble," Jupiter muttered, loud enough for Booker to hear.

"Fuck off," he mouthed back, and went after Popi.

He tried to think of several reasons for his actions that wouldn't get him into any more hot water as he dragged his sneakered feet through the house. By the time he entered the kitchen, Popi had a large portion of homemade lasagna, steam rising from the plate as Popi placed it on the counter. "Sit."

Seeing absolutely no way around it, Booker did as he was told and reached for the fork. He dug into the food for something to do to avoid looking at the man who filled a glass with white wine and sat opposite him. Booker could feel Popi's stare, it held the weight of his disappointment. Booker didn't need to see to know that. Popi had always used that look and the silence to make them all understand they'd pissed him off. It was a genuine talent. No shouting, no hitting, just that look that said they'd caused him to feel disappointed by their behavior.

The silence stretched so long, Booker had cleared his plate before he chanced a look at Popi. The years had been kind to him. Despite being in his sixties and his hair silvery-white, his face hardly had a wrinkle. His eyes were clear and piercing as they held Booker's.

"I'm sorry."

Popi took a sip of his wine. "For what?"

"For whatever Dad told you," Booker hedged, searching Popi's expression to see if he could suss what exactly he knew. He gave nothing away.

"Why don't you explain what happened to me?" Another sip of wine and a smile that made Booker shift in his seat.

"I... we... went to speak to the asshole and tell him to stay away from my family." That summed it up if he discounted standing on his father's nuts and trying to rattle his teeth from his head. Minor details.

"Didn't Frey and I express that we wished for you and Derick to leave that man for the lawyers to deal with?"

The quiet question caused sweat to gather under Booker's armpits. He could feel his T-shirt sticking to his skin. "It was just—"

"That you both thought you could hoodwink me and Frey and do what we expressly asked you not to do?" One brow quirked up. Another sip of wine and Booker was sweating so hard he was going to need another shower.

Booker ran his hands through his hair, then scratched at his beard, trying to figure out the best way to answer. "I... yes."

He sagged, his shoulders slumping as he rested his arms on the counter, reaching a hand out to Popi, giving him begging eyes. "Popi, I was worried for my family. I wanted to make sure that fucker didn't think he could hassle my mate and daughter. They've all kept away after they cut ties after that night..."

Booker took a deep inhale and then released a shuddery breath at how the past was there, reminding him of things that no one could change. "To come back now when I'm truly happy and attack my family. What if he'd done what he'd tried to do to you, and I wasn't there to stop it?" Booker shuddered. That fear had materialized during the hours he'd spent in the air, trying to get back to Frey. Then to find out his father had laid hands on Frey—hurt him? His nightmares were back to being a reality, and as much as he'd promised Frey to let the lawyers sort it, he could not settle without having his opportunity to tell that fucker to stay away.

"He's a coward at heart. Greedy and manipulative, it's why he targeted Frey and not you. We will deal with him, so he doesn't harm any of you." Popi took the hand reaching out for him and squeezed it.

It helped settle Booker like it had always done, that quiet support. His suspicions about paying off his father, yeah, he'd known all along. The greedy fucker had taken Dad and Popi's money and without knowing, done Booker an eternal gratitude. His chest ached with the love he had for this man who'd chosen to be his family. "I love you, Popi."

"My sweet boy." Popi sniffed, placing his glass on the counter. Releasing Booker's hand, he slid off his seat and rounded the counter.

Booker twisted, and Popi came to stand in front of him. Even seated, Popi had to tilt his head back to meet Booker's gaze. His hands cupped his bearded cheeks and gave Booker the sweetest smile, one filled with the affection he displayed every day since Booker had become part of their family.

"I love you, too. You're my big brave son and have been since the moment you saved my Silas, stepped in front of your father, and took those punches." His fingers gently ran over Booker's cheeks, wiping at the tears running down them. "But more than that, your heart is so big and generous. You love deeply and protect those who are vulnerable. That is who you are. Don't let that A-hole make you think differently. *Act* differently."

He tugged Booker's head towards him and kissed his forehead. Their gazes held. "You wanted to protect your family, but doing it from a jail cell isn't the answer. That man wanted to provoke you, for whatever stupid reasons he has, and he succeeded. Violence is never the answer. Your Dad and I disagree on this, but he now knows my thoughts on how he handled this without discussing it with me or Frey. I understand why you felt the need to protect, and your Dad is the same, which is why he went with you."

Booker got Popi's argument, he truly did, but... "Popi, he touched my mate with violence. Laid hands on him and hurt him. Same as he tried to do to you. He needed to know I wasn't going to tolerate that." For Booker and his animal side, it was as simple as that. "And you don't need to worry, I didn't hit him."

Back was the one arched brow. "You didn't?" Popi searched his expression, and Booker held his gaze. "You aren't lying."

Popi pouted, and Booker's brows drew together in confusion.

"I was hoping for one good punch at least."

Booker burst out laughing and hugged Popi against his chest. "Popi, you're so... naughty."

Popi giggled. "I know, but you are not to tell your dad."

Booker kissed the top of his fragrant hair, continuing to chuckle. "I won't, but I want brownie points for it."

"That's my boy."

Chapter Forty-Eight

Derick

Walking into the bedroom, Derick eyed his husband, who was stripping in a way that suggested he remained annoyed with him. Derick understood it, but he didn't have to like it. His need to protect his family had come the moment he'd held Silas in his arms. It had expanded with each new son. They might not have been his biological children, but that made no difference to the love he had for each of them. The man who he'd claimed as his mate, against all the odds, got it. But that didn't mean he wouldn't make Derick suffer a little more for going against his wishes and paying a visit to that scumbag.

"How did it go with Booker?" he asked, clicking the door closed behind him as he continued to watch Lane's ass sway seductively to the closet. A sight he'd never tire of or stop finding arousing. He adjusted himself before going to sit on the bed, knowing the teasing and driving him crazy with lust could continue for days, as punishment for not talking about his plan to support Booker. He held back a sigh and took off his loafers. Would he change what he'd done? No. But talking to Lane first would have been a wise move. He removed his socks and, standing to remove the rest of his clothes, he watched Lane as he continued to torment him with his sexy, lean body. Despite his age and love of cake, Lane's body still enticed Derick to taste, touch and devour it in hungry bites.

"What did you say to that A-hole?" He looked over his shoulder, beautiful eyes pinning him with a look that said he'd pay for any bullshit.

Derick hated to disappoint this man as much as their sons did. Lane had a wonderful ability to make them all feel like crap for actions he didn't approve of without so much as a cross word. He envied his husband for it. It was also something Lane had used in business and balanced out Derick's rougher edges.

"All I did was explain that I've got insurance, evidence of what he's been getting up to with a certain omega across the other side of town. And if he didn't want his wife to read about it in the local tabloids, he needed to stay the fuck away from Booker, Frey and Emmy."

Lane's shapely brows arched. "So you didn't lay a finger on him?"

Derick heaved a sigh at how much he'd wanted to punch the fucker's lights out but resisted because of the very man coming towards him, giving him a searching look.

"No. I told you, I wanted to, but it's always better to go with something they value more. And hitting him would have only given me satisfaction for a few seconds."

It was the truth. As much as he wanted to ram the asshole's teeth down his throat, seeing Booker crush his balls had to suffice, not that he was going to tell Lane that. Booker had the right to make the man suffer, if only a little. "That fuckhead is all about pride. To take that away from him would be the worst thing..."

Derick gave Lane a devilish grin and tugged him to him, wrapping his arms loosely around his waist, inhaling his warm scent. "That and take back every red cent we paid him to sign the adoption papers. The law is very clear, no money should exchange hands when it comes to shifter children in adoptions." His nostrils flared in anger at how the fucking law makers had no issue selling divergent children.

Lane reached up and cupped Derick's face. "Don't. I can see exactly where your thoughts are heading. We have made a wonderful family despite what society deems 'appropriate or correct'. We will continue to support divergents anyway we can. It's who we are."

"How did I get so lucky, my love?" Derick murmured before taking Lane's mouth in a hot, hungry kiss. His heart beat for this man. He'd taken it the moment Derick had laid eyes on him and in the forty years they'd been married, nothing had changed.

Lane groaned and eased back, his arousal painting Derick's thigh. His lips were glossy and his skin wore a flush of desire.

"You were always good at fighting dirty." Lane gave him a seductive smile, eyes gleaming with wickedness. "I'm not sure I've forgiven you yet."

Fingertips trailed down the silver hair covering Derick's chest until they rested on a nipple. He gently squeezed, then licked at his lips, making Derick's system hum with anticipation right as Lane twisted the budded flesh painfully.

Derick moaned in pleasure, arching into the touch, wanting more, then the fingers let go, leaving him needy. He groaned anew when Lane took a step back, then another. His arousal poked towards Derick, one he wanted to taste enough that he'd beg if he had to. But that wasn't part of this game. "I believe I prefer you lying on the bed... tied up so you can't interfere."

Heat poured through his body like lava rolling straight down to his throbbing shaft, which bucked in total agreement at what his lover planned to do.

Lane tapped at his lower glossy lip, his hooded eyes roaming over Derick's body with a satisfaction that made Derick's heart tremble with love—with need. Yet, he remained where he was. He'd played this game many times and his love would give him what he wanted... but only after he'd made him suffer in the best possible way.

"Spread eagle, tied up and blindfolded... yes, that will do nicely. For starters..." Lane all but cooed at him, getting Derick walking to the bed, his heavy cock bouncing as his eagerness matched his anticipation of what Lane would do to make him beg.

Fuck, he loved his husband, and hoped his boys, those who remained single, would be as lucky to find someone who matched their souls.

They all deserved that.

Epilogue
Alphaholes

Jupiter: *What's this about Ziggy chasing down a guy at the lake in his snake form, then getting a date with the police officer after he saw him? All the PAs are gossiping about it. It seems our little snake has some hidden talents I might need to explore!*

Booker: *Leave it be, Jup!*

Jupiter: *Why? Oh, that's right, bears don't like snakes.*

Booker: *That's got fuck all to do with it. Just don't be your usual asshole self, okay?*

Silas: What the fuck are you talking about, Jup?

Jupiter: *Get with the programme, Silas. Ziggy was your PA for weeks before he came to me, surely you saw his hidden talents? I'm looking forward to seeing his sexy snake.*

Silas: You fucking look sideways at him and you'll have me to answer too!

Rue: Okay, Silas what's with that? It's not like you're dating him. Ziggy is free to date whomever he wants. And if he chooses Jup then it proves he's got no more sense than all the other airheads Jup dates.

Jupiter: *I don't date Rue and the last guy I fucked has a PHD in physics, so fuck you.*

Laken: *Rue, give the fuck over. Stop being derogatory about who Jup dates. And Jup, if I were you I'd step away from the fucking grenade. It's gonna blow up in your face.*

Jupiter: *Thanks, I think, Laken. But can you stop being so dramatic. And once more I don't fucking date! I'm with Rue, Ziggy is a free man to FUCK whoever he wants.*

Kodi: *Takes a seat to watch the fallout.*

Kari: *Come on Kodi, stop being a dick. Don't wind up Silas or Jup, you know how much he enjoys it.*

Dad: *Why do my sons feel the need to talk shit? Maybe it's time you all went to Silas's ranch for the corporate team building seven day package he has? In fact, now that I think about it, it's a perfect idea. Silas, you can arrange it. Maybe it will help with all this testosterone being thrown around.*

Jupiter: No way Dad, I'll hate ranch life. All those smells!

Silas: Scared you'll get some dirt on you? Big wuss.

Laken: It doesn't smell as bad as Emmy's diaper.

Booker: That's my daughter you're talking about!

Kodi: It's the damn truth. Whatever you're feeding that little girl could be classed as a damn lethal weapon when it's unleashed the way she does.

Booker: You say that to Frey. I dare you.

Laken: Let's get back to this supposed trip. I'm far too busy to take time off.

Dad: *It's not a request. You need to make the time. All of you, end of discussion!*

Silas: *Then if we're going, so are the PAs...*

Taylin: *I second that because I'm not leaving Hollis behind.*

Booker: *We have Emmy to consider.*

Dad: Lane *and I will look after her. We managed you eight. I'm sure we can cope with Emmy for a week.*

I hope you enjoyed Booker and Frey's story, they'll keep you on your toes in future books. If you are interested to find out who is next brother to fall and learn love doesn't come without pain, then read on for a snippet!

Silas's Sweetheart

Silas

His hand cramped as he held his phone, staring at the screen, reading what Jupiter had written over and over. It ripped open his chest and allowed his heart to fucking bleed all over the damn place.

What have I done?

It didn't matter how many times he asked the question, he still couldn't come up with an answer that made the ache in his chest take a fucking run off a cliff and give him some peace.

To know that Jupiter was only down the hallway and was a wind up merchant of epic proportions didn't stop Silas wanting to go shut him up with a fist to the face. The edge of the phone case dug into his palm as he remained glued to his seat, breathing hard. Where was the brother code of keeping away from someone they'd dated?

He doesn't fucking know, does he?

Shut up! His animal side had made its choice, and Silas op-posing him had not gone down well. Though he still couldn't quite figure out why he'd done what he'd done. That was a question he still couldn't find the answer to. Or not one he was willing to look too closely at when it uncovered insecu-rities he hid from everyone except Popi, Dad, and Booker.

What a fucking mess his life was.

He flicked the screen open and ran over the conversation, torturing himself once more. Was Dad's suggestion a good one? Could that give him the chance to show Ziggy...

What could he show him?

He dropped the phone, making it clatter on the desk in front of him, to scrub his hands over his face.

Man the fuck up. Booker's words ran through his mind. *You are one of the best fucking men I know. Stop fucking hiding behind society's fake fucking beliefs about divergents. I saved your fucking ass that day in the alley because you are my best friend. One of honor, of courage. Do fucking you. Show him who you really are, the man I love. He won't run from you if he's everything you think he is.*

Silas released a shuddery breath, inhaled and blinked hard, swallowing past the ball of emotion in his throat. Pick-ing his phone back up with a renewed determination, he searched the chat names for Ethan.

> **Silas:** Hey Ethan, can you give me the next free dates for the seven day corporate team building package, with enough spaces for sixteen?

Ethan: Yep, who's it for?

Silas: Me, my brothers and the PAs...

Ethan: LMAO...

Silas: I expected nothing less. Just get me the dates and prepare for Armageddon!

Ethan: Oh the fucking joy... can I play with Jup?

Silas: If you want to end up kneeling at his feet worshiping him, then go for it, my friend.

Ethan: Maybe not... but it would be interesting to see if I could tame the wild beast.

Silas: It's your funeral.

> **Ethan:** *It just might be fucking worth it.*

Silas grinned for the first time since seeing Jupiter's name pop up in the notification. Ethan was as bad as Jupiter for conquests. He loved a pretty face as much as the next man, but they seldom held his attention for long.

Silas closed the chat, but it might be fun to watch those two go head to head...

His door opened, and Booker strode in, wearing a look of concern. His suit jacket was missing, and his sleeves were rolled up, looking like he was ready to fight. "Want me to go shove his head up his ass?"

Silas sat back, eyeing his brother with amusement, his chest warming with affection. "The kinky fucker would probably enjoy it." Silas's lips transformed into an evil grin as he met Booker's stare. "Nope. I think a week on the ranch will be enough payback, don't you?"

Booker's laugh reverberated off the walls as his head tipped back and he roared in obvious pleasure at what they both knew was Jupiter's idea of hell.

It took five minutes before he calmed down enough to wipe his eyes, though he continued to chuckle. "You're right, he fucking hates the country. It's damn perfect!"

All Silas had to do was hope that it wasn't Ziggy's idea of hell, because he was out of time.

How did someone win back a heart that they'd already cast aside?

Coming summer of 2025... if you want to get to grab the chapters early and as they come hot off the computer then why not join my patreon :)

Other Books by the Author

A Little Christmas Cllie (coming dec 2024)

Series
Assassins To Order With Lisa Oliver
Marvin – Marvin and Ajani in Audio

Ben – Ben, Teilo & Nico in Audio

Duron – Duron & Beaumont

Conrad – Conrad & Kylo

Dancing With the Devil – Wyatt & James

Tangled Tentacles Series with Lisa Oliver
Alexi #1in audio

Victor #2 in audio

Todd #3 in audio

Markov # 4in audio

Kelvin # 5 in audio

Obsessions Series with Lisa Oliver
Demon's Obsession

Controller's Obsession out 4th Dec 2024

Christa's Obsession out Feb 2025

Secretary's Obsession out March 2025

King's Obsession out May 2025

Little Paws Haven Series
Little Treasure he Hides

Little & Lethal

Enforcers Little Warrior coming 2025

Divergent Omegaverse Series
Alphas Divergent Omega
Taylin's Temptation due Oct 2024
Booker's Bliss due Jan 2025

Spin off Series in the Divergent Omegaverse Darling Ranch
Ranch-Down coming Feb 2025

The Potters Creek Series
A Christmas Wish (book one)

The App Series
The App: Daddy kink (book one)
The App: Littles (book two)
The App: Puppy play (book three)

The Flamingo Bar Series

Always More (book one)
The Little Side of Me (book two)
3 Is the Magic Number (book three)

La Trattoria Di Amore Series

Puzzle Pieces (book one)
Dominated but not Subdued (book two)
Made to Submit

The Playroom Series
Mine, Body and Soul: Part One
Mine, Body and Soul: Part Two
Mine, Body and Soul: Part Three
Ferron's Journey: Damaged Part One (book four)
Ferron's Journey: Hidden Part Two (book five)
Ferron's Journey: Revelation Part Three (book six)
Mine, Body and Soul Trilogy
Ferron's Journey Trilogy
Spinoff Love's Heart Print

Dark River Stone Collective Series
The Light Beneath the Dark (Book One)
When Darkness Turns to Light (Book Two)
Running From Darkness (Book Three)

The Billionaire Playground Series
Property of a Billionaire (Book one)
Reluctant Billicnaire (Book two)
Billionaire's Muse (Book three)

Heart Stones Series

Blood King

The Manx Cat Guardians Series
Where it all Began: Origins (Book 1)
Seeing Beyond the Scars (Book 2)
Destiny Collides Past and Present (Book 3)

Searching for a Soul to Love (Book 4)

The 12 Disasters of Christmas (Book 5)

Laws of Attraction (Book 6)

The Teacher's Boy (Book 7)

Boxset

Weird & Wacky Shifters

All he wants is a Fingerling

Alphas Fingerling Surprize

A Boy Called Blu

The Rhubarb Effect spin off from Weird & Wacky Shifters

Sticky For You

Rhubarb 2 Go

Ravished By the Rhubarb

Embracing The Stalk

Audio Books

Mine, Body and Soul, Part One: The Playroom Series

Mine, Body and Soul, Part Two: The Playroom Series

Mine, Body and Soul, Part Three: The Playroom
Series

Daddy Kink: The App (book one)

Always More: The Flamingo Bar (book one)

When Fake Changed Everything

Ferron's Journey: Damaged Part One

Ferron's Journey: Hidden Part Two

Ferron's Journey: Revelation Part Three

Romance books in a mixed series of M/F and M/M by the Author under a different pen name Jayne Paton

Smith's Corner
Delilah & Dallas (book one)
Layla & Levi (Book two)
Ash & Alora (Book three)
Fox & Faith (book four)
Storm & Stone (book five)
Hunter & Holden (book six)

Crime and Thrillers by the Author under a different pen name J Paton

Headspace
Chozen: Dark MM Crime Drama (Headspace Book 1)
Chozen: Dark MM Crime Drama (Headspace Book 2)

About the Author

Eccentric cake lover who has a passion for words of all kinds. I'm Jayne or JP, I live in the Isle of Man. A tiny place in the Irish sea where all the magic happens. I'm a confessed bookaholic and if I'm not writing I love to snuggle with a book or two...if you catch my drift.

If you're interested in keeping up to date, then I've a few places you can do that, and they're listed below. My website is where you'll find all the different Me's there are, LOL. As I travel this path into the future, I'm going to be writing in different genres so to stop there being any confusion I'll be writing under different pen names.

If you would like to give me any feedback or just have any questions, go ahead and friend me on Facebook, and I would be happy to answer anything. I hope you enjoyed this book and if you would also like to leave a review, then I would love to read your thoughts. Even if you just want to rate it, I'll be grateful

Thank you for being a part of my dream.

Newsletter Sign up

Goodreads

Tumblr

Bookbub

Instagram

Twitter

Facebook

Website address

Facebook Author page

JP Manx Minx's

Patreon